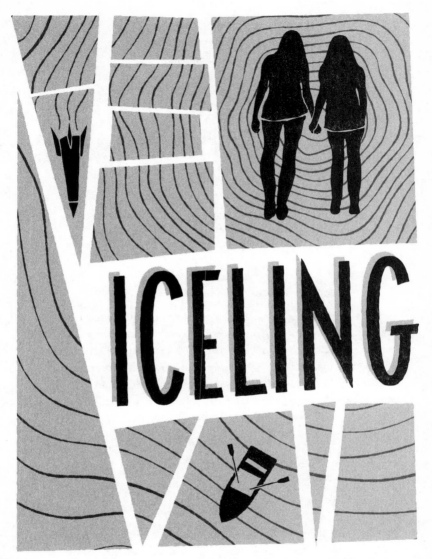

ICELING

SASHA STEPHENSON

RAZORBILL
An Imprint of Penguin Random House

RAZORBILL

An Imprint of Penguin Random House

Penguin.com

ISBN: 978-1-59514-769-1

Printed in the United States of America

1 3 5 7 9 10 8 6 4 2

Design by Anthony Elder

ONE

SO, HERE WE are, Dave and I. The two of us, alone in my room, with no adult supervision, ostensibly engaged in homework. My sister, Callie, is downstairs watching a thing on the Internet about carnivorous plants. Or at least that's what she was doing the last time I checked, about forty-five minutes ago, which is usually how long I tend to go without checking in on her.

The thing about Dave is that he's tall, like, six two, and he's got these real broad shoulders, and he's always wearing these baseball hats but only for teams that don't exist anymore. He's better than me at social studies, and I'm better than him at reading, writing, and most of the sciences. We actually *do* do homework together sometimes, but that's not what we're doing right now.

"Did you hear that?" Dave says, pulling away from me for a moment. And I do hear it: Downstairs there is a crashing and gnashing, a weeping and moaning.

Oh no, I think, and I run downstairs.

On the floor I find Callie, her eyes wide open, her legs curled up into herself while her arms flail around, as if she's trying to dig her way through the air. For a second all I can do is stand there, looking at her on the ground, making sounds. Like what, I can't even try to say.

Dave's been around Callie plenty of times, but he's never seen her like this before. I don't think I've ever even seen her like this before. Callie gets these fits sometimes, and I'm usually pretty good at calming her down, but this one is a bit scarier than what I'm used to. And I think I need to get Dave out of here and help my sister.

"Dave, I'm really sorry, but I have to take Callie to the hospital and—"

But before I can finish, Dave is picking Callie up off the floor. He's telling me to get my keys, and I do, and then I'm grabbing our coats and closing the door and clicking the dead bolt to lock it. I head out to the driveway and see that Dave's already got Callie in the backseat, strapped in and everything. And then there's Dave in his car, backing out of the driveway to clear the way for me, and then he parks by the curb and sits there waiting to watch us go off, and he looks at me, and I know it'll be okay.

Well, "okay" isn't the word. But I know that Callie's big fit and my leaving Dave so abruptly isn't what's going to hurt whatever it is we have together. I smile at that, and then I don't, because I don't really *know* what this is with me and him—I don't really know what I want it to be. But, as I'm sure you can imagine, I have bigger things to worry about right now, like my sister, Callie, and her weirdly giant fit.

Weird for Callie, that is. Lots of people these days have fits, sudden loss or acquisition of new language, mild levitations. Last month *60 Minutes* ran a piece on a group of children in India who went to bed knowing only their native language and woke up speaking fluent French. When I was little I knew some kids who claimed they could move things with their minds, but I never saw any of them pull off that comic book trick with my own eyes, so the jury's out on them. But the other stuff is real, and this is just how things are around here on earth these days. You read an article about a mother lifting a car to save her baby, and there are way more explanations than just "adrenaline rush sparked by maternal instincts."

Callie's pale green eyes lock with mine. She's looking at me like she wants to say she's sorry about all this. And also that this hurts and she doesn't understand it either. She's looking at me like "Yes, we both hate this," and I want to tell her, "I know, I love you, it's okay." And I do, I say it out loud, and then I tap out the words with my eyes just for her. I turn my head from the road for a moment and blow her a kiss. I think she tries to too, but she can't make her mouth work right right now, so instead she just keeps looking at me with those sorry eyes.

You'd think after sixteen years of Callie not talking, I'd be used to it by now. You'd think after sixteen years of having a sister who can't speak, or read, or even *understand* any language at all, nights like these wouldn't bother me much. That the way Callie is wouldn't keep surprising me day after day.

Dad says Callie is "non-lingual." Me, I'm not so certain. I keep trying different languages and cadences with her to see if anything clicks. It never does. We have this thing between us that Mom calls language, but it isn't that. It isn't a language. It's more that we have this way of reading each other. Of being very specific with our eyes and our faces, our postures, our vibes. We have these signals, almost, or at least I think we do.

But if Callie can talk to anyone, it's plants. Not that plants are people. I know plants aren't people. But she's always been good with them, ever since she was small. She seems so calm and just generally *at home* around them, with her hands in the dirt, her eyes shut—not tightly, but just softly closed. As if when she's with them, they help her remember some other home. Which is weird, considering she was born in the Arctic.

Or at least the Arctic is where Dad and his research crew found her, along with a hundred or so other infants, in a ship, all alone. Not a parent or any other human in sight, just a hundred or so babies all alone in the Arctic. I shiver, and it's not just from the thought of the cold.

I look at Callie in the rearview. Her eyes are still sorry, but her face is going toward the window, and for a second I think she's watching the lights of the highway count us down to the hospital. But then I realize she's looking at herself and her sad and sorry eyes.

"Hey, kid sister," I say. "Callie?" I say. She almost turns around.

The fits have been getting worse. Mom calls them "conniptions," but there's no way I'll ever say that word out loud where anyone could hear it. Whatever they are, they're getting worse, and they're happening to my sister, who can't ever tell me what it's like to be her. Whenever I look into her eyes I feel like I can almost see it, except I know that's just me wishing I could tell a story about a time and place where everyone can be understood, where we are all able to really get to know another person and hold them close and find real comfort in that, and then we all have a pizza party and build a tent in the living room and make a scale model of the solar system and hang it from the ceiling and then go to college and then get good jobs, and the economy is stable, and the government is just, and the story only ends when nobody is scared of being alive anymore.

Stories are pretty great if you don't mind crying sometimes.

Callie's eyes are full of something I don't have the words for, and the lights of the hospital are just ahead.

TWO

IN THE HOSPITAL, everything is fine.

Callie looks at the lights and the door, and after we find a parking spot close to the entrance she seems to pull it together enough to help me help her up and out of the backseat and into the lobby. I open the door for Callie, because the child locks have been on for the past few weeks, and if you were to ask me why, then I'd tell you a story about coming home one day and finding Callie sitting in the backseat of my car. Or another story that's different but the same, about coming home and finding Callie furiously packing and unpacking suitcases. And anyway, the child locks have been on for the past few weeks.

Callie grows calmer with each step we take toward the automatic doors, and I can't help thinking that it might not be fair for me to assume that she's actually pulled herself together. I can't tell if this is a situation she even has the ability to pull together, whether or not her growing calm after the worst of these fits is her attempt to control something uncontrollable, something big and terrifying that grips her in a scary part of her brain she can't ever do a thing about. I want to ask someone about this, but I don't really know who or how to ask in such a way that won't make them look at me weird, or even worse, look at Callie weird, the way they'd look at someone who they think should be taken away to be observed in an environment away from "outside factors." Because I'm pretty sure I fall under the category "outside factors."

"Outside factors, kid sister," I say to Callie, and she smiles a bit but doesn't look at me. I should talk to her more, I think. "I should talk to you more, huh?" I say, and she smiles a bit more, and I smile back. Finally she looks at me and then again over to the hospital, but her smile's gone now. Her mouth took it back and instead gave her an expression I don't know how to read.

"Sometimes," I tell her, "I think we're like different editions of the same book."

I know that this doesn't make any sense, but it maybe sounds nice.

AND SO HERE we are, in the hospital.

As a government-mandated condition of caring for an Arctic Recovery Orphan (which is the official term for Callie and the others found in the Arctic when they were infants), there are regularly scheduled check-ins with what my parents call a "caseworker." What Callie's particular "case" is is something I couldn't tell you if I wanted to. I would, though. Want to. But nobody asked me. Or told me. Nobody tells me much of any use, at any rate.

Anyway, here we are in the lobby, and Jane, Callie's caseworker, is walking toward us in a professional hurry, walking quickly yet in such a way that it's clear she doesn't want anyone to think she's walking toward anything urgent, which only makes everything look even more urgent, and nobody is comfortable about any of this.

"Hi, Lorna," Jane says. She's coming out to greet us now, walking down a hallway I've never been allowed to enter. She's wearing a white lab coat, but otherwise she's dressed like a vaguely stylish but relatively severe woman who is somewhere between older-than-college and probably-younger-than-my-parents. "I have to say," she goes on, "it's a bit surprising to see you so soon after Callie's last check-in." She puts her hand on my shoulder a beat or two after she finishes her sentence, as if she had to think of the gesture before making it. Either that or I just don't like her and find everything she does slightly annoying. "I have to ask: Is everything okay?"

"Oh, sure. I drove here at eleven o'clock on a school night because things are just swell" is what I don't say. I stare at her for a minute, then I tell her, "Callie had a fit, and it was not the smallest?" Jane nods and looks from me to Callie. "She was watching this carnivorous plant doc on YouTube," I continue. "And then all of a sudden I heard her, having the fit, from upstairs with my door closed. When I went down and found her, I got worried enough to get her in the car and come down here." And I stop there, because that is roughly as honest as I am willing to be with Jane.

I know that with doctors you're only hurting yourself if you don't tell them how bad you're really feeling on a pain scale of one to ten—if they don't know how bad you're hurting, then they don't know how to treat you. But the thing about doctors is that after you tell them your symptoms, they tell you what's going on and what they need to do to fix it. And that's not something I feel like I get with Jane.

"Oh dear," says Jane. "Well, let's take her back and see if we can't figure out what the trouble is. Poor Callie, we love her so. She's just one of the sweetest girls I've ever been able to work with."

"Great," I say, then catch myself. "I mean, I like her too," I say.

"I'll need her back, though. I've kind of gotten used to having her around the house."

Jane just looks at me, and I look right back. She smiles, then takes Callie by the hand and goes through the doors and down that hall, and once again I'm not allowed to follow.

I go back to the lobby and sit down in a waiting room chair. I text Dave, Dad, and Mom, in that order. Dad gets confused by group texts, which I learned in a pretty awkward way that I'd rather not go into, so Mom and I agreed that we would not do group texts, for the sake of all of us.

Everyone has something to say in response, but mostly I don't care. Right now, all I care about is Callie and about getting home and going to bed. I tell my parents I can handle it, and Dad responds with nothing but confidence, and Mom responds with a hesitant OK, but call us if u need us and we'll be right there!!!! I text Dave a whole bunch of kiss emojis and tell him again how I'm sorry, and he tells me not to even think about it, there's nothing to even be sorry about, and I almost believe him.

The main question people have for us is how Callie, non-lingual and subject to fits, spends her days. Well, one of the perks of my mom's position as a tenured college professor is that she usually ends up teaching, like, two classes a semester. There are office hours, but she shares a lab with Dad in our house, which means there's pretty much always someone at home with Callie. And when there's a blue moon and all of us have obligations outside the house at the same time, there's a never-ending supply of grad students looking to get on my parents' good sides.

I scan the hospital waiting room. There are a couple of coughing children sitting near me, along with a whole handful of parents whose expressions range from worried to bored. Suddenly, two more teens on the other side of the room start having mild seizures, and I'd say they were Arctic Orphans too, except they look like they're too old. One of the parents seems to think everything's totally fine, nothing to worry about here, and the other kid's parent is totally freaking out. But from the way she's freaking out, I can't tell if it's more that she's embarrassed, as if she's hoping nobody else sees this, or that somebody will come to help very, very soon. Then I start thinking that maybe it's both of these things. That she's hoping somebody's going to come and say to her child, "I know this is scary and hard, but it's okay, and it'll be okay." Wouldn't it be nice if there were someone who could just come up to you and say that, and you would believe them, and it would be true?

The freaked-out woman is starting to put me on edge, so I look away and see, sitting across from me, Stan.

Stan is like me in that he has a brother who is also an Arctic Recovery Orphan, whose name is Ted, I think, but I'm not 100 percent sure. Ned? Anyway, I can't remember the last time I saw Stan, but here he is now, in gym shorts and new but dirtied Nikes and a hoodie. We've been together in this waiting room enough times that I smile and wave at him now. But we've never really talked before, and never outside the hospital. For some reason there isn't, like, I don't know, a listserv or a message board for people like us. It's not as if the government or whoever makes up the rules for our sisters and brothers has actively tried to make sure that none of us ever meet, but it's also not as if anyone's ever encouraged it.

I've seen Stan, like, three times, and I've never seen his brother before. Once, *once*, maybe three years ago, I remember he and I were sitting with our parents in this very same room, waiting for Callie. Jane, her caseworker, came out alone, and Stan and I both stood up to greet her, and his eyes fell a bit when she came over to us instead of him. That's how I figured out who Stan was and why he was there. Later I saw Jane talking to him, and I heard her say "conniption," and it is not like everyone just goes around saying "conniption" like it's a fashionable new turn of phrase. So it's always a bit weird to see him here, I guess. Seeing Stan could mean that his brother and my sister are having seizures at the same time.

I want to ask Stan if his brother's getting weirder too. And also about Jane and what he thinks of her.

See, Jane always talks to me in this sweet, concerned, authority-figure voice. But her eyes are cold. She'll be smiling at me and calling me "dear," but she'll look at me with these eyes that let me know that my life or death would mean nothing to her. Maybe I'm just being melodramatic or projecting because here she is, this stranger who is in total control of Callie and what happens to her during check-ins and after she has fits. And because I know all about what's involved in caring for and about Callie, knowing that is a little terrifying to me. And I've seen how her posture changes as soon as she walks away from me, like she only cares about making me see her as kind and nurturing for as long as I'm in her line of sight. Anyway, suffice it to say, I'm not her biggest fan.

"Hey," I say to Stan, after we catch each other's eyes. "How's yours?"

He kind of coughs and kind of laughs, and then he takes down his hood as if to let the world in a little. "Been better," he says.

"Mine too."

"Sorry to hear it."

"Mine too."

He smiles at that, which is nice, but he does it in this way that makes me think it's been a while.

"So," I say.

"So."

"Is he getting worse? Than usual?"

He takes a breath and holds it in a bit.

ICELING

"I know how weird it is to talk about them. You know, with any-one besides family. And Jane," I say. He looks at me like he agrees, so I lean in, and I decide I'm just going to go for it. "But my sister *is* getting worse, and I don't really have anyone to talk to about it. She's been having fits more and more, and, I don't know, maybe I'm just being paranoid, but I feel that if I talk to my parents, all they'll do is worry and maybe just make things worse, and if I talk to Jane . . . I don't even want to know."

"Ugh, Jane," he says, then pauses to think. "Jane is either, like, a vice principal desperate for you to like her, or she's completely terri-fying and her whole life is a front.

"Ted's," he starts, but then stops. "I don't know how your sister is," he says, restarting. "I used to like to think that, like . . . that they were all the same. But now I feel like maybe they're not." He pauses, looking more thoughtful than I would have assumed he could. "Ted is pretty aggressive. My dad has us, like, wrestle, to let his aggression out. We can play football. We can't really play basketball. When I say 'football,' I mean my dad throws me passes and Ted tries to tackle me. And when we play 'basketball,' it's just layups and dunks. And his fits," he tells me, "have been getting rough. Dad feels as though this means we should work harder to give Ted outlets."

"And what do you feel?" I ask.

Stan shrugs. He makes a face, and then another one, but I can't read either and don't know if I want to try to right now.

"With Callie," I say, giving him a break from talking about Ted, "what's scary is how quiet and under control she is until something just, like, grabs her."

So I go on and tell him how her body is calm, but her eyes look to me like she wants to escape. But maybe "escape" isn't the right word. It's more like she's running from something, but she doesn't know what it is, or if she does know she's afraid to think about it, and she *can't* escape it, and it's everywhere. And it's like I think that maybe when I'm feeling like everything is calm and under control, maybe it actually isn't. I tell him how sometimes I feel like maybe she's *always* fighting this thing.

I stop talking, and he just looks at me. I don't know what to say. I want to ask him for his number, so we can keep talking like this. Before I can think more about it, I'm handing him my phone to have him put his number in it. Just as he's finishing up, I hear someone saying something about needing a turkey wrap on rye with pastrami instead of turkey. Someone else says, "That's not a real thing," and then the first person responds, in vaguely threatening overtones, saying something along the lines of "You know what will happen if she finds out failure is even on the table as an option."

All of which seems pretty extreme for a hospital, let alone a dinner order. Who gets that serious about dinner? Then Jane comes striding through those doors to that hallway.

She beckons me over, as if I'm simultaneously her best friend and a worker minion over whom she can exert some ominous administrative authority. I got my phone back from Stan just before she walked through the doors, but she's still looking at it in my hand like she wants to ask me about it. But she doesn't.

"Lorna, dear," she says instead, "has Callie been acting . . . strange? Lately?"

Whenever Jane calls me "dear," I feel like a deer, in that I feel like she is trying to trap me or track me. I am not completely certain about this metaphor, but I *am* certain about this feeling.

I try to look thoughtful before telling her no, and then I put on a face of sincere determination to make sure she knows I have nothing more to say on the matter. "Things are fine, you know, other than the fits."

"She hasn't seemed . . . I don't know . . . anxious to travel or leave the house or anything like that?" Her face, while she's saying this, looks totally inquisitive, but like she's acting. Like she wants this answer from me, an answer she already knows, and for a minute I want to give it to her.

"I mean," I say and then stop, because I haven't thought my answer through, and I'm starting to think that I need to start being more cautious around Jane. "No."

"Okay!" says Jane. She says it like *Wow, what a relief!* And there's this flicker of something on her face for an instant. As if she's silently trying to tell me how no is totally a good answer to give and I did a great job giving it. "Well, long story short, Callie's *fine*. Nothing to worry about! I know it was scary, but it was nothing major. We still don't know exactly what happened to those poor children abandoned up there like that. All of us involved just shudder to think . . ." And her words trail off as she actually shudders here. "Anyway. It's clear your sister loves you very much, Lorna. You're such a genuinely calming presence to her." She puts her hand on my shoulder again, just a beat faster than last time.

THREE

"SO ... SHE'S FINE?" I ask. "I can see her?"

"All of Callie's treatments are closed to friends and family," Jane says. "You know that, Lorna."

Right. I do. Because of "the rules."

So, pretty much right after the babies were brought back from the Arctic, the government came up with a guide for adoptive families about the care and treatment of Arctic Recovery Orphans. Some of the more memorable selections are as follows:

> *-To ease the transition to American culture, and to ensure companionship, only those adoptive parent(s) with at least one existing biological child no more than one year older than the Arctic Recovery Orphans (AROs) are eligible to participate in the Arctic Recovery Orphan Adoption Program (AROAP).*
>
> > *-Before taking AROs on extended (three days or lon-*

ger) trips or vacations, doctors and caseworkers must give medical clearance and assign in-network care providers in areas of travel, in case of emergencies.

-All adoptive parents must sign a medical waiver stating that the government-appointed caseworker—not the adoptive parents/legal guardians—will serve as medical proxy and/or in loco parentis decision-maker regarding all medical issues and emergencies.

-Make sure AROs stay hydrated, as they will easily become dehydrated, exhibiting such symptoms as fatigue, jaundiced and flaky skin, and a generally depressed disposition.

-Conniptions are common and expected in AROs. Conniptions, however, should always be reported. Not all conniptions are alike, but common symptoms are as follows:

- The ARO appears to be in distress.
- His or her eyes may be rolling up in his or her head.
- His or her limbs may be flailing about.
- He or she may be exhibiting behavior that warrants outside attention.

And then there's this particularly instructive section:

-To prevent any ARO from becoming the topic of gossip or conjecture among curious, confused, or otherwise uncouth strangers, be up front about who the ARO is and where he or she comes from. Inform interlopers that your adopted child is an ARO and is therefore a victim of trauma. Inform them that even though your adopted child cannot speak, they are nevertheless a human being and should be treated thusly. [I can never tell if this one should freak me out, or if I should

be glad that someone came up with the idea to dole out a polite, reasonable line to use in these uncomfortable but inevitable situations. Although referring to everyone else as "interlopers" is really weird, and also, you wonder what had to happen for someone to come up with this idea/polite line in the first place. Right?]

-*Sunlight is a must!* [I'm kidding. I think. Although there is another pamphlet, and it says something like "AROs require plenty of personal space and privacy—the same amount as your biological child—and a private bedroom with access to windows. And also, please have a garden."]

-*All Arctic Recovery Orphans must attend monthly medical check-ups at their designated hospitals. Friends and family members are strictly forbidden in the exam room during check-ups.*

So, yeah, Jane. I know the rules. And I want to see my sister.

"Most of these rules seem just as arbitrary to me as they do to you," says Jane unconvincingly. "But we do need to follow them. Though, honestly, you probably know more about the history behind those rules than many of my colleagues." She means because of my parents. "When your father found those poor babies . . ."

Yes, Jane, I *know*.

But I like the way I tell it better. It's the 1990s, and it's very cold. My mom and dad are part of a university-funded expedition, but my mom can't make this particular trip due to me being a baby that she just had. And so! It is very cold in the Arctic, on their ship, en route to this remote Arctic island that has been exhibiting some completely bizarre seismic activity. Suddenly, off the portside bow, a crew member spots another ship. They try to signal to it; it doesn't respond. My dad and a couple of others board the ship, and they find it completely abandoned. Except for hundreds of infants, who happen to be totally and completely silent, just huddled there with no parental supervision or guidance, just a bunch of really quiet and totally alone babies, on an abandoned ship, in the middle of the Arctic.

So my dad and his team haul the babies on board. And then, as if this day wasn't already full of sadness, most of the babies end up dying. From the state and style of the boat, the scientists deduce that it probably came from some Balkan state and that someone had hurried all of the babies into it before pushing it off to sea in some desperate attempt to give them a fighting chance at a life. But that's just conjecture. I guess wherever they came from was a place that was already full to the brim with some fate worse than death at sea. Because whatever's happening around you that makes you think putting a hundred babies into a boat and setting it adrift, unmanned, into the sea . . . whatever makes you think that *that* is the safest alternative . . . whatever that is must be horrifying.

And so my dad and his team shelter and feed and care for the babies that live. And soon they notice that something seems off. Though they seem to be able to see and hear, and they understand what food is, and they understand blankets, they don't react to normal stimuli. Other than some screams, they're basically totally silent. Which to me and based on what I know about babies doesn't seem so odd, but to these scientists it was something worth getting alarmed about.

So Dad alerts the sponsors of the university-funded expedition, and he wrangles permission to bring the babies to the United States, where they will be processed into adoptive families that meet a very specific set of requirements, some of which we've already discussed.

Jane is still going on with her version of the story, but I think she's wrapping it up. She gives a heavy sigh and tells me Callie will be right out, and then she is, escorted by a familiar-looking doctor in a lab coat that matches Jane's. I want to say bye to Stan, but I also can't tell if we're not supposed to know about each other. So what I do is I text Stan: stan it's lorna. this is me saying goodbye, like a spy, because of jane. i hope ted's ok. :/ Stan almost looks up at me, but instead he makes a small smile and texts back: Good thinking. We r real spies now. And thanks. Me too.

And then there's Callie.

I almost feel bad about throwing my arms around her in front of Stan, considering all he's maybe had to deal with. But I do anyway, I hug her close, and I smile, and I feel her hug me back a bit too. Which is not her usual thing, but man, it is nice right now.

I put my arm around her shoulder and say, "How are things, kid sister?" She sort of looks ahead, and her face doesn't look too sad, or too hurt, and I smile at her, and we make tracks to the door, which will lead us to the parking lot, wherein is parked the car, which will take us home.

I look over at Stan, who has to wait around for Ted a while longer. He waves, like *It's fine to go, don't wait up for me*, is how I choose to interpret that. As we're heading to the door, I hear Jane say, "Ted'll be with you in a moment, Stan. We gave him a little something to cool him down a bit, nothing to worry about." I look back at Stan one last time before we push through the doors, and from the look on his face, this is not the first time that a conversation with Jane about Ted has ended this way.

Only about a mile into our journey, it starts to rain.

"It's raining," I tell Callie. I glance at her and watch my words wash over her like the rain does over us, here, now, in the car, just gliding off and sliding to the floor in a puddle to be stepped in.

FOUR

IT'S BEEN A few days since the hospital, and Callie's calmed down a bit. Mom and Dad are acting a little off, walking around the house as if trying not to wake a sleeping monster, whispering furtively. Why they would whisper instead of text, I have no idea. I ask Callie if she thinks that Mom and Dad whispering instead of texting has something to do with them being old, and a general reluctance to change or grow or adapt. Callie smiles at me and puts an entire Ritz cracker in her mouth.

"What was that, honey?" asks Mom from the other room, thinking I was talking to her.

"Oh, nothing. I was just talking to Callie. Just remarking on progress and its wants," I tell her.

"Well, look at you," she says, entering the kitchen.

"We have something to tell you, sport," says Dad, coming down the stairs behind her.

"But first," says Mom, "do you have your fake ID on you?"

※

ABOUT FORTY OR fifty minutes later we're sitting at their favorite restaurant, this Italian place, which is great since I gave up being a vegetarian around the time I realized that idealism wouldn't save me from my own feelings, and their chicken parm is amazing. I'm looking over the menu like I have any idea about wine, or like there's any chance I'm going to order anything other than chicken parm. We're in the back, behind a wall that separates us from the rest of the restaurant, with Callie vaguely boxed in, like we usually sit at family gatherings. Callie's going to have the salad, I know, and is right now really into eating all of those breadsticks that are basically sticks.

Me, I'm trying really hard to be nonchalant about Mom's nonchalance about my fake ID. Was she just assuming I have one because she knows all of her college students have had one since freshman year? Or did she actually *find* mine in the laundry or something? I'm starting to worry that all of this is just a trap and a prelude to a big punishment, and then they start in with it, using their sincerest voices. Their change in tone causes Callie to look over at me, smile, and then put an entire dinner roll in her mouth.

"Kid sister," I say to her conspiratorially, "did you just make a joke? 'Cuz of what you did earlier, with the cracker?" Callie stares straight ahead, keeps mum. "And did I just ruin the joke by explaining it?" Probably I did, and I could swear she's nodding at me. "I did," I say, and then the parents begin to speak.

"Honey, we are just so proud of you for the other night."

"Just the proudest, sport."

"Really."

"The way you took care of your sister shows true strength of character. Port in a storm, good in a crisis."

Callie starts nodding again, assuming she even stopped in the first place, after I ruined her joke. Mom and Dad are looking at me and smiling, and so is she. Or that's *why* she's smiling, because Mom and Dad are. I can look at it however I want, right? Because I'm special and important and reliable and basically the world's best big sister.

"Tom, what are you getting?" Mom shifts topics when the server arrives to take our orders. The server smiles at us, but especially at Callie. Everyone here loves Callie. She's cute, she smiles, she's quiet, and she has never had a fit here. When we were littler, I used to think we should just live here and then she'd be fine forever.

Dad gets the oxtail ravioli in a bone marrow sauce, Mom the linguine with lobster. I get the chicken parm, and then they ask for a Montepulciano or something, and we get wineglasses all around. Except Callie. Obviously. I order Callie a few salads, because Mom's doing her thing of sort of talking around her, and Dad's doing his thing where he includes her in the conversation, even though, you know, no language.

The appetizers and the first of Callie's salads come. Do I take some of Dad's fried calamari? I do. Does Callie take them off my plate? She does. Does anyone else notice how adorable this is? They do not seem to.

"Listen, sport," Dad says halfway through dinner. "We have an announcement. There's a research expedition coming up. In the Galápagos Islands."

Wait. Are they going to invite me? They could be inviting me! Visions of beachside accommodations, giant turtles—there are giant turtles there, right?—begin to fill my head, then Dad speaks up again.

"There's all kinds of weird stuff going on down there in terms of seismic/meteorological confluences."

"The amount of activity is *ridiculous* for that area," Mom adds. "It makes hardly any sense. We could almost explain it away as some kind of wandering pressure system, but that doesn't really explain the seismic stuff, and we haven't seen something like this in *years*, and I've never even seen it up close."

I start to tune out a bit, because I know for a fact that I'm not going to follow any of this, and they haven't invited me yet, which means the chances that they will are growing slimmer by the second. *No vacation for us, kid sister*, I mouth to Callie, who has already finished her salad.

"But anyway, sport," says Dad, "here's the thing."

Wait. Are they going on this trip together?

"We're going on this trip together," Mom says.

Because they never go on trips together. Because one of them always stays home with me and Callie. Those are the rules. I mean, Callie isn't some *freak* or anything, but she's special, and she has needs and thrives best in certain conditions, so when these trips happen one of them always stays home with us.

"And we feel totally confident leaving you home with Callie for a few weeks."

Well.

I pour us all a bit more wine, and they smile at each other and at me, and for some reason I'm feeling a little weird right now. I think about how we've watched movies together where the parents go out of town, and almost immediately the kids start running through the house drunk and naked, and then Mom says something like "What kind of idiots would leave their kids alone and expect something like this *not* to happen?"

Maybe Callie's the reason they're so cool with this? Like I wouldn't dare have a party at our house because doing so would be uncomfortable and scary for my sister? But honestly I kind of think they just haven't even thought of it. Like maybe they've waited my whole life to do something like this together, and now, for the first time, they can, because I'm just barely grown up enough to take care of stuff. They're talking about something else now, but I'm basically lost in these thoughts, and it takes me a minute to focus back on them.

"Anyway, sport. We just want you to know. And you too, Callie!" Dad says, looking at Callie, then looking at Mom.

"That this is just one of the many reasons why we know we can always count on you, always, no matter what," Mom finishes.

"For real and for always."

"Exactly."

"Thanks, guys," I say. "And, I was just wondering . . ."

"Yes?" says Dad.

"Well," I say, finishing my glass of wine, "I was just wondering, since I'm the world's greatest big sister and all, when am I going to get my trophy, and my certificate, my cash reward . . ."

Mom laughs, and Dad says, "Your certificate's at the print shop, kid," and Mom finishes his glass of wine.

※

ON THE WAY home, Callie naps next to me, though it's impossible to tell whether or not she's actually sleeping.

Dad looks back at us in the rearview and asks, "How's Callie been?"

"She's been fine," I tell him.

He looks at me in the mirror and makes his face into the shape of a question, and that question is: *Really?* And it is real skeptical.

I tell him that since the hospital she's been fine, if not *better* than fine. I tell him that if I were worried, I'd let them know. It works okay, I guess. His face unfurls from its question, and we keep driving.

But the more I think about it, it's weird as hell that they're going on this trip together. I keep thinking about this even though all I want, just for a minute, is to pretend it isn't there, so I could just enjoy this happy family feeling a little bit more.

And I'm tired. And maybe I had a little bit more wine than I should have. And then I hear something.

"We just worry is all," Dad says quietly.

Mom is asleep in the front seat, or so it seems. Then, more to himself, I think, than to me, Dad says, "That day . . . that day, it . . . just. It just wasn't what we were expecting to find out there. But mostly what I remember was the sky. My God. It was purple and yellow, and it smelled like lightning, but I couldn't see any. Do you know what lightning smells like? Don't. Don't know that. And the clouds were so low and heavy and with a mind of their own, opening a hole in the sky to let the light in," he says. He says this to whom, I don't know.

"How did you guys find the boat?" I ask.

"The boat?" he says, as if just remembering that I'm in the car with him. "The boat. The boat was . . . just *there*. It was just there. In the middle of all this, there they all were." He pauses. "I can't imagine what it would be like to come out the other end of whatever they came out the other end of. I can't imagine what it would be like to be . . . to not have the words . . . to not have *any* words to put to your experiences."

Then he tells me—or himself, I still can't tell—"You're a good sister, Lorna. You've got a good heart even if you like to keep it under wraps sometimes. There's nothing wrong with that, but just be careful."

He tells me, "I love you, sport."

And then we're home.

FIVE

I MAKE PLANS to see Dave tonight, this time at his house so I don't have to do the same old dancing-around-my-parents thing that both of us hate.

Can't wait to see you, he texts, and I tell him, same, with the hearts-for-eyes emoji.

I got the sense at dinner tonight that we were all scared that Callie was going to have another fit while we were out. They've been ramping up, getting more intense and unusual ever since that night Dave was over and we had to go to the hospital. Also, it wouldn't have been the first time she would have had a fit while we were out to dinner. But it didn't happen, and there was a feeling of relaxation during the whole car ride home, and it wasn't just that we all had something to drink at dinner, I don't think.

But then as soon as we got back, Callie ran to the garden and stuck her hands in the dirt and wouldn't budge until two in the morning. I sat there with her, rubbing her back, until I started dozing off a little. And then I dozed off a lot. I fell asleep basically on top of her, my arms draped over her back, and she woke me up, gently poking me in the cheek with her dirty fingers, staring at me with something like worry. When I opened my eyes, she closed hers like she was asleep too. "Bedtime, kid sister," I said. She smiled, as if she understood me, as if she'd only just had the idea to go to sleep now, as opposed to at nine thirty when we first got home and instead of running upstairs she ran to the garden to tend to the dirt in the ground.

I go back to my contacts list and open a new text window. hey, I text Stan. how's yr arctic brother? Having never texted Stan before, or ever even talked to him before the hospital the other night, maybe it's weird to just ask him about his brother, right out of the blue. But Callie has been acting stranger and stranger, even for Callie. Even before the hospital and definitely a lot more since that night, she's been running outside to the driveway and getting into my car. She'll just sit there in the passenger seat, looking as though she's waiting for me to get in and take her somewhere. Which, okay, fine—she does odd stuff sometimes, but usually when she gets back from the hospital after a bad fit, she's great! Things go back to "normal" for a while. But this time, it seems like she's getting, for lack of a better word, worse. And if I tell Mom and Dad, they'll just want to take her back to Jane, and since that just seemed to make her worse, or at least not make her better, this time . . . Anyway, I'm starting to wonder if maybe Stan's brother might be getting stranger too. And if he is, well . . . then what does that even mean? And who else can I talk to about this? Stan is literally the only person I know who would have any idea what this is like.

My phone buzzes almost immediately after I press send, and for a second I think Stan must be a weirdo who just stares at his phone all day, but then I see it's not from him, but Dave. Let me know what you want me to get for dinner, and then the pizza, donut, bento box, and question mark emojis. all of the above pls, I text, and Dave says, On it.

I switch back to Stan's window and put my phone facedown on my desk and wait. I don't know why I feel anxious, but I do. I can't stop thinking about the night at the hospital and how it was weird in a way I can't put my finger on. I decide to stop thinking about that and instead think some more about Dave and about why I don't want him to meet my parents, because it can't just be that they'll like him, right? *Spite can't be, like, the only thing going on here,* I think to myself hopefully.

And then the phone buzzes, and this time it's from Stan. Hi Lorna. Um. Ted's OK? Things are OK?

oh, cool. glad to hear it. callie's fine too, I type.

And then some time passes, and I stare at my phone, because apparently texting with Stan is roughly as awkward as trying to talk to Stan while seeing if he'll look you in the eye. Or, it's not that it's *awkward*, it's just that I just get the feeling that Stan has even more of a guard up than I do. And from what he was telling me about his dad having him wrestle with his brother to calm him down, and basically being a kind of a human tackle dummy, maybe there's good reason for a boy with a brother like that to not talk so openly about things. And I *was* kind of freaked out by all that stuff, honestly. It seemed pretty weird to me. But then I looked over the rules again. I'd be embarrassed to say how often I do that, but I do. Anyway, there is this bit in there that basically says that our Icelings are special and that we should learn to understand their specialness. It wasn't clear if that was a suggestion for the parents or for us, the siblings, or for the person who was writing it. The emphasis on the *need to understand the individual specialness* of each Iceling . . . it got me thinking about how I really just have no idea what Callie's been through. Let alone what Stan or Ted have been through. And about that whole nature versus nurture thing. About whether it's our biological imperatives or our home lives that shape us. But why is that even up for debate? Of course it's both. Why can't we just say it's both?

Anyway, maybe the wrestling has to do with what Ted's individual specialness is. Ted's loud. For someone who has no access to language, of course. And Callie—Callie's quiet. And anyway, the rest of that section in the guidebook is about establishing a baseline for behavior. Like: Understand the individual specialness of each Iceling, so that if they start getting weird, you'll know whether it's just "their way" or if it's the kind of thing to notify an authority figure about. This was something that no one ever really went over with me. Also, the guidebook doesn't call them "Icelings." I do. I'm the only one who calls them that. And anyway, look. Over there. My phone. It buzzes.

Actually is it weird if we talk some time?

I call him, right here and now, because that seems easier than waiting to see what happens next.

"Lorna," he says.

"Stan," I say.

"Hi."

"Hi."

"So."

"So."

"Well."

"Stan," I tell him. "Look. I know we don't know each other that well, or really at all, but it's just that I don't have anyone else to talk to about this. You know? Not that your 'this' is the same as my 'this,' or that I get what you're going through, or that you get what I'm going through. But we both have these siblings we can't talk to, but then we also can't really even talk *about* them with anyone else. You know? I just feel like if I were to talk to my friends about Callie, like, *really* talk to them about it, they'd just stare at me and assume she was a total freak. But then if I talk to my parents about it, or Jane, then I feel like there'd be . . . consequences. To that." I pause, but in such a way where Stan knows that there's still more I have to say. "I feel like you're the only person I can talk to about Callie," I continue, "and that maybe *I'm* the only person you can talk to about Ted, and nothing bad'll happen because of it."

Unless the government's listening. HA HA HA, I think but don't say.

Then it's quiet for almost a minute, which I know because I check my phone to see if he's still there.

"Hi, sorry," he says at second fifty-three. "It's just . . . ugh, man. Yeah."

And then it's quiet again.

I'm about to just plow through with my own plan and start talking about Callie when he starts talking again.

"So my mom left a couple of years ago. We were on a trip, me and Dad and Ted, and when we came back she was gone. So that sucked. But I got pretty okay at cooking. Which is nice? Ted is just . . . he's aggressive as hell. He walks around the house like . . . well, not like he wants to *fight*. But like he's convinced that, at any moment, someone's going to want to fight him. Does that make sense?"

"Kind of?" I say, but then I think that yeah, that actually makes a lot of sense.

"So, like, hands in his pockets, but really shoved in there. And his eyes aren't exactly . . . *furtive*, but I can see them trying to take in the whole room, all at once. He doesn't like to be touched or anything. I think 'bristles' is the word you could use for what he does when anyone tries to touch him. Yeah, 'bristles at contact.' That's definitely something I read in some file of his somewhere. And. Um. What are . . . Callie's? Fits like?"

"They're . . . well . . . I guess it depends. The one that I took her to the hospital for the last time I saw you was weird. A lot of the time, she'll just start making fists, really tight ones, with her fingers digging into her palms. And then she'll hit her thighs while kicking at the air or whatever is around, and sometimes she falls down, and her mouth is open. I used to think it was her version of a scream, but without any sound. But now it's more like . . . I think it's like she's try-ing to get something out. Or something's trying to get out of her, but I don't know which. And I don't know what, and I don't know why. A few weeks ago, she was out gardening, and I found her out there with her hands in the ground, just trying to dig herself a hole. But her eyes were almost rolling up in her head, and her mouth was shut, like she was trying to keep it that way, or like something had tripped a trap."

"Tripped a trap?" Stan says.

"Yeah, like a bear trap or something. Like something came along—whether it should or shouldn't have, I don't know—and her mouth was a trap, and she had to snap it shut and keep it that way so whatever came along couldn't get out. That's what it looked like to me, anyway. But then the other day, I was up in my room and I heard this noise from downstairs, so I go downstairs, and there's Callie, my sister, on the ground, her eyes wide open, her legs curled up into her chest while her arms flail at the air, like she's digging her way through the air. And she was making sounds like nothing I've ever heard from her before. And then suddenly she was up on her feet and just . . . shaking. Like she was *being* shaken. And I almost feel like if that last part hadn't happened, where she stood up, I might not have been able to get her in the car to the hospital."

"Seems scary."

"It was. I'd never seen her like that before."

After a pause Stan says, "Ted runs into things. We've got punch-ing bags in basically every room at this point. Dad's tried to get him to run at them on purpose, and it sometimes works. The only thing that actually helps is if I can get him in a nelson. You know, with my arms coming up under his shoulders from behind, and I grab around the back of his neck, and then I try to . . . sit on him, more or less. Immobilizing him seems to help—calm him down, I mean. Not just get him to stop moving. But it always has to be me that does it, I think, for it to work. Dad used to try, and he could never calm him. Mom tried once, and he thrashed so hard he broke her nose. His arms sort of thrash around, and he just finds something to run into. His jaw goes all slack when he does it. Like he's hypnotized. And I don't know if he'd stop if I didn't stop him. I came home once to Mom sitting at the top of the stairs, watching him. 'It's been four hours,' she said. Then she said it again. Then she stood up. Then I had to wrestle him to the ground, and Dad came home and took us to the hospital.

"Ted," Stan said, sighing, "isn't the easiest little brother in the whole world."

"Our Icelings seem pretty different," I say stupidly.

"Icelings?"

"Oh yeah, sorry. So that's a word I made up. Like a portmanteau of 'ice' and 'sibling.' It just . . . seemed better than calling my sister a capital-*O* Orphan, you know?"

"Yeah, I do." Then a pause. "It's still not very . . . humanizing, though, is it?"

"No," I admit. "It isn't."

"That's probably right," he says quietly.

And something in me sings out, because this is it. This is the thought I have but that I ignore all the time, because I don't ever know what to do with it. And because I don't know that I'll ever be okay speaking that thought aloud, I just say this: "Not that they're not human! Just that . . . I mean, *something* must have happened, right? And we can never understand it or know it, because we don't know what it's like to think or do anything without language to do it with.

We have parents we know are ours, who've been talking to us since before we were born. And we go to school, and most of the time we learn things, and when people talk to us we have some idea of what to do or say in response. And for the most part, we know what's expected of us." I stop for a second, making sure he's still there and that it's safe to go on. "And they don't. Not at all. They don't, and we have to see that every day. And they have to see whatever they're seeing every day. And know that all we can do is try to be, like, *mediators* between them and the world. But nobody can be careful enough to do this job right."

"Yup. Pretty much Suck City."

And he's right, it is.

But even if Suck City's where we're both living, at least now we know that we're neighbors. We can start a neighborhood watch program. Maybe even elect a new mayor, who supports better education and immigration policies and has socially progressive views. Or maybe we start up an underground militia to bring about the revolution, the one where everything finally works out, and there's income redistribution, and women make as much as men. And there's free education and healthcare for everyone, and everyone is finally okay with being scared of things that are different. I don't know. I'm just wishfully thinking about the possibilities of life in Suck City. The point is: Stan and I know we're not alone in this anymore. And that's kind of amazing.

We tell each other we'll call or text if anything weird happens or if we just need to talk. Which I have a feeling will be relatively soon. Because I feel like we've both barely even seen the tips of the giant icebergs of our feelings about our lives with our Icelings. I know that I feel as though Callie is my sister. And I love her. And something happened to her that I don't understand, and all I want, all I've ever really wanted in my life, aside from a Barbie house and a boyfriend and a car—none of which were as cool as I thought they'd be, except the car—is to understand and be understood by my sister. To look in her eyes and see her looking in mine and to hold that feeling like that. I can see it; I know it's in there. But it moves around. And I can't tell who understands whom. And Stan and Ted. It seems like Stan just feels like he's only there to keep Ted under control. Like that's all his dad wants or needs from him, and all Stan ever seems to feel is that it's his responsibility to prevent more bad things from happening. And I have no idea what any of this means, or what to do with the way it makes me feel, or the way it makes Stan or Callie or Ted feel, for that matter. But here they are.

Here are my feelings.

SIX

MY PARENTS LEAVE for the Galápagos in two weeks, which is apparently all the advance warning they think I need before they leave the family home—and Callie—in my capable, responsible, and wholly trustworthy hands.

So while I still have them here, I'm mostly just out driving all the time with my best friend, Mimi. The thing about Mimi is she's amazing. And so cool, and she wears animal prints always and to the extent that when she's not wearing them, I get very seriously worried. I like that with Mimi, and I guess also with Callie, I know what my job is. I love it. I know how to be around them. With Mimi, my job is to be quiet, and to listen, and to participate when called upon. I drive, and she talks about her future, in which Mimi's decided she'll go to school in New York and intern at *Rookie* or somewhere like it.

"The thing is," she says, "wherever you end up, you're probably just going to be updating mailing lists and getting coffee. But at least at a smaller place, unlike, say, *Vogue,* it could probably turn into something more. Not in terms of, like, money or anything. But experience. And making contacts with people who are above you and know what you should do next."

We see a group of dudes walking on the sidewalk, and Mimi rolls down her window and we start dog calling. Dog calling is like cat calling, except you tell random guys on the street about how you think they'd make great father figures, or that they seem like really responsible men who would probably stay at home in order to help you advance your career, or that they look like they really know how to cook for a lady and make her feel like gender is just a concept and like she is a wonder of individuality, just a pearl of competence.

"Hey, baby!" Mimi says to the entire flock of guys. "I bet you have a good relationship with your parents!"

"I bet you're a great listener!" I shout from the driver's side. "I bet you have a really nice heart!"

"Don't lie—I bet you have a favorite bedtime story that you're dying to tell the child we'd raise together!"

"Wow, good one," I tell Mimi, who winks at me.

"Hey! You should smile more! I bet you have a real nice smile!" I shout as we're driving past, leaving them in the dust.

"So," says Mimi, "how's Dave?"

"Lord, Mimi," I say, sighing. "Can we just be two girls having a conversation that isn't about boys?"

"Sure," Mimi says, powering down her window and yelling at a new guy: "I bet you understand that gender roles are a social construct!"

"I bet you're comfortable enough with yourself to not project a bunch of weird, assumed desires on other people, thus allowing you to communicate with others on a real and sincere personal level, culminating finally in a fulfilling partnership that will last as long as it has to until something else happens totally beyond everyone's control!" I shout across Mimi.

"Damn," Mimi says. "That was something. But seriously. How's Dave?"

"Ugh," I say. "What did he tell you?"

"That you won't let him meet your parents in any sort of official boyfriend capacity."

"His exact words, huh?"

"Verbatim."

"Look. I *like* Dave. I think he's great. But."

"But . . . ? But what?"

"I don't think I . . . love him? I don't think he's the kind of guy I can picture myself, like, being with forever. He's great, and he's cute, and he's basically sincere, and he's kind of smart. But I don't know. I don't like the idea of committing to him, for some reason. I don't feel like he's *that* for me. Like some sort of blinding crush. I don't feel crushed, and I want to. And maybe that's shitty of me. My parents will love him. Because he's great. He's so great! But I don't love him, and that's shitty of me, and there's no way to tell him that. I don't know how to tell him that, and I don't know how to introduce my parents to this totally great guy who I'm really into, but not *super* really into. Because then what happens when *they* fall in love with him, but then one day he's gone, and I'm in college, and they're all, 'So how's Dave?' And then I have to be like, 'Oh, I don't know. Living a wondrous life full of love and promise and finding, I hope, getting emotional fulfillment from whatever and whoever is capable of giving him the sort of emotional fulfillment he so richly deserves!' And they're all, 'What a wonderful life!' and then I can only agree, and then this conversation happens again and again, and per usual all it does is make me feel like I did something wrong by trying to be honest about my feelings."

"Lorna," Mimi says after a pause to make sure I'm done talking, "you realize that, to some people, worrying about something like the intricacies involved in introducing the guy you want to bang to your parents, and the repercussions it could have, like, *years* down the line sounds a little weird. Right?" And I'm about to say, "Yes. Yes, I know this, this is why I keep avoiding your questions about Dave," but before I can, she says, "And this is why I love you," and then I just sort of stare at her.

"You just have this . . . purpose!" she goes on. "This, like, *unshakable* purpose, Lorna." She pauses, and I just keep my eyes on the road, because I'm not super comfortable with people saying nice and smart and precise things about me to my face, so if I stare at the road I can maybe pretend like it's not happening. "It just seems like you really understand what you want out of life, or at least have an idea of the kind of life you want to live. Or at the *very* least the kind of person you want to be. I mean, do you even realize that you're a beacon of light shining in a storm full of awful people who do things like wait for social cues to determine what they're going to do or say or how they're going to be? You're a *person*, Lorna. And you know your life. You know it deeply, even if you don't think you do, and you live it every second of the day." Mimi pauses, and despite myself, I look at her quickly and smile. "I've known you since the first grade," she says, "and it's been like this since always."

And so screw you, Mimi, because what do you say to something like that?

"What the hell, Mimi?" I say. "What am I supposed to say to that? Look at you. You just spent this whole drive telling me about all the things you're going to do to get to the life you know *you* want to have. And you even have backup plans for those plans, and you read about what you want to do, you know the names of the people who've done it and feel totally comfortable approaching them with questions. You figure your shit out all the time! You're amazing to me, and I'm just lost in my own little world, and then you tell me all that, and now I feel like I know even less what to do."

"Look, here's how this will go. I think you're great. You think I'm great. So naturally both of us are going to resist the idea that we're great, and then it'll get weird, and then . . . and then your parents will call you."

"Huh?" I say.

"Your parents, they're calling you now. I can see it on your phone. You probably need to take that, so maybe instead of doing anything, you should just know that you're the best? And then drop me off at home?"

And that is exactly what happens.

I TEXT DAVE when I get home.

> hey bae

> (what)'sup?

> nm u?

> Same. A/S/L? Want 2 chat?

> 42/male/boca

> Hot. Into it.

> thought you might be.

Sometimes I can't tell if we're flirting or just finding new ways to not talk about serious things. Either way, I stare at my screen and the blinking ellipses keep flashing and dying, flashing and dying, so I put my phone in my back pocket where it will later tell my butt when I'm wanted. I check in on Callie, who is sitting upright and on her knees, her long and light blond hair tucked behind her ears. She's examining, really deeply, some large potted plants Mom recently installed for, I'm guessing, just this purpose. She's been doing a lot of this kind of thing— this withdrawing into herself is how I see it—ever since that night after our dinner out, when she sat in the garden until the small hours, her hands worrying around in the dirt. It's not like Callie's ever been some kind of exuberantly social party girl, but this kind of deep, deep withdrawal—it's different, and it's happening more than usual. Sure, she is quiet and really into plants, but considering her total lack of language, she's actually pretty engaged and engaging. So it's weird watching her just sit around quietly staring at plants nearly all the time.

My back pocket buzzes.

How was the dog calling, asks Dave.

vaguely empowering, mostly rewarding.
mimi has gone pro at it. i need to up my
game tbh.

You could try something like "Nice pants,
want a healthy relationship based on
mutual respect and understanding?" or "I
bet you'd make a great stay-at-home dad."

I smile. The thing is, I meant everything I said to Mimi about how I feel—or maybe don't feel—about Dave. But when he says stuff like this, how am I not supposed to want to kiss him on the lips while smiling? And can I want that and also want boundaries? Either way, I text him ugh yr the best, because it's basically true, and he texts me back a blushing emoji, and all in all, Callie and her plant-staring considered, today is a pretty good day.

I get so caught up in this fine feeling that when my butt buzzes again with a message from Stan asking how Callie is, I just text back fine! But then I look back at Callie, who is still looking at her plant, and I ignore the flashing ellipses on Stan's side of the screen and start again.

actually, I text, callie seems maybe a bit weird? like withdrawn. like more so than usual. idk.

Ted keeps walking up to this punching bag in our house. And then he sends me a photo of a boy, Ted almost definitely, standing with his nose up against a punching bag. He's got the same sandy blond hair that Callie has, and her same weird pale skin, but his face is sort of squatter than Callie's. And he's not too tall. Actually, he and Callie are maybe the same height, about five eight.

I type a response: 1) what's rocky there training for? 2) is ted 5-8?

Stan texts back What? and then, Yeah, he is, but also . . . what?

I text him a video of Rocky running up and down the Philly museum steps, and then Weird. Callie is too.

Stan texts back a picture of a Post-it that reads, "ADRIAA-AAAAAN," and I laugh.

"LORNAAAA!" Dad calls, and then it's dinnertime.

At dinner we take turns telling each other what we did all day, except for Callie, who has never told us anything about her day, ever. But the dinner table is quieter than usual tonight. Normally, Mom and Dad will offer up weird trivia about some totally freak weather phenomena they've just discovered or have been tracking. Like when they told us about that time they were on this island they described as "like the state of Indiana, but in the ocean," where they went to see about these sinkholes that would open up before lightning storms, and they were trying to figure out whether the sink-holes were, like, presaging or predicting the storms, or if they were somehow concurrent but unrelated events. Or the time Mom went up in a weather balloon because the lightning sounded like it was singing. Or when they had to call a friend in the archeology depart-ment because a sinkhole revealed a small city or village, but nobody wanted to go in there until a degree-carrying academic gave them the okay.

Anyway, dinner's more entertaining, and less effort for me, when they're working, and tonight we're really struggling to come up with any riveting conversation.

Callie has a salad in front of her that's full of all kinds of exotic greens. Dad's been getting pretty good at picking out exotic-looking seeds for Callie to grow into exotic-looking lettuces for her salads, and Callie's getting pretty good at eating them. I spear a bite of salad from her bowl and make a big show of eating it.

"Sharing is caring, kid sister," I tell her. Callie just looks at me the way I would try to look at someone if I was feeling hurt and con-fused. She looks down to her bowl and over at me, and she looks like she's about to cry, and I feel utterly terrible.

Which is when she grabs a pinch of my green beans with her hands and grins at me.

And then she gets up, bolts from the table, and runs out to the greenhouse. I look over at Mom and Dad and ask, *Should we do some-thing?* with the arches of my eyebrows, but they look back at me with the faces of two people who are used to this and whose flight leaves first thing in the morning. "Don't worry, sport," says Dad. "She's fine."

"Will you clean up, sweetie?" Mom asks. "We need to get to bed pronto if we have any hope of making this flight tomorrow."

"No problem," I tell them, then give them both hugs good night.

I peek out the window to make sure I can see Callie, and once I know she's safe, I text Stan: callie ran out to the greenhouse during dinner.

Ten minutes later, he texts back: Ted ran into the greenhouse during dinner.

wait. for real or are you being funny?

4 real.

I can't help but laugh a bit. wtf, I text.

IDK, he texts. I want to be worried but right now who knows.

And I know just what he means. It isn't like what they've been doing is anything other than what they've always been doing. It just seems like recently there's more of it, all the time. I want to worry about it, but I don't really know how. Or, I guess what I mean is, I have no idea how worried I should be.

So I text back yeah, because, well, yeah.

I GET BARELY any sleep and then wake up early to see Mom and Dad off. They're in the driveway, waving, and I'm waving back, and Callie is next to me and kicking out her legs like a Rockette, but not in any sort of rhythm, which is awkward and adorable, and I decide here and now that this is just her awkward and adorable version of waving. Mom and Dad blow kisses, shout "Be good!" one more time, then get in the car. We watch them drive off into the distance.

And here we are.

I close the door and smile at Callie, who is holding a sleeve of Ritz. She smiles at me too and takes one cracker out, real dramatically, then moves it toward my mouth. I open my mouth, take it, and eat it, and she keeps smiling, and I smile bigger, because I have a sister, and I can't ever hear her voice, but she's still my sister, and she's here, and it's just really, really nice. "Nice" isn't the word, though, not exactly. I'm tired and thinking too much, so I just hug her, and she makes this kind of sighing sound that feels very warm. And I just hold her like that, and she holds me the way she knows how to, and then the doorbell rings.

I open the door to see Mimi, and standing behind her and nearly a foot above her but still acting like he could hide, Dave.

"Uh," I say. "Hello? Fancy seeing you here?"

"You mean you're surprised to see us here, at your house, immediately following your parents' departure for parts unknown?"

"The Galápagos," whispers Dave.

"For the Galápagos unknown?" tries Mimi.

"'Galápagoses unknown' is probably more accurate," whispers Dave.

"Dave," I say, turning to look him right in his sheepish eyes, "you're really not helping your case by helping her here."

"His case?" Mimi says.

"Yup," I say, "the case against Dave."

"There's a case against Dave? What are the charges? Being too sweet and wonderful?"

"Actually, yes," I say. "Supplemented by suspicion of aiding and abetting what I can only imagine is a house party, to take place at *my* house, about which nobody told me, at which minors will be served alcohol."

"You left out that there'll be good times had by all!" says Mimi, with such sheer joy that I actually consider closing the door on her face.

Seriously, though, why would she do this? After everything I told her about Dave and my family and how overwhelmed I am about having to take care of Callie?

Dave must be able to see all of this on my face, because before I can think anything meaner about Mimi, he says, "She just thought you could use a break is all."

"That is *exactly* my thinking here," Mimi says.

I look to Callie, who is calmly chomping a cracker. "Ugh," I sigh. "Fine. How are you getting the booze?"

"My brother, duh," Mimi says.

"Okay, and how many people are coming?"

"All of them." She says this as though she is the literal embodiment of nonchalance.

"All of them?" I say. "What the hell does that mean?"

"It means . . . all of them," Dave says, but he says it like what he really means to say is *I'm sorry*, and it's the right thing to do, him saying it like this, and I'm grateful.

And anyway, even if the whole city shows up, they're probably right. I do need a break. I'm supposed to know this!

"Aren't I supposed to be the one to know if I need a break?" I say.

"Right, because you're the queen of going easy on yourself," says Mimi.

"You're too busy looking out for Callie and other people's feelings is all," Dave says. "Which is why it's our job to keep tabs on this kind of stuff." And once again I feel like a terrible human because I don't know how to let this sweet boy, who says all kinds of sweet things, into my life.

And instead of saying that out loud, I just give in. "Well. I guess we'd better get ready?"

SEVEN

MIMI WASN'T KIDDING—I'm pretty sure everyone I've ever met in my life so far, plus about two dozen strangers, is currently inside my house. Callie's in the greenhouse, and Dave, Mimi, Mimi's brother Mark, and I are going to check on her in shifts. I set alarms on everyone's phones, because I'm basically the world's best and most reliable big sister. Mimi's with her right now, which is why I'm out here in the living room, relaxing and having fun, because everybody knows I am the queen of going easy on myself.

And then I spot a major party foul: This boy I don't know is in the corner of the dining room, singing a cappella to some girls I *do* know, and this move just won't fly.

"Dave!" I call out, to no response. "DAVE!" I call again, still seemingly in vain. "Will someone please get my man? There's a party foul that needs attention!"

That got his attention—though whether it was me calling him "my man" or saying "party foul" I can't be sure—because here he is now. "Dave! And you're wearing a . . . football helmet?" Where did he find a football helmet?

"Babe," he says to me.

"Man," I say to him, and I grab the face cage and pull it down, and I kiss the top of his helmet like they do in shows about football on TV. He grins at me, and I point to the sans-instrument-crooning offender in the corner.

"Mother of God," Dave says. "I had no idea it was this bad. Wait here."

"Dude," Dave calls to the boy as he makes his way toward the dining room. But the boy keeps on going, like he maybe thought Dave was talking to someone else, but then Dave just stops and stands there right in between him and the girls.

"What?" says the boy, pausing his song because he finally gets it now, though still not completely, because it's clear by what we'll call the tone of his voice that he's pretty sure that this interruption is super unwarranted as regards his performance.

"Dude. Buddy. There is no a cappella serenading at this party unless it's a joke or you're asking your girlfriend to dance. And maybe not even then. It's just the policy. And anyway, Lorna says you should leave." He points to me, and I point to the boy, and I do the thumbs-down.

"What? Who's Lorna?" the boy says, still incredulous.

"This is Lorna's party, you jerk! Ugh!" says one of the girls he was singing to, and then another one steps forward and dumps her drink on his head.

"Oof," says Dave. "Buddy, you should maybe consider going home and changing into some dry clothes and maybe thinking about your life and the choices you made that led you here."

"Here?" the boy says.

"Here," says Dave. "Where you got a drink dumped all over you.

And where you are now leaving. Come on, let's go." Then Dave moves to pick up the boy and sling him over his shoulder.

"Hey, man, there's no need for all that," says the boy, trying to dodge Dave and flinging his eyes around the room in what I recognize as embarrassment.

"Yes," says Dave. "Yes, there is." But before he can reach again to hoist him over his shoulder, the boy is gone, out the door and into the night. The only music in the house now is coming from my parents' fancy speakers, and I sigh in what is actually sweet relief.

I chance a look at the rest of the party.

Two of my high school's most famous couples are sitting on the staircase. Both couples are arguing pretty intensely, but I can tell that only one of the pairs, Gordie and Eve, will be broken up before the party's over.

"And another thing!" shouts a voice from above, but then we never get to hear a word about the other thing, because a moment later the owner of the voice—an editor on the student paper named Stephanie—falls down the stairs, her body tumbling between the couples' arguments, then landing, really impressively, with most of her beer unspilt. She goes for the extra point by proceeding to take a sip from her cup while waiting for someone to help her up, so she can tell them the other thing.

One unexpected thing about being a little bit drunk at a party in my parents' house while they're out of town is that it turns me into a neurotic mother hen whose mind is filled with guilty, fearful thoughts and imaginations of the most awful possible outcomes of the night. Thoughts like how this is maybe a terrible idea that will only end in tears, with the house burning to the ground, and Callie the bride in a shotgun wedding. Or like realizations about how much you hate the idea of disappointing your parents, or being disappointed in yourself for worrying about disappointing your parents. Or about how you could just walk away into the night, right behind the beer-soaked a cappella guy, and start a new life somewhere in, like, New Jersey, where nobody would ever go to find you, because who would ever want to go to New Jersey? But of course I won't go to New Jersey—Callie would hate it there, and we'd have to find her an all-new doctor and an all-new Jane—so the only thing I can do is say to myself, "Be cool."

A kind of quiet LCD Soundsystem song comes on, Dave's favorite, and I know he must have plugged his music into the speakers. The varsity lacrosse goalie tries to change the song, and Dave runs over and tackles him. I go to high-five Dave and I kiss him on his neck, which is no longer helmeted, and the song picks up right where it left off. It isn't quiet anymore, and as it crescendos I try to press myself against him as closely as I can, and everyone is dancing.

In between two weirdly synchronized dancers, I spot a kid sitting on the floor by the fireplace reading *Infinite Jest*. Ugh, how pretentious. Not to be reading *Infinite Jest*, I get that that book is important to a lot of people, but to be doing it at a party is just . . . ugh.

"Stay home next time, kid!" I shout at him. He looks up at me and then around the room, like he's startled, like he didn't realize there were people here and a party here and that these things were literally all around him, and then goes right back to his place in the book.

For some reason the sight of this guy doing something so out of place at a party causes the mother hen mode to kick in again, and now instead of focusing on dancing with Dave, I'm trying so hard to ignore the constant rattling off of things that could go wrong. *Shut up, Lorna! We're having fun!* So much fun! Fun like . . . damaged-furniture and cracked-picture-frames fun. Or shameless-strangers-going-upstairs-to-hook-up-in-my-parents'-room fun, or in-my-room or in-Callie's-room fun. I keep dancing, but my heart's not in it, because now all my worries are focused squarely on Callie, even though I know she is still in the greenhouse, with Mimi. But I know I'm still going to go check on her soon because now all I can think about is what if some jerk like Adam or Rick or Dan—oh God, please not Dan, who has not once in his life brushed his teeth—makes a pass at Callie, and then Callie freaks out, and then Adam or Rick or—ugh, God, please not Dan—calls her a freak, or freaks out, or other worse things than that? Or what if some other, even more massive jerk tries to get aggressive with Callie, Callie who can't consent to anything in any way and maybe doesn't even understand at all the sorts of things being asked of her . . . and then I stop thinking about anything at all, because I see Mimi on the other side of the room, dancing close with her crush when she's supposed to be with Callie.

I stop dancing and shout in Dave's ear. "Where the hell is Callie?"

"Huh?" says Dave, not hearing over the noise on the dance floor, which has gotten wild and crowded.

"Callie!" I scream, trying to make my way toward Mimi.

"Oh, shoot, I forgot to tell you," says Dave, pulling me out of the living room and into a quieter hallway. "She's with Mark! Mimi told me to tell you, but I totally forgot. I'm so sorry, Lorna."

I sigh and press my palm to my racing heart, feeling a little relieved but not quite calm yet. Mark is a very nice guy, and since he brought the booze and is the only one here who's technically an adult, he's more or less our chaperone tonight.

Dave goes to get me some water, and then the song changes to the highly danceable anthem everyone's been belting out of their cars all summer. The dance floor is really flooded now, louder and sweatier than I ever thought my parents' living room could get.

And then I hear someone shout: "WHOA, WHAT THE HELL!"

And the whole night is shattered.

Callie, I think, my voice in my head getting worked up past mother-hen level and straight to human-mother-worried-about-her-baby-trapped-under-a-car-that-is-on-fire-level. Dave is at my side before I can even turn my head to lock eyes with him, and he strong-arms us a path straight though the loud, sweaty, messy crowd to the greenhouse. We get there and *why the hell are there people in the greenhouse?* I will call the cops on my own party just to get them out of here if I have to, and *what the hell.* Oh. Oh no.

Callie. Standing in front of something there isn't a word to describe. First all I see is a massive amount of Popsicle sticks that had been, I'm guessing, intended for use as splints to prop up some plants. I get closer, pushing past the last few people standing in the way of me and my sister, and then I'm standing right there in front of this thing, and my cup falls out of my hand to the floor.

Because Callie has built what I can only refer to as an *island.* An island of Popsicle sticks and blades of that super-strong grass she grows, intricately braided into whole sheets on top of this island the size of a small sofa.

"Holy shit," says, of all goddamn people, Dan. Now he's going over to it or to Callie, who is still working, layering in more sheets of woven grass, her hands trembling and then not trembling, not at all. Dan's leaning down to touch the island, or Callie, and that voice in my head snaps to attention and forces its way out of my mouth.

"OUT!" I shout at him, and he just puts his palms out toward me and spits out a string of "Whoa, bro, cool down, bro."

"Get the hell out of my house, *bro!*" I shout again, pointing at the door, giving him the meanest eyes I can. He's frozen where he is, in anger or confusion or both, and I shout, "Get. The hell. OUT."

Callie keeps flinching at the noise: from the party, from the people, from the world, from me. But still she keeps weaving blades of grass into those sheets and layering them up and up. I forget about Dan for the moment, because then I see there's a part of the island that looks like it's shaking, like something is loose and trembling, or trembling to be loosed. And then I realize that Callie has bent some of the Popsicle sticks supporting that section, and there are these tiny little blossoms peeking out in between the trembling and the shaking. Without thinking, without taking my eyes off the miracle or curse unfolding before me, I take out my phone and start texting Stan.

callie is building a goddamn island??????

I send him a picture, which is when I see that everyone else has their phones out too, taking photos of Callie and her island.

"WHAT PART OF 'GET OUT' DID YOU NOT UNDERSTAND?" I scream. Dave starts physically moving people out and asks Mark to call a whole fleet of Ubers, because the party's over. Mimi's back here now too, helping Dave with crowd control, and slowly the greenhouse empties until all that's left is me, Callie, and her island.

Stan texts me back: I know, and then a blurry photo of what looks like an island, like this island, but way uglier, and Ted looming over it.

come over, I text him. bring ted.

OK, Stan texts. And then a couple of seconds later: What the hell, texts Stan.

"Who are you texting?" Dave asks, returning from the house.

"Is it Stan?" Mimi asks.

"Who's Stan?" Dave asks, and I don't totally know what to tell him. All I can do is just look from Callie to him to Mimi and then back to Callie, who is still weaving grass, building her little world up layer by layer.

"No. Seriously. Who's Stan?"

EIGHT

I EXPLAIN TO Dave that Stan is a guy whose brother is also an Arctic Recovery Orphan sibling while we wait for him to show up.

"We see each other at the hospital sometimes. His brother has a lot of the same . . . quirks that Callie does, which means we've both been in the hospital more often than usual lately, so we've been comparing notes. About them and about what it's like to be in a family with them."

"Oh. You mean you talk to him because there are things you can talk to him about that you can't talk to me about?"

I want so badly to just yell the honest real-talk answer: *"Yes! But that isn't a reflection on you, you handsome dummy!"* But I'm not rattled enough or drunk enough to mess everything up by being all open and honest, so instead I say this: "Dave, he's had a hard time of it, way harder than me and my family, and he needs a friend." And then, because I can't help myself: "And there's also the fact that he's not as cute or smart as you, and he's never been allowed in my room, unsupervised or otherwise, and the only thing you need to worry about when you meet him is making everything weird by acting all jealous and aggressive, because you are my guy, you dingus."

"Hey, that's adorable, charming, and all-around-dreamboat dingus to you," Dave says, and how he says it is like he's almost but not quite convinced that the situation here is fine.

I put my arms around him and rest my forehead on his chest and say, "Mine." His muscles loosen up a bit, and he pulls me closer, and I know he's at least a little happy right now. But this lasts only a moment, because as soon as I've made Dave feel better, the part of my brain that doesn't want me to use the word "boyfriend" or introduce him to my parents wakes up and starts stirring, and now all I can think about is that it's lame as hell that right now I have to worry about Dave's feelings while my own feelings and whatever is going on with Callie have to sit quietly until they get called on.

But before I can let the monster completely take over, the doorbell rings. Mimi jumps up to get it before I can, then returns with Stan behind her, and a looming and lurking Ted bringing up the rear. And then I see it side by side: their identical heights.

"Hi," Stan says to me, then turns to look around the house, his 360 gaze making me realize how trashed the place is. "You're having a party?" he says, his face fallen and sad, and I feel terrible, but then the monster whirls around again to remind me that this is just one more person whose feelings I shouldn't have to take care of.

Dave puts his arm around me, which only makes my cheeks burn hotter. "*Had* a party. Kinda. Yeah. It was a totally last-minute thing, I didn't even know it was happening until earlier today." Stan nods, playing it cool. "Anyway, Dave, this is Stan. Stan, Dave."

"We're together," Dave says, reaching his hand out to Stan, and my cheeks are completely and totally on fire.

"Hey. Stan," says Stan, and then they shake hands without smiling, and it's at once so masculine and childish that I could throw up.

"This is at once so masculine and childish that I could throw up," I say.

"Um," says Stan.

"Uh," says Dave.

Mimi falls down laughing, and I smile real fast at both of them. Ted starts shuffling around impatiently behind Stan, and that's when I see what he's holding: a ham-fisted sculpture that looks *exactly* like an uglier and ham-fisteder version of Callie's.

"Come on," I say, and we all go to the greenhouse. Ted leads the way, holding his easy-chair-sized island over his head far more cautiously than anyone would ever hold an actual easy chair over their head. Callie follows, and I'm struck again by the fact that they are exactly the same height, with the same skin and eyes and hair. I'm used to weird, but, like. This is maybe *actually* weird. At least a little. Right?

We step inside, quiet and cautious, entering like we would a haunted house. Ted stops short right in front of Callie, and they're looking at each other like they know each other. Like they know something about each other, like their lives are linked by some sort of shared secret. I don't mean they're fawning over each other, and they're not bristling at each other either. They're not retreating, not advancing. They're just ... they're sharing something is what it looks like. Like they're maybe acknowledging this shared thing between them, because I swear I can feel a palpable sense of relief and understanding here in this greenhouse. I look at this, and I'm so happy for Callie. I'm just so happy to see this peace flashing in her eyes, to know I was right: She *can* feel connected to people, and in a visible, real way. And then I'm immediately sad too. I feel something crushed within my chest as I realize she has never looked at *me* like that. It takes no time at all for the shame I feel about that thought to crash over me like a wave, washing me with sadness and happiness both.

I know Callie knows me, and she maybe even loves me. But I'm not someone she can share *this* with. She's my sister, but I still don't *know* her. I'll maybe never really know her. And she'll never really know me. But I have to swallow all this down, because all I want to do is cherish this, to be glad for her, so I banish the shame and the sadness and the portion of the happiness that led to this whole mess, and I turn all the energy I have toward trying to be a good sister.

"Wow," Stan says, as if coming up for air from his own personal emotional storm. "Callie's island is . . ."

"Decidedly un-ham-fisted?" I finish for him.

"I was gonna say 'deft,' but sure, that works."

Ted has set his island on the floor next to Callie's, and the two of them kneel in front of their creations. Stan and I take a few steps toward them. Dave and Mimi hang back by the door, and I'm grateful to them for knowing that this is a time to give us some space. Mark's long gone and I don't much blame him, and so I just text him thank you thank you thank you.

We stand there, Stan and I, watching our siblings moving their hands over these mountains and plateaus. Their hands tremble in time with and over their trembling fields, the bit that seems to shake and bloom so gracefully on Callie's island, kind of violently on Ted's. Their hands move closer together, until they're almost touching but not quite, and I look down again and stare at the small mountain ranges, the long expanses broken up by cracks and tears in the sticks and grass, by shallow dips that look like riverbeds long dry and frosted over. There's a ridge ringing a field and around it what could be a stretch of trees with low branches. I look over at Ted's, and there's the same ridge ringing this shuddering expanse. His is this thin, thin, *thin* layer of paper that seems to shudder and shake with every molecule of air that moves around it, while Callie's is almost . . . dancing, and I can't figure out how. Ted's trees are actually Popsicle sticks and pens and pencils stuck in hard with some paper on top like a canopy, whereas Callie's are also sticks, but the canopy is woven, and some of the sticks are split up and splintering off into branches. But still. It's the same place. And that trembling expanse, with small flowers almost poking through on Callie's . . .

Oh my God. Dad's story.

They're building their home.

They're building their memory of home.

"Stan," I whisper without knowing why. "Everyone. Can you help us get these guys back in the house? I think I might know what's going on. Or at least part of what's going on. And Stan and I have some stuff to talk about."

"What kind of stuff?" Dave asks. I can tell he's wary of Stan, and I don't have time for his wariness right now, because my sister has just built a smart-car-sized memory of the place where she was born out of grass and sticks, and Stan's brother did the same thing but with paper and spit as well as sticks, and Dave, the major thing you have going for you is that you're so understanding, so how are you not getting that this is all that matters to me right now?

But I don't say that. What I do say is "The fact that our Arctic-born siblings just made these models, simultaneously, despite being totally isolated from each other."

"Yeah, okay," he says, but not without giving Stan one more warning look, and then everyone helps shepherd our siblings and their sculptures back into the house.

Dave, Stan, and I sit in the kitchen, while Mimi flits around trying to find some food for Ted and Callie. Ted and Callie are sitting down and basically just staring at each other, raising their hands one at a time, like they're trying to figure out a math problem using sign language.

"Okay, Stan," I say. "What do we do?"

"What do you mean?" says Stan.

"Uh," I say and gesture first toward the greenhouse and then at Ted and Callie. "You know, the whole 'Our Icelings built, at the same moment, in two different places, incredibly intricate replicas out of whatever materials were handy of what is almost definitely an Arctic island, which strangely seems to replicate what little we know about the one where they were abandoned' thing? That's more or less what I'm referring to when I ask you what we should do next."

"Are you asking whether or not we should report it to Jane?" Stan asks.

"Well," I say. "Does a situation like this really warrant reporting?"

"Good point. They don't appear to be in distress," Stan says.

"They're not showing any symptoms normally associated with fits or . . ."

"Conniptions?" Across the counter, Dave says the word he knows I refuse to say, and he winks at me, and it's cute, but I get these shuddering chills anyway.

"Nope," says Stan, "I definitely don't see any fits coming on. Their eyes aren't rolling up into their heads."

"No arms or other limbs flailing about," I say.

"They're being supervised by those responsible for them."

"I think we've exhausted the list of report-worthy criteria and can conclude that this isn't anything we need to bother Jane with."

"Unless there's some 'Weird, Spontaneous Art Projects and the Dangers They Pose to Your Orphan' pamphlet that I missed, I'd say we were in the clear," Stan says.

"I have seen no such pamphlet, and as such I definitely agree," I say.

"So then what?" Dave says, leaning on the counter between us now. I turn to him and give him a look that's more accusatory than I meant. "What? Don't give me that look. I care about Callie. And I obviously care about you, and you care about Callie more than anyone. And what happened—what's happening—tonight is crazy and basically unprecedented. In that it's unprecedented. So what are you all going to do about it?"

"Dave's right," I say. "All of this is too weird to be just a coincidence."

"I agree," says Stan, and the way he says the words makes them feel heavy as hell.

"And can we also agree that these . . . structures are probably totally definitely replicas of an Arctic island?"

Stan pauses, looks to Dave and then to me. "I believe I think we can," he says.

"Okay," I say. "Well, I'm really curious about what any of this means. And I want to try to figure this out."

"Me too," says Stan. But then Dave says it too, just a nanosecond after Stan started speaking, so they're almost exactly in unison, like two cheesy actors in a bad sitcom. Mimi loses it immediately, falling to the floor laughing again, and I only hold a straight face for about ten seconds, and then everyone's laughing, and it's almost enough to make me ignore the strange shuddering feeling seeping into my bones.

NINE

STAN AND I sit at the dining table trying to figure out what to do, while Dave walks around picking up cups and putting them into a giant trash bag he's hung from his neck.

"Reporting this is out."

"Turning them in is out."

"Cutting open their brains in the name of science?"

" . . ."

"Cutting open their brains in the name of science is definitely out."

Dave takes a break from cleaning to see how we're doing. I give him a kiss and squeeze his hand, but my heart is only barely in those gestures.

"Maybe it doesn't mean anything," Stan says.

"Maybe," I say, though when I turn to look at Callie and see her worrying—practically praying—over her island on the kitchen floor, I remain completely unconvinced of Stan's theory.

"Maybe," Stan says, "when you're an Iceling, this kind of behavior is totally normal. Maybe building sculptures of islands is the Iceling equivalent of playing hearts or watching YouTube videos."

"What if it's not, though?" I say.

Stan looks stumped, and I let out a big sigh. Suddenly, Callie raises her hand like she has a question.

"Callie?" I say uselessly. "You okay?" But she just continues to raise her hand as she stares at mine.

"I think she wants you to raise your hand," says Stan, one eye open, resting them in shifts.

I raise my hand, and Callie's eyes sort of light up a bit, and then she stands up and comes toward me and grabs it, takes hold of it. She leads me over to her sculpture and places my hand on the trembling field.

My hand is there, over the trembling, dancing field. My hand is trembling too, and now Callie's hand is holding mine, and hers is trembling too. And right now it feels like the whole world is trembling.

I look up to see that Ted has, meanwhile, done the same thing with Stan: raised his hand, then took Stan's and led him over to us. Stan and I crouch across from one another, our siblings pressing our hands down against these buzzing fields, as if asking us to read them like braille.

Suddenly and simultaneously, they pull our hands back from the fields, then bring them back down again. They keep doing this, holding our hands down to the fields, pulling them back, bringing them down again, over and over, as if they're trying to make us point at the sculptures and then at them. It's three or four in the morning at this point, and I know something is happening, but per usual with my kid sister, I have no idea what, and I don't think I've ever been more frustrated about the language barrier. Their eyes are getting worried, and Stan and I are getting worried too, and the more worried we get and the longer the night draws out, the less sure we are about what we're supposed to do.

And then they're gone.

They run out of the house, leaving the front door gaping open, and we follow. We run to the edge of the driveway and look up and down the street, but we don't see them. I spin around in a panic, and there they are, sitting in the backseat of Stan's car.

"Road trip?" says Stan.

"So it seems," I say.

✳

CALLIE AND TED are still in the car, and I'm in the kitchen, putting on a pot of coffee and telling Dave that Stan and I have to take the Icelings somewhere. I tell him I'm sorry and that I don't know what else to do, but that I have no reason to think we'll be gone for a very long time.

"I get it," Dave says. "But don't you think you at least need to tell your parents? They'll be worried. Or, like, leave a note? You know, *Dear Mom and Dad, Callie made a weird sculpture, so we drove to the Arctic. Back in a few days!* Or something like that."

"No way," says Stan.

I glare at Stan, because he's snapping at Dave, and Dave is only trying to help.

"We can't tell them, really," I say sweetly. "All they'd do is freak out and call the hospital and then come home and then their trip would be ruined, and Callie and Ted's trip would be ruined too. And if the hospital finds out . . . I don't know what they'll do. They might take her away, I don't know. I know you know I need to do this. She's my sister, Dave. She's my family. And she needs me. I need to figure this out. For Callie, but also for myself."

"Well," Dave says, grinning a little bit, "who am I to get in the way of you finally figuring out what'll make your sister happy?"

"No super-heroic guy I'd ever hang around with, that's for sure."

And then he takes me in his arms and kisses me, and I just want to collapse in them, right here, right now. And I do. But then the coffeemaker makes that spitting noise that sounds like Dad in the morning when he has a cold, which means our caffeine is ready and it's time to go. I kiss him one more time, then tear myself away. Stan and Dave find and fill some travel mugs, while I go grab a phone charger, three changes of underwear, and some other essentials and throw them in my purse, the big one, because we don't know exactly how long we'll be gone or even where, exactly, we're going. But because we suspect the far north, I also grab both my and Callie's warmest winter jackets and two of Dad's for Stan and Ted, and I throw them in the biggest duffel bag I can find, along with a bunch of random hats, scarves, and gloves. I feel like I'm forgetting something but I don't have the time to worry.

We head out to the driveway. Stan packs the trunk and gets in the car, leaving me and Dave alone to say goodbye. Dave pulls me in for another hug and then he tells me he loves me. I say, "I know," and I make my eyes as serious and as sad as I can, and then we kiss, and all of this makes my heart feel so heavy. I join Stan in the car and buckle up, making sure Callie and Ted are strapped in as well, and I blow Dave a kiss. He smiles and puts his palm against the glass, and I match it with mine.

THE SUN IS up. We're on the road. We're drinking coffee. The radio is spitting out a song that I hated when I first heard it at the beginning of the summer but that has grown on me in the strangest, rarest way. Stan's turning onto the freeway, headed away from where our homes are.

I allow us about an hour of pure, destination-less driving before I ask the big burning question of the day. "Any idea where we're going?"

"Nope," says Stan.

I nod, mostly because if I really think about it, this whole trip was mostly my call, but what I really want to do is press him on this. I really, really want to say something like *Well, let's make a plan then!* But Stan beats me to it.

"Probably we should have wondered about that sooner? Like before we left?"

I let out a weak snorting laugh, then find I have nothing else to say.

"But," Stan goes on, "I figure if all this noise is about the Arctic, then we can just take 476 up through New York as far as those two let us. And we just keep going, maybe into Canada? That's cold, and north. The Hudson Bay, maybe. I don't know." And then he kind of sighs, and under his breath I think I hear him say, "Shit," and this is my cue to start dealing with other people's feelings again.

"No, that's good! It's something! That's more or less what I was thinking, but I never take 476, and that's totally a better route. Less traffic. We do that, what you said. That's what we'll do. West-ish and north. It's a plan!" But then a few minutes pass, and while I'm looking back at Callie gazing sweetly through the window, it occurs to me that Canada is a whole other country entirely, isn't it? Quietly, I say, "Uh, don't we need passports for Canada? Or if we don't, won't we at least maybe have to deal with Customs? When we cross the border?"

"Oh. Damn," says Stan. This is rapidly turning out to not be the easy road trip romp I maybe imagined it would be earlier. "You're right."

The car slows down, and we grind over the rumble strip as Stan pulls over. I hear Callie fuss in the backseat, so I reach back and put my hand on her knee in a pathetic attempt to calm someone who doesn't necessarily even understand that when someone puts their hand on your knee, it means they are trying to comfort you, and it's polite to pretend that it's working.

Stan pulls out his phone. He starts zooming in and out on the route he mapped out. "I don't want to deal with New York City, so . . . how about we just get on 80, and then take that to 84 and go through New England? They've gotta give us some kind of clues once we start making our way up there, right? And if they don't, then, well . . . maybe this road trip isn't what they want after all, and no harm done?"

I smile and nod at that, though my stomach sort of falls into this sad, anxious somersault when Stan suggests that maybe this isn't what they want from us after all. I don't really know why—it's not like I *want* to drive up into some forbidding, freezing, unknown territory with two non-lingual kids and a guy who is basically half a conversation away from being a stranger. But I still can't shake the feeling that turning around after coming this far—even just an hour away from home— would be equivalent to giving up entirely. It would be my hard and fast proof that Callie and I were never meant to understand each other.

"We can keep checking the map as we go to see if we're near any islands that seem like they'd be anything like their sculptures. And if we end up near the border then . . . I guess we'll figure the rest out from there. Right?"

"Right," I say.

"Hooray for plans," says Stan.

Hooray for plans, I think. There's movement in the backseat as we pull back onto the highway, and I turn to see my hand is still on Callie's knee. I remove it, sensing for no good reason at all that she doesn't want it there anymore.

THE HIGHWAY IS about to split. We have to make a choice.

I'm about to ask Stan which way he thinks we should go when suddenly Ted reaches up from the backseat, lurching his big arms forward. He grabs the wheel and tugs it toward 276 EAST, which will eventually head to 295 and north, bringing us onto the on-ramp headed way up there, to the vast unknown or whatever comes closest to that. Stan looks at me, and I look at Stan, and our eyes sort of shrug, and on we go.

And for the first time in my life, I feel like I'm doing something for Callie. Really doing something, not just spotting her while she negotiates the space around her, or trying to help her in the garden but really probably just getting in the way, but *actually* helping her find something. Something real and important and that's for once a part of *her* world, not mine. I can do something, right now, for my sister, for once in my life. I catch her eyes in the rearview mirror, and she's looking right at me, and she's smiling.

TEN

IT'S PAST NOON. We've been driving north since we left my house at dawn. The last sign I remember paying attention to was for an exit toward Providence. After he got us on 95, Ted stopped reaching forward as much, so we've decided just to stick with it. The fact that we ended up going through New York City wasn't exactly thrilling to Stan. And I'm not exactly thrilled—though not exactly *not* thrilled—about the fact that when we match Ted's route with the moving maps on our phones, it seems to suggest that we're headed up to Nova Scotia.

But all I notice now is that I'm hungry. I mean, I'm that kind of hungry where thinking about anything other than the fact that I'm hungry is nearly impossible. Probably we're all hungry. There is no way I am alone in this. And come on. Of course I packed snacks. But we already ate them.

"Stan," I say, pointing with a trembling finger at a sleek, chrome roadside diner. "Look. Oh man, look what's coming up ahead."

"Are you hungry?" says Stan.

I nod vigorously, because I don't even have the energy to say, "Duh."

"I guess I could eat," he says, and then everyone applauds. Even the radio.

THE BEST THING about roadside diners is that they have got those large and deep booths, the kind you can hide in with your siblings who don't respond to language and who aren't always great at responding to new and outside stimuli. Plus, their menus usually have a lot of pictures you can just sort of point at, which is great when, again, you're traveling with two people over whom language just washes like rain on a raincoat covered in grease.

Did I mention how hungry I am? Or that there are complimentary rolls on the table, brought to us by some kind of goddess named Betty, who smiled and said she would keep them coming? Betty the goddess takes our order, and we don't even wait until her back is turned to pounce on the rolls and tear into them. It's not at all pretty, it's kind of an animals-at-the-watering-hole type of scene, but I couldn't care less about table manners right now, because these rolls are maybe the most delicious things I've ever tasted.

We order chicken fingers and mozzarella sticks and French fries and cheeseburgers and grilled cheeses and a few very large salads, because Callie doesn't go as crazy over greasy diner food as the rest of us do. After downing a few rolls each, the clouds part, and the lights shine down from heaven or the ceiling, because the food has come, and we eat.

We approach our main courses the way we approached the rolls, which is to say *hungrily*, and with *vigor*. I only slow down once I feel my hunger has been about 40 percent satiated, at which point

I take a break to sip some water and look around the diner. It's about three-quarters full. Whenever I'm with Callie, I'm always watching out for people sending dirty, confused looks our way, but the patrons here don't seem to be all that fazed by our unusual siblings. Most of the families look like they're on trips, which I surmise based on the way the parents seem really good at tuning out whatever frequency their kids' voices seem to exist on.

There are a few couples, young and not so young, leaning across the table in various poses of affection or malice. There's a group of what I assume to be long-haul truckers lined up at the bar, drinking coffee, with their pants hanging off various points of butt or no butt, their guts or no-guts hanging a bit over their belts, their T-shirts hiding what they can, but—let's face it—a T-shirt only has so much to work with. They all have mesh-back ball caps. One of them has what looks like a map tattooed all over his forearm.

Satisfied that no one's out to get us or even gawk at us, I turn back to my food and go in for another round. When we're all finished, Betty, the manifestation of grace on earth, clears it all away, like a battlefield medic.

Stan leans back in the booth, clearly full and satisfied. He looks at Ted and Callie and then back to me.

"Did you notice how they, like, touch the ground when we get out of the car?" he says.

"Yeah," I say. "Weird."

"Yeah. They like grass better than asphalt, it seems."

"That thing with them and soil."

"Yeah."

"It's definitely weird. But honestly that's not even close to what I'm thinking about. I mean, I'm kind of excited," I say. "About this 'journey of discovery' or whatever it is."

"Why the air quotes on 'journey of discovery'?"

"Oh," I say. "Um. I was being ironic, I guess? I don't know why I felt weird calling it that."

"Oh," he says. "So you were being 'insincere'?" He puts his hands up and curls his fingers in scare quotes when he says "insincere."

"No! I just..."

"Because," says Stan, "it's not like I'm comfortable calling this a 'journey of discovery' or whatever. But probably that's what it is, right?"

"Yeah. That's probably what this is. And it's really weird to think about! I mean, I never really thought I'd see where they came from. You know? And not just with Callie, in the context of a *journey of discovery*, but in general. I *still* don't fully believe it. That we could—that *we* could—learn so much about Callie, about Ted, about these people we spent our whole lives growing up with, our siblings . . .

"So I guess it's more that I'm being . . . cautious. Trying not to jinx it. I mean, it's not like anyone's going to give us a map to their past, full of explanations and a backstory and a whole pile of solutions to the questions our perpetually mute siblings inspire. But I just . . . I guess I just resigned myself to the fact that I'd never get to share anything with Callie. Especially not something that mattered."

Stan's looking at me like I have one too many heads, so I take a pause to sigh and figure out what it is I'm trying to say. "I guess I don't really know how to put this. But it's like . . . this is the first chance I've had that I can think of where I can do something for her that won't just *help* her, you know, with day-to-day things. It'll be something I can do for her and also *with* her, that will be a shared experience. It's not like I'm helping her get around on the first day of school back when we were kids, or showing her how to be around people, or sitting with her in the garden. Whatever this is, we're going through it together, as sisters. I've never had anything like that. With her or anyone else. I've spent a lot of time *wishing* I could share something meaningful with her, or that some kind of *miracle* might happen that would just turn everything around. Like . . . maybe one day Callie just starts speaking. And we stay up all night and share everything forever. And it turns out I've mostly done right by her. Sure, not all the time. She'll tell me that there's some stuff I should really work on. But she knows my heart was in the right place. But I never thought any of those wishes would come true. Or that I'd *actually* get to do something for her that was real. And *this* is real. This isn't a story I tell myself to feel better about things, it's an actual thing that's happening.

"And, well," I go on, because all of this is hitting me just now, hours after Callie and Ted made their islands and we set out on this crazy journey, "I've wondered a lot about what things would be like if Callie hadn't . . . been around. If I didn't spend my days thinking about how she might view the world, trying to think of ways to make it easier on her. I hated having those thoughts. Having those thoughts made me hate myself. I don't know what happens next, but I know *something* happens next, and whatever it is, I just hope it means that I don't ever have those thoughts again. I don't know what I'm saying or even fully what I mean. It's just . . . this feels like something new. Like something is happening. Does that make any sense?"

"No, no, I get it," Stan says, and I immediately feel calmer. "It's really hard to deal with Ted sometimes. You know? I need to watch out for him pretty much all the time. I need to watch out for authority figures who might not realize that it's not that Ted's a problem, it's that someone abandoned him in the Arctic when he was a baby, and so he doesn't understand language and is maybe in a constant state of shock or something, but we have no way of knowing because, once again, he cannot speak. And when he gets confused he gets upset, and when he gets upset he gets tackle-y. And then I need to watch out for everyone *else*."

He looks away a bit, and I follow his gaze to Ted, who fidgets and then looks around. Stan looks back at Ted again, sort of nods downward, and then points to the bathrooms, and Ted gives him a kind of "hello" sign, then heads back to the men's room. I wink at Callie, because it's not until now that I realize how lucky I am to have the sibling with the big bladder—we had to pull over at least a dozen times on the way here so Ted could go relieve himself.

"Callie's got a big bladder," I tell Stan. "Not like Ted over there. Right, kid sister?" She's shredding up her paper place mat and arranging the scraps into something beautiful and unnamable.

Stan, though, isn't listening to me. He's still watching Ted and looking an awful lot like he has something to say but isn't sure if he should say it. And then he goes for it.

"He's never, like, hurt anyone," says Stan, still looking toward the bathrooms, even after we both watch Ted get in safely. "Or done anything really out of the ordinary. Out of the ordinary for Ted, I mean. You know?"

I do, and I think about that rule from earlier, about determining the baseline of behavior for each individual Iceling.

Stan goes on. "The most alarming thing he's ever done—that has ever made me think he wants or needs *something* really urgently—has been, like, running into walls. So building this thing and figuring out a way to tell us to take them somewhere ... I know it's awful of me, but I keep thinking maybe this means there's something out there he can do. You know, some purpose he can serve, some way for him to be independent. And maybe then that means ... for a time ... or for once, or just ..." And he kinds of trails off a bit and looks out the window.

"What?"

"Sometimes," he says, still looking out the window, "I think about how, if Ted weren't *Ted*, I could maybe have my own life that *didn't* revolve around just keeping my crazy brother from getting tackle-y all over the place all the time. And I could maybe have friends, who

I could actually spend time with, or invite someone over—not just to my house but *anywhere, ever,* and not worry about Ted, or my dad, or my dad's reactions to Ted. I mean, this is good, talking to you. But you only know me through Ted and Callie."

"Stan—"

"It's fine. Or it's not fine, but it's whatever. It's awful and it's self-ish, and maybe I'm awful and selfish. But I can tell Callie isn't a burden to you, Lorna." And I look over at Callie, at my sister, and I don't know what to tell him. Because I know what he means, but I also don't. "She's not like Ted," Stan goes on. "I mean, I don't mean that he's a *burden*. But, like, for instance, you have a boyfriend. You have friends, you have people over, you have parties where you don't worry about your sibling tackling someone because the music is weird and not what he thought it would be. Or, I mean. I don't even know if that's what he'd do. Or if that *is* what he would do, I wouldn't know *why* he'd do it. I don't really know why Ted does the things he does when he does them." And I can tell how much this kills him when he says it.

Stan leans in, kind of looks down at the table or his hands in front of him, and his voice gets quieter. "His whole life. His whole life, and Callie's whole life, they've just . . . they've been trapped, basically. Right? Those researchers found them, and then the government just stuck them in homes, just decided on the families they'd grow up with. And the whole time they're just stuck in their own heads, to-tally unable to talk to us about what it's like for them. And then we just stick them in hospitals when things get too weird for us! And in the hospital Jane just sticks them in closed-off spaces and guarded areas where they can only leave when someone else decides, and they have to be there alone without the people who they know and may-be trust." Stan leans back in the booth, looking exhausted. "Wow. I guess the short version of all that is that I agree with everything you said. And I guess my feelings about this are more complicated than I thought. Which is I guess what happens when you don't spend a lot of time thinking or talking about them much."

I want to hug him. Because yes to that whole last bit, and that whole other bit too. But still, when he was talking, I'm sure I made some kind of sour face at him, because I could feel myself judging him for thinking those things. For feeling like his brother was a burden. He's right that I would never think of Callie like that. Except that I do, a little. And she isn't even anything at all like Ted.

So "Yeah" is all I say to Stan. "Yes."

"We're supposed to be doing this, right? We can do this much for them. Who else is going to? Our parents?"

"Probably not."

"Their caseworkers?"

"Definitely not."

"The government?"

"One hundred percent no."

And then, of course, my phone rings.

POP [snow-capped mountain emoji]

"Sorry," I say to Stan. "I have to get this."

He puts up his hands in an "Of course, no problem!" gesture, and I turn away, into the booth and toward the window, and focus on a tree in the distance. I take a deep breath.

"Hey, Pop!" I say. It's important, when misleading your parents, to appear cheerful yet vaguely callous.

"Hello, daughter of mine! We have landed! How goes the sister-watching?"

"Swell," I tell him. "So far no fits." Totally true. "She's had a lot of garden time." Counting the way she's been crouching down and examining the ground at rest stops, that's maybe not a total lie. "Overall, things are good here!" They are, mostly.

"Well, okay then. Glad to hear it. We just wanted to check in and let you know we're here safe," says Dad.

"How's Mom? How're the Galápagos?"

"*Hot*," says Dad, and I can hear him smiling at himself. "And the weather is pretty warm too." There it is.

"Ugh, yikes," I say, pretending to be grossed out by the affection my parents have for each other.

"In all seriousness, your mother's doing well, and the islands are beautiful, except I'm mostly staring at the ground and at readouts. So it's great, for me. And it's too hot for a suit, so, again, having a great time!"

"Good!"

"Uh-oh, sport, it looks like I need to go check on something. Your mother sends her love! Can I say hey to Callie?"

"Sure," I say, immeasurably relieved. I only barely had to lie.

I pass her the phone, which she doesn't take—never has—so I just hold it there up to her ear and give Stan the "shh" sign with my finger to my lips to let him know he still needs to keep quiet. I hear Dad's goofy voice through the speaker and watch Callie's eyelids flutter—*in response to Dad*, I tell myself slash need to believe. Dad's voice hums on for a few minutes, then cuts off. I wait about thirty seconds for Callie to offer some kind of response, knowing she won't, and then take the phone from her ear. The home screen is up, meaning either Callie hung up on Dad or vice versa, but I'm happy either way not to answer any more of his questions.

I put my phone away and sink back into the booth with a sigh of relief—but this feeling lasts for about two seconds, because then I hear what I can only describe as a kerfuffle coming from the direction of the bathrooms. A baby starts wailing, and everyone in the diner turns to look.

"What the hell's the matter with you? Watch where you're going!" A man is yelling at Ted, who looks to me like a cross between scared and sorry and furious, and while I'm trying to come up with a name for what I think I see in his eyes, there's Stan right there in the middle of it, and I didn't even see him get up from the booth.

"I'm so sorry," says Stan to the guy. He's gesturing down at something, and that's when I see the stroller and realize where the baby screams were coming from. From the way Ted is standing and the position of the stroller, which is pressed flush against the diner counter in what looks like a tight squeeze, I conclude that Ted must have bumped the stroller into the counter, upsetting the baby and the baby's dad even more.

"Can't *he* say he's sorry?"

"No, no—he can't speak." Stan looks at Ted, sadly, and then reaches out to him and claps his hand on his shoulder. Ted's face twists into this sad kind of smile-grimace. The man looks on, and the look on his face *almost* changes. *Almost.*

"He needs to learn to look where he's going."

"Yes. Totally. I agree."

"Because he could have killed my baby!"

"You're totally right, sir," Stan says, and I'm surprised he's conceding to everything so coolly—especially since it doesn't seem plausible at all that Ted even came close to hurting, let alone killing, that guy's baby. But then I realize Stan's not done talking yet. "If my brother had paid better attention to his surroundings, he'd totally have seen the stroller with an infant in it parked right in front of the bathroom door, where lots of people frequently pass through at high speeds."

"Are you serious with this right now?" says the guy, and now the baby is wailing even louder. *Me too if he were my dad*, I think, sending waves of pity over to that poor kid.

"Yes, absolutely. And I will personally make sure that the next time my brother goes to the bathroom he checks at least three times for strollers with babies in them parked directly in front of the door."

A small crowd is gathering, craning their necks to get a better look at Ted, and I'd really rather they didn't. I'm torn between going up to join Stan and staying here with Callie, trying to shield her from view with my body, against I'm not sure what. People are starting to talk about manners and bad parenting and then about what the hell is going on with all these kids who don't know how to talk.

Um, what? "All these kids"? What are they talking about? Who do they mean? I want to ask what they mean, if they've seen any others, but then there's a hand on my shoulder and I think better of leaving Callie to go get involved with a bunch of people who don't seem like they'd take too kindly to a girl like her. I look up, and there's Betty, our waitress, our angel.

"How're you kids doing?" Betty asks. "Can I get you all the check?"

"Yes, please," I say, then turn to Stan and wave. He's no longer the center of the argument, thank God, so I tell him to get the hell over here, please, in gestures. He catches my meaning and drags Ted back to the table.

Betty brings the check, which has a smiley face at the bottom, and I notice she left off all our drinks. Stan and I pay, and I leave her a huge cash tip, and then we're off, leaving the angry diners to fume and scratch their heads.

ELEVEN

WE'RE BACK ON the road, still headed north. It's my turn to drive for the next four hours, which Stan and I have decided is the longest either of us seems to be able to manage before the road and its accompanying signs and markers all start blending together.

I keep my eyes straight ahead on the road, and at the sides of my vision I watch the trees chase the retaining walls and the retaining walls chase the trees into some sort of small space in the distance where the highway will stop, where everything we know will just disappear. I see Callie in the rearview watching me, and I start to smile, but my face is too tired, and anyway she doesn't smile back. I must be wearing my anxiety on my face, because all of a sudden Stan pipes up and tells me he thinks that I should rest and he should maybe drive for a bit. I make a lame attempt at reminding him that my shift isn't quite up yet, but he insists, and I can't find the energy to pretend I have any real powers of concentration left.

So now I'm in the passenger seat watching it all with full vision, as one sign for the interstate swallows another until, poof, we're in Maine. I think of this poem I once read, about how one train can hide another, and this feels a lot like that. One thing is right in front of you, and directly behind it is another thing, and then they're gone, but then there's something else, let's call them clouds. So there are clouds, and they're in the sky, and then the clouds in the sky swallow up the sky, and then everything's just sky, and the power lines keep running along around the sky's knees, and cell phone towers keep trying to punch their way up into space. All of which is to say, it's a good thing that Stan took the initiative to take over the wheel.

It didn't take being around Ted for too long to learn that he's startled by sudden movements, so when I get the urge to check on Callie, I glance up to the rearview mirror instead of turning around. I look at Callie's reflection instead of her real self, and then I look at Ted's reflection too, and I think about how different the two of them are, but also how identical. And then I think about the first time I realized things were different for us, for me and Callie. I was older than a person might think, because it turns out that most people are fine—almost happy—with a kid who doesn't ever speak. Especially a cute and affectionate kid like Callie, who sometimes smiles for no reason but in ways that can accidentally make your whole day better. So I was as old as nine or ten the day that some office lady came into my classroom to take me to the vice principal, who then took me to the nurse's office, where Callie was sitting alone on the cold linoleum floor. She'd been having a fit for nearly thirty minutes. It was already starting to become common for kids to have seizures and brief telekinetic explosions back then, but for something like that to go on for thirty minutes was not something the nurse felt was normal—or that she was equipped to handle. I remember the nurse's face: pure terror. I have no way of knowing what went on in there before I got there, but I have an idea. And it must have been bad, because I remember the nurse talking to my parents in her office later that year, telling them that she was worried the event was going to have some sort of brain-damaging effect on Callie. But it didn't. According to Jane, the CAT scans came back completely normal, the same as before. Callie has gotten regular CAT scans ever since she first got rescued, and no matter how bad the fit, there's never been a blip. But after that day, the school sort of made it clear that they felt they couldn't handle Callie and that alternate arrangements had to be made.

I've never told this to anyone before. Obviously my parents knew the facts of the matter, but still, I've never told anyone about it from my angle, or confessed that that was the first time I looked from myself to Callie and saw something fundamentally different. But I guess if something is important and awful enough for you to carry around inside yourself for long enough, it'll eventually find a way to get out. I guess my "something" has chosen now to come out, because that memory has come back to me with such force that before I know what I'm doing, I'm saying it aloud to Stan.

"Lorna," he says, once I'm finished. "I'm sorry." I bite my lip and don't look at him. "And I'm also sorry that I have nothing more helpful or creative to say than 'sorry.'"

"Ha," I say, letting him know that it's fine. I'm fine. "I doubt anyone does. There's not exactly a step-by-step guide for how to talk about non-lingual adopted siblings that someone found abandoned in a boat in the Arctic. You know?"

Stan nods and gives me a long, thoughtful pause.

"So you're saying," he says, slowly and seriously, "I would not find this as a volume in the *Chicken Soup for the Soul* series?"

"Oh, my bad, you're right. There *is* a guide. *Chicken Soup for the Teenage Soul of a Teenager Whose Sibling Is Totally Non-lingual and Was Found Abandoned in a Boat in the Arctic.*"

"Ah-ha—so *you're* the one who always has it checked out of the library!" he says, and we both laugh, which feels great.

"So," says Stan, once we've laugh-sighed our way into silence again. "They were still calling it the 'special class' when Ted was there, which is a horrible, awful name, and I can't believe a professional educator would allow it. Anyway, this one day, when Ted was maybe eight or nine—and *huge* for his age—there were some workers out on the playground pulling out a tree to make room for a new jungle gym. Some genius—the same one who thought of 'special class,' probably—thought it was a good idea to go ahead and hold recess outside anyway, with just the jungle gym part of the playground off-limits. But of course that rule didn't deter Ted—he didn't even know there was a rule. So Ted sees the guys working out there, and he starts to have a fit. It was a short one—like, weirdly short—and it wasn't anything out of the ordinary. His eyes were rolling up, his hands were opening and closing, and his entire body just got really stiff. One of his teachers came to get me—I was just over on the playing fields for gym class—and as I walked over toward him, I saw it all happen. His body unfroze, he shook his head, and he stood up, like nothing happened. But then he turned. He was looking at the workers, who were pulling up a tree to clear out the ground for the jungle gym. And then something came over him, a different kind of fit. And this is where it gets fuzzy for me, because all I could do was start panicking and running toward him. The roots were starting to surface, and the tree was out of the ground, and Ted lowers his head and just . . . went at them. He pummeled them with his little-kid fists, and it didn't do much to the huge dudes removing the tree, but it made an impression on everyone, I'll tell you that much."

"Jesus" is all I can say, and a bright, clear image of Ted as a child, violently lashing out on an elementary school playground, crops up in my mind with a fierceness that lets me know it'll be there for a while.

"Yeah," Stan says quietly, his eyes straight ahead on the road, where they've been the whole time he was telling the story. "Ted's on the . . . aggressive side. Sometimes I wonder if all the wrestling my dad has us do isn't so much so Ted can have an outlet but more, like, my dad seeing if I have what it takes to help contain him. I truly don't know—my dad is a weird enough guy for an idea like this to either be right on the money or so far from his mind that he'd find it insulting that I'd even suspect it. But I wonder." Stan pauses, and I let the moment be a silent one. "Anyway," he says after a short while, "Ted was asked to not come back. Just like Callie. I guess a nine-year-old kid built like a twelve-year-old, prone to seizures and who doesn't speak or react when spoken to and who sometimes freaks out and tackles or hits things and people, is not exactly . . . easy. The saddest part about it was that even though I was just a kid too, I still got the distinct feeling that the main sentiment around school after Ted was gone was sweet relief. Everyone was glad to not have to worry about him anymore. And just . . . it's not always easy having to live with people looking at your brother like that.

"And I get it! But just . . ." And his voice drifts off as both of our gazes wander into the rearview, where Ted is clumsily braiding Callie's hair.

It'd be great if we'd passed the Walt Whitman service plaza right then, so we could think about how we contradict ourselves and contain multitudes or whatever, but this is real life, and real life doesn't get to line up in convenient metaphors.

Suddenly, my phone buzzes. "Sorry," I say, taking it out of my bag.

"What? Don't be sorry. That's silly," Stan says.

His response makes me think of Mimi, who's on a personal crusade to erase "sorry" from women's vocabulary, so I smile.

I look down to see a text from Dave: Hey.

hi from the road, I type, a novel about road trips, featuring a stranger and two silent siblings, and yrs truly. who misses you.

Aw shucks.

How're you?

How's Callie? Are you any closer to her Secret Origins issue?

Was that a bad joke?

I thought it was a pretty good joke. I could explain it if that would help?

All of these come buzzing in one after the other, but I don't look down, because in the mirror Ted's *still* trying to braid Callie's hair, and it's mesmerizing, but then what's more mesmerizing is the way Ted suddenly drops Callie's hair and turns to stare straight ahead and to the left, right at the back of Stan's head.

My phone buzzes again, breaking the spell, and I look down.

That always makes jokes funnier, when you explain them?

dave! hi. sorry. no, no, i get it. that's funny! we're doing really well. stan has all this money from an inheritance from his favorite grandma, which is sad but also really nice because all our food and gas is taken care of. callie and ted are ok. they're traveling better than I thought they would.

Amazing, texts Dave. And what about you? How are you?

I do a 360 scan of the car. Stan is dazed and looking tired behind the wheel, and now I can't look at him without thinking about that playground story with Ted. Ted's in the back, still staring at Stan, and Callie is next to him, looking so content yet so far away from me it makes me want to cry. I decide to answer Dave honestly.

> i don't know. i mean, it's not like i thought
> that just by doing this, everything would
> make sense, or that callie would all of a
> sudden start to talk, or that we'd make
> some big breakthrough once i got to know
> more about her past. but i guess i also
> maybe did think those things a little.

No response just yet.

sorry, I type, that was maybe a lot.

No blinking ellipses.

hey, I type, noting he didn't tell me not to say "sorry," wondering if he's trying to give me a taste of my own medicine by not answering, getting mad at myself for thinking these things because Dave's the best and I don't know why I'm always looking for reasons to push him away. you can text back whenever, but it's my turn to drive soon, so I won't be able to respond. but i miss you. i would kiss your whole face if you were here.

There they are now, the blinking ellipses, come to restore my faith in chivalry and Dave.

> Ah, sorry! My mom needed me. This whole

> trip seems like a lot for you. Take care of
> yourself. Please? And drive safe.

> A whole face's worth of kisses right back
> at you.

I send him a dozen emojis with hearts in their eyes, then close my own eyes and allow myself to feel just a bit calmer, until Stan pipes up from the driver's side.

"I don't know where the hell I'm supposed to go," says Stan.

I look up to see at least four exits going in every direction up ahead where the horizon is.

I'm setting up a logic puzzle in my head and trying to pull together an educated guess when suddenly Ted reaches up from the back and across the seats and turns the wheel. We zigzag for a terrifying few seconds, but then Stan regains control and rights the wheel, and I look up just in time to see us sailing through one of the northbound exits. In the blur of it all, I catch a hurried glimpse of Ted in the rearview mirror. His hand is still on the wheel, but he's not looking at the signs or even the road in front of us. He's looking intently at Callie, who stares back at him too.

"Jesus, Ted!" Stan exhales, getting into the rightmost lane and slowing to sub-speed limit. "You okay, Lorna? Sorry about that."

"Don't apologize. I'm just glad someone's stepped up as navigator." I turn to look at Ted, and though he meets my gaze, I can tell he's staring straight past me. He just seems to be pulled somewhere, like he's trying to lead us along to wherever somewhere is.

I'm flipping around the radio stations, and all I hear are commercials and the same songs over and over again. Because we're willing to do anything to distract ourselves from our own anxiety and lessen the tension of Ted's arm shooting out from the backseat to nudge the wheel north again, Stan and I start a game where we see how many times we can hear the same song within an hour, and you'd be surprised how high our scores go. Then Stan tells me about a thing he read about how Elvis Costello once said that we can blame DJs who keep replaying popular songs for the mistaken belief that radios broadcast "frequencies." We skip through stations, trying to play a new game to see how many times in a row we can hit the song's chorus, which is to me the best part of any song, and I don't care how obvious or unoriginal that opinion is. That big rushing moment, the epiphany electric, on fire. You know the part I'm talking about.

"What if there was a song that was just all chorus?" I say.

"You mean a song whose main purpose was just to give the people what they want, all the time, and then never walk away from it?" Stan says.

"Yeah."

"How long do you think a song like that could last?"

"As long as people would listen to it, probably."

Some cheesy Top 40 track comes on, and Stan turns it up in a way that suggests he's trying to be ironic but that he actually really likes it. Me, I just like the song. He's drumming his hand on the steering wheel when, with a horrifying jolt, he slams on the brakes and sends the tires screeching.

"HOLY SHIT," he calls out, then starts muttering more expletives and puts the car in reverse. He has one of those mounted gear shifts, which has taken some time for me to get used to, so while I'm scrambling around to try to see whatever's freaking him out, the gear shift's right there in the way. I turn around, and I see Ted and Callie, both of whom are also freaking out, but in an almost negative way, if that makes sense. As in, they are so calm—eerily, unsettlingly, cult-member calm. And now I'm starting to freak out too, I can hear my own heartbeats and maybe everyone else's heartbeats too, and the sound is deafening. And then I hear this noise, a real noise, from outside this car full of our terrified hearts, and I turn. And then, lo, a bear.

There is a bear. A giant, frothy-mouthed bear, crouching in the road, right in front of us.

It starts to stand. And it's so big and so close that it can reach the front bumper with its paws, which it does, and sort of pushes itself upright. The car is continuing to reverse. I can't look away from the bear, which is now opening its mouth.

"Stan," I say.

He just keeps muttering curses, and I want to tell him to get it together, if not for us then for our siblings, but then the bear roars at us, snarling with its whole head, spittle flying at the windshield, so I don't—can't—say anything at all. Stan hits the wipers.

The bear bellows. It bares its teeth and snarls and roars, again and again. Stan's eyes are wide open, and though I'm practically frozen where I sit, clutching that bar above the passenger door, he's maneuvering the car to try to get us as far away from the bear as possible. I'm yelling at Stan to back up faster, like way, *way* faster than he's going, and oh my God, please just faster can we get away faster, and I look back to Callie, and I reach out to just touch her, to let her know I'm here. Just as the car starts to pick up, I hear a small clattering noise in the backseat and the creaking of hinges and then the rush of air, and then I see Ted, who is out the door and on the road.

Ted looks like Brad Pitt with a crew cut and a broken nose and two chipped teeth, and he's, like, five eight and built like the kind of house you don't want to fall on you. He's moving, striding, quickly and determinedly, right over to the bear. He bends forward at his waist, like his mind is just a few steps ahead of him, or like the world's a few steps behind, and his arms are widening out to the sides, and his legs are just moving and moving—and then he leaps. He leaps right onto the bear's back.

He's on top of the bear, and he just starts pulling its front legs back toward him, and then we hear this awful, strange cry escape from its mouth. And now I'm terrified that the claws will get him, will slice open his arms, or that he'll kick the bear in the face and its jaw will snap shut on his leg like a trap, with blood and sinew everywhere. I want to turn away, but I can't, I need to throw up, but I'm terrified of opening the door, so I just stay frozen and let the nausea sink in deeper and deeper. Stan starts muttering something, and at first I think he's gone delirious with shock, but then I start to make out words in the sounds: "You can do it, you can do it, come on, Ted, you can do it," he says.

He's not watching the bear anymore at all; he's watching Ted. Only Ted.

And Ted has picked up the bear.

Ted lunged at the bear's stomach, and we saw the wind get knocked out of the bear as Ted hoisted it up over his head. Ted's whole body is now trembling with the effort, and then he snaps himself upright, and he shakes it, and its legs smash together, and it gives a yelp.

The bear's front legs are dangling and bent at painful angles over Ted's head, and now Ted, with the bear, is running full bore at the highway barrier.

"Stan," I say. "What's he . . . is he going to . . . *throw* the bear over the guardrail? Stan?"

Stan doesn't respond. He's watching Ted and muttering, and I want to yell at him to snap out of it, but I'm also completely terrified that if I disturb this situation, if I let the bear know there are other people here who are weaker and more terrified than Ted, then the bear'll eat Ted, and then Callie, oh God, Callie. I look back. She's watching everything with her hands over her eyes, her fingers splayed wide like slats in a window blind. Ted's still carrying the bear, and it still looks to me like he's preparing to throw it far away from us, but I'm having lots of trouble believing in a reality as insane and backward and illogical as the one that's apparently right in front of me. But it's all I have to believe in, and so I do. I hope he throws the bear over the divider. Because the bear will recover from a fall like that, he'll just get up and scramble away and out of sight, and then Ted will dust himself off and get back in the car, and he'll just sit in the backseat blankly and calmly like nothing ever happened, and we'll drive off, trembling, completely terrified, and just so relieved to be alive.

But that isn't what happens.

What happens is: Ted rams the bear's head into the barrier. He runs at full speed, somehow managing to distribute the bear's weight so that the bear is in front of and forward of his body, almost like a lever. This doesn't look right, not even a little, and now it definitely doesn't look like Ted was ever planning on throwing it. Instead, he keeps pushing forward. He gathers momentum until there's nothing left to gather, and all that's left for him to do is ram the bear's head into the highway barrier.

But then he doesn't stop. He finds more slack to pick up. He just keeps moving, pushing into the dirt with his legs while the bear shudders, goes limp, and makes the saddest, most terrible sounds. The sound of all life leaving a body that big. These are not sounds I am ever going to forget. Teeth are falling like loose change. Ted's face isn't exactly calm, but it's also not incredibly expressive or full of fear or pain either. Like a guy in a weight room. Like he's exerting a lot of concentration and effort, but without any actual feelings attached to it. I can't help but think Ted looks a little monstrous.

Suddenly, we're moving.

Slowly, Stan is inching us forward. "Ted!" he calls. "TED!" he shouts again, but louder. "TED!" he screams and opens the car door.

Ted looks up, and just like that, he walks back to us, his footfalls strong and deliberate. His face still has that look of almost frighteningly dedicated concentration. His jaw is clenched so tight I can see it through the filters of the dirty windshield and the tears welled up in my eyes. His eyes are focused on something beyond us, and he's still moving like the world's a step behind, leaning forward, as if pulled—no, tugged—along. Beyond him the big bear twitches, and I realize I'm holding my breath.

Stan gets out of the car and walks to Ted. He isn't shouting now, he's saying, calmly, soothingly, "Ted. Hey, Ted." When he gets to him, he says, "Whoa," and Ted still doesn't look at him. Stan puts his arms on Ted's shoulders, and it isn't until he stops Ted in his tracks that Ted's eyes seem to see him. "Ted, whoa, hey," Stan says, and Ted's jaw slowly unclenches. While Stan leads him back to the car, I coach myself to start breathing again, slowly. I look back at Callie again, bracing myself for how frightened she must be, but her face looks placid. She's just sitting there, quiet and still. She's looking ahead, north.

WE'RE DRIVING AGAIN. It's quiet as hell.

I never thought of hell as being quiet before, but I'm starting to think, of course, that's exactly what it would be. Hell is probably just you and whatever demons are crawling around in your head, locked in a small, quiet room, damned to whisper to each other forever. Neither of us moves to put on the radio, even though I think we'd both rather listen to anything other than the sound of us coming to terms with what just happened.

After a few miles we reach a rest stop, and I don't even need to tell Stan to pull over. We park, and I tell him I'm going for a walk.

"Okay," he says, and then, more quietly and without making eye contact, "Just stay close? And maybe be back soon, please?"

I nod and I walk a bit, making sure I can see him and Callie and

SASHA STEPHENSON

Ted, even though all I want to do is walk into that crowd of people and disappear, get lost, or at least just be surrounded by people who didn't just encounter a bear that climbed over a highway divider to stare at you through your windshield, like your body was a jar of honey it wanted to eat. Who didn't just see a strange kid kill, with nothing but his body and fury, that bear who would have otherwise killed you. I realize my breath keeps catching, keeps getting held, and that my heart is trying to kick its way out of my chest and run someplace safe.

I stop and watch Callie lying in the lawn across from the parking lot. She's smiling, her fists bunching up around the grass. Without thinking, I take out my phone and call my dad. I'm totally terrified, completely scared, and possibly definitely traumatized, and I don't know what to do, and I want to talk to my dad.

TWELVE

THE PHONE'S RINGING.

And it rings again. And again.

When it rings *again*, I check the screen to make sure I pressed the listing for Dad with the satellite emoji next to it, which signals the number for the super-high-tech phone my parents use on expeditions, the one that can always reach them. After confirming that I do in fact know how to operate a smartphone contact list, the line rings again one more time, and then starts in on the next ring when Mom picks up.

It's not that I don't love my mom. And it's not even that I don't love talking to her, or as though my mom hasn't talked me through upwards of fifty, actually probably more like one hundred, crises. It's more that, where Callie's concerned, Mom's always sort of thought of her as more of a specimen she's objectively interested in than, say, a daughter. Dad and I, we see her as a necessary part of the family. Or at the very least I know that Dad makes sure we all know that he's on

Callie's side, and he has shown what could easily be called compassion toward his younger daughter, in addition to his first and favorite. But anyway, it was Mom and not Dad who answered the phone, so I prepare to put the kind of cheerful voice that might get me past the gatekeeper and into Dad's ear.

"Hey, Mom!"

"Hi, Lorna, sweetie. Is everything okay? Did something happen to Callie?"

"No, no, Callie's fine! Everything's just dandy. How're the turtles?"

"Turtles?"

"Whenever anyone says 'Galápagos,' all I can think of are giant turtles everywhere, possibly speaking, catering, bringing drinks, floaties, et cetera."

"Cabana boy turtles is what you're telling me you imagined?"

"Yes."

"Well, that's certainly a fun image," she says, and then we both go silent for too long for either of us to keep pretending that everything's normal and fine.

"Lorna?" Mom says.

"Yeah?"

"Are you going to ask me to fetch your father so you two can talk about whatever it is you two talk about?"

"Mom! I'd never even *dream* of asking you to do a thing like that!"

"Well, I take it all back then," says Mom.

"I forgive you," I say, then take a deep breath away from the speaker. "But now that you mention Dad . . ."

"Aha! Well, sorry, sweetie, but your father is unavailable right now. He's out at the research site, and he'll be mostly unreachable for the better part of the rest of the day. The sinkholes and the lightning storms are at it again, but there are also these strange clouds that keep gathering. You get the feeling they'll shake with thunder at any minute. And beneath them, the earth and the sea are trembling. As if they're in concert. It's so bizarre, honey. And absolutely amazing. Your father claims he's seen something like it before, but it was back when we didn't have the instruments we have now, so the data is practically nonexistent. It'll take us at least a week to figure out what to make of it."

Perfect. My eyes wander over to the car. Stan, Callie, and Ted are just sort of standing there, waiting, looking freaked. Even Ted looks freaked out, like maybe everything that just happened finally, right this moment, caught up with him. And the idea that he maybe didn't know what he was doing is pretty scary, and the idea that he is just now realizing what happened is honestly even scarier to me right now. So I just go for it.

"Well, Mom, since you and I are chatting and all . . ."

"Yes, honey?"

And all at once, I can't even help it. It just spills out of me. I tell her about the party and about how it wasn't my idea but I still let it happen, so I'm sorry for that, but I think I kept it under control okay, and don't worry, the house is fine, and everyone made it home safely and responsibly. But how the party came to a screeching halt when we discovered that Callie made this model of an island. I describe to her the vibrating expanse of the sculpture, with the almost blooming blossom things, the way it trembled, the way Callie's hands trembled over it. My voice catches on the words and feelings that are coming up from my chest and propelled out of my mouth, into the receiver, up to the satellites, and then into my mother's ear.

I power past these trips and falls and tell her about Stan and Ted, who they are and how they came to the house after Stan and I found out that Ted was also building an island at the exact same time Callie was. I tell her how, after a lot of careful debating, Stan and I decided to take our siblings and go, to figure out what they needed. Because they'd built those sculptures of what seemed like exactly the island where Dad was when he found them, and they kept pointing to it and trying to get in the car, and in the end, all we could think was that they wanted to go there. Home. To *their* home. And then before we knew it, they were running to the car, and then they were in the car, and so we figured that was it, they wanted to get in the car and go somewhere, so we drove. We just drove. It was the only thing we could think to do for them.

I tell her about the diner, how I decided, or I guess already believed, already *knew*, that I wanted—that I *want*—to do this because of Callie. Because of craving that closeness and feeling of sisterhood and finally, for once, maybe being able to do something for her. I talk about agency, how Callie and Ted and everyone like them seem so trapped in these bodies without language, with no way to ever really tell anyone anything, ever, not about themselves, or the weather, or the weather inside of themselves. Nothing. Not a thing, not once, not ever, not never.

And then the bear. Oh my God. I tell her about the bear, and I just barrel through it because I can't even stand to think about it or to have her ask me about it. So before she can ask I tell her not to, and I tell her that we're fine, but we're all really rattled. Even Ted looks rattled now, like he wasn't prepared for any of this, for his actions, for the bear, for the highway, for this life.

"But," I tell her, "they *are* trying to go somewhere. I know they are. It's like they're being pulled, and they're pulling us in that same direction. They need to go home, to *their* home, they know that we can take them there, that we can do this thing for them. Mom, this is a chance for me to do more than just chaperone her around a world she isn't equipped to engage with." And now my throat is closing up on me, and the words are sort of hiccupping out. "This is me enabling whatever it is she feels to be her sense of purpose. I'm sorry," and I start sobbing and trying to talk through it, which barely works. "I know this sounds crazy. You're probably freaking out. But this just feels so important. And I'm responsible, remember?" And I take a moment here, because I'm crying. "You and Dad said it yourselves. I am. I'm a good kid, and it's not just because I know how to work around things. It's because I have no real interest in trouble, and I don't invite it. How often do you get to do a good thing, like a genuinely good deed, for someone you love? Mom. I'm scared. But I'm mostly happy because I can help Callie." And I start wiping the snot from my nose and the tears from my face and trying to do that thing from earlier where I try to remember how to breathe.

It doesn't work, though. My heart is racing all over again, and I just wish it would stop, but it won't. The line is insanely quiet. I have no idea what is coming, and I am terrified. I keep breathing into the stark silence, but I know she's still on the phone, because I can hear something gathering inside her.

Then, suddenly: "Turn around, Lorna," she says. "Now. Right now. Get in the car, then turn the car around, and go back home. Please. Please, Lorna."

My eyes dart to Callie, and my heart starts jumping even more. *What?*

"What?" I say. "Mom, did you hear anything I just said?" *Oh God oh God oh God.* I shouldn't have said anything! Unless, "Is it because of the party? Because the house is fine, and locked up, and I called the cops to let them know we wouldn't be home in case of burglaries, and I set timers for the lights, and . . ." Ugh. Of course it's not that. Obviously, Lorna, come on. "Is it the thing with the bear? Because we're fine! I was just scared, so I wanted to tell someone about it so I could feel less scared. Which I do now! Thank you! Talking to you has really helped. It was nothing. Mom, I just—"

"Lorna. I need you to listen to me. I need you to take a deep breath and listen to what I'm about to tell you, which also happens to be something people could kill me for telling you. Okay?"

"Okay," I say softly, and now I feel my heart is actually in danger of stopping. Everything's stopped. The whole world feels like it's slowing down, and now I'm stuck here, in this moment, for probably forever. What the hell is she talking about?

"Listen. Your father"—she snorts a bit, or else breathes hard through her nose, I can't tell—"your father believes that this group of orphans Callie belongs to are peaceful and naive and innocent. But there are many people, many of them in the government, who do not feel this same way. These people believe that Callie and the other children like her are a sort of living weapon. A force to be used against us. Against people."

"What? Mom, are you kidding me with this? That's *insane*—"

"Lorna! Let me finish! This is important, you have no idea how important. Because of Jane. Jane—well, Jane isn't Callie's caseworker, Lorna. Jane is the government liaison who was assigned to monitor Callie and Ted and three other Orphans. This is why it's always the same hospitals, always the same doctors." She pauses for a moment, and my chest feels crushed, like the bear from Ted's fury.

"Lorna," she starts again. "Lorna, if you take Callie and that boy, Ted, if you take them back to the place where they were discovered, which is where I'm almost certain they're trying to get you to take them, if you do that, the consequences will be very, very bad." She gets quiet here, and she does not elaborate on what she means by "bad." "We've been playing with fire for years by having her here, in our family, in our home, and if you do this . . . If you do this, Lorna, baby, there will be hell to pay."

"Stop!" I shout, panic engulfing me now. "What the hell are you even talking about? I—I don't believe you. I don't believe a *single* word you say! Where's Dad? I want to talk to Dad. Please. Now. Put Dad on please. Now."

"I *can't*, Lorna. I told you—he's not here, he's at the site, and thank God he is. Please. *Please*. Please do not take them back there. Please. Please listen to me, and do as I said, and I promise that Jane won't harm you. Or Callie," she adds.

Then, after her longest pause yet, during which I'm not talking because I'm shaking so hard and she's not talking because her desperation is so thick I can feel it through the phone, she says, "Whatever you do, Lorna, please: Please don't die for Callie. Please. Just please promise me you won't die for her. I know you love her, I know you love her like she was your own sister, I know that. But do not get between her and the government. Please. Please don't die for her. She's not your blood. Please, Lorna—"

I hang up. I don't know why I didn't do it sooner, but what she said about Callie, about how she's not my blood . . . I just couldn't hear any more of it. I look over, and Stan is waving at me. Somehow, blindly and floating like in a dream, I make it there, to the car, and he starts the engine.

"What happened?" he says.

And then I just start weeping and shaking and shaking and weeping.

THIRTEEN

WE'RE STILL GOING NORTH.

Stan's driving again, and I'm just staring out the window, thinking that if I don't make a sound, then I can maybe draw all the sounds around us right into me. And then I could drown out the echo of everything my mother just told me.

Weeks pass like this, but then I check the clock on the radio, and it's only been an hour.

Another ten minutes pass, and that feels like a whole day, and I just want to crawl out of my skin. I feel like my guts want to jump out of my mouth and like my bones want to crawl out after them and head off in another direction entirely, like south, or east, or west, or anywhere but here, and then whatever's left of me will just be here, in the car, existing. What Mom said. I. I can't even form thoughts right now, the only things echoing around spookily in my head are a few disjointed words, some underwater sounds. I'm narrating all this to myself to try to give any sort of structure to anything at all.

"Lorna . . ." says Stan, tentatively, quietly, and the sound of my name pulls me up out of myself. A bit.

I don't say anything, though, because I'm still trying really hard to draw all of the sounds into my body. Except I don't actually have the capacity to manipulate sound waves. Or to pretend that that phone call never happened. Or to deal with any of this at all right now.

So I stop trying to deal with things. Because obviously I can't. Stan is still waiting patiently for me to be ready to speak. I need to tell him about the phone call. Of course I need to tell him. It's all trying to get out anyway, so why not, why not just weep all over the passenger seat, and on Stan too.

"I talked to my mom. I was hoping for my dad, but I got my mom instead. And, um . . ." And of course I can't stop my face from trembling here.

"It's okay, Lorna, just—"

"It's *not* okay, Stan, okay?" He flinches when I snap at him, and I immediately feel bad. "I'm sorry. Just listen. Please?"

He nods, and I thank him.

"I wanted to call my dad because he's the only one who cares about Callie like I do. I think. Jesus, I don't know anything anymore. Hold on." I blow my nose into my sleeve as hard as I can to mask the fact that I'm choking down sobs. "Anyway," I go on, "my mom picks up instead, because my dad is out at the research site, and we talk, and I tell her . . . everything." Stan starts a bit in his seat, and his eyes go wide and panicked. "I know, I know, but please, just wait, okay? I told her everything.

"And she completely freaks out. She does a one eighty, and it's not even that she's mad, she's just *freaked. Out.* She said the *government* is after Callie? That Hospital Jane is a *government liaison*, and that the government thinks they're weapons. She kept telling me, over and over, that we shouldn't take them back there, that they were definitely trying to get us to take them back up north, where they came from. She said not to get between them and the government, or we'll basically die." And now I'm just full-on crying and not even trying to stop or hide it. "*What the hell*, Stan? What the hell are we supposed to do with this?"

"Jesus," says Stan quietly.

And I look back at Callie and Ted and see them sitting there quietly, one sweet and one brooding, and I wait for the world to end around us.

And then nothing happens. The world doesn't end. Ted yawns. Callie yawns. Then I yawn, and I realize we're no longer moving. Maybe the world did end.

Either way, Stan pulls over. We're sitting here in a car on the side of the highway while all around us other cars with other people in them pass us by, their lives untroubled by the kinds of trouble we're dealing with in here. The sheer incomprehensible impending disaster that my mom's phone call painted the world to be. Because I know my mom isn't messing with me. Because my mom has never really ever messed with me, and on the rare occasions she attempts a joke, she uses this voice, like she shifts her voice so I know she's messing with me, like she always wants me to know where she stands. My mom is a dedicated research scientist. Her whole life is about gathering data and then sitting down with that data and finding ways to see what the data is trying to tell her about the universe. She's told me that the world is a series of narratives and that all you need to do is listen to the story it's telling you. That science isn't about deciding which story you like best; it's about listening to all the stories as they're told. When you're little, you test the hypothesis. You have an idea, and then you try to figure out if your idea is right, and if it's not then you change your idea to figure out what the right one is. You don't change the data to fit the assumption. When you do that, you fail the science fair.

Which is all just to say that I believe her. Every word she said. Which is totally and compellingly terrifying.

"Are you sure..." starts Stan, after an uncomfortable span of silence. "Are you sure you heard her right, or—"

"You mean, did her voice come through over the completely clear satellite connection?"

"*Or* are you sure that this wasn't maybe your mom's idea of a joke?"

"Please," I snort. "My mom's jokes aren't, like, *jokes*. I mean just that she doesn't invent stuff. Her 'jokes' are always, like, facts that strike her as ridiculous. Like the kinds of things you see on the insides of Snapple caps. And anyway, the main reason I know she wasn't joking is because when I was listening to her, something happened. On my end. Where I put everything together—that night at the hospital, the party, this trip, the bear—and I feel like it's all true. The government, the danger." Stan has his head in his hands now, and he's slumped against the steering wheel. "I'm sorry, but I don't know what else to think, Stan! Either my parents have been lying to me my whole life or they've just decided to choose the scariest and cruelest possible moment—when their terrified daughter calls them looking for comfort—to start lying to me and messing with my head. I mean, which one is harder to believe?"

"So your parents are government agents," says Stan.

"*What?*"

"I mean, think about it. If what your mom said was true, then for them to even *know* all of this... They'd know this because they were contracted, right? Maybe? The government wouldn't just tell *anyone* something like that. Right?" He's looking straight ahead and setting his jaw all rigid, and he smells like sweat and fear, like scared wet salt on a knife, and I'm sure that I must too.

"Well, then, that means your dad's one of them too," I say.

"*What?*"

"If my parents are in on it, like you said, and if this is really happening, then . . ."

"Lorna—"

"Stan, I just saw your brother smash a *bear's head* into a highway wall. My mother just told me to let my sister *die* because the government thinks she's a weapon. Callie, who is *right there*, in the backseat, weaving a crown out of grass as we speak, a *weapon*. Because apparently my parents, and probably every single other parent who adopted an Iceling, are not who they say they are and don't work where they say they work, because they actually work for the government." My sobs come out in short choking bursts now, until I'm still deeply crying, but there's no sound or water, and my face is just twisting itself into all these distorted shapes.

He takes a deep breath. "You're right," Stan admits. "My dad's probably on the inside of this too. He's been looking at Ted this whole time like he might be a weapon, not because he has a kind of anger problem, which could happen to any teenage kid, but because he knows how they were found."

"*We* know how they were found too. My dad was the one who found them. He told me all about it."

"And did he tell you the government has thought Callie is a weapon from the start and that he worked for the government too? Did he tell you that they were monitoring their every mood and moment? Did he tell you we were probably—shit, I'm sorry." He stops as he looks up at me, noticing that I'm sobbing. Cool. This is great. This is the most fun road trip in the history of the whole world. Four stars, would embark on again. "I'm sorry, Lorna. I know I'm being a jerk."

"It's fine. This situation is sucky as hell, but you're fine. You're not being any more of a jerk than anyone else would be, considering we just found out our parents probably work for the government, and the government thinks Ted and Callie are deadly weapons. And so our parents have also definitely been lying to us, about stuff way bigger than the tooth fairy or the democratic process, for our entire lives."

"So our parents have been in cahoots with the government about our weird Orphan Icelings, about our *families*, our whole lives. And according to your mom, they have some sort of nefarious plan for them. So we just need to figure out what, if anything, we can do about it. Right?"

"So you think we should take them to their home, right? No matter what? Even if that's the one thing my mom said not to do? We're taking them back to where they were found—really found, wherever that is. That's where we're going. That's what we're doing."

And then I look to the backseat, where our Icelings are. What do I do here? How do I ask if this is really what they want? How do I make them know that if we keep going north, a serious threat might be lying in wait? Do they already know and don't care? Or are their minds as free from suspicion as their faces seem to suggest?

I look back at Stan, and he's just staring straight ahead, looking as perplexed as I feel. Then I feel a hand on my shoulder, and I turn around. Callie, reaching out to me. She touches my tears, which makes me start crying again, and then she just nods over at the road, like *hey, let's get going, sister*. Stan and I switch shifts. I turn the key and then signal to merge. And lo, we have merged.

So that was that. Second star to the right and straight on 'til morning, or 'til the government blows us up and our parents pull off their parent masks and are complete strangers, and everything around us crumbles and burns.

FOURTEEN

SO BASICALLY EVERYTHING is completely terrible and also a total disaster right now.

This is how it feels, for me, at least, to be alive, in Maine, which is huge, by the way.

Dave keeps texting me, and now that I know what I know, I have no idea what to say to him anymore. It's not as if I feel like I'm talking to a stranger now, but rather like he's talking to a stranger whom *neither* of us know. I just keep answering that everything is fine, then tell him about the clouds I can see from the car, or type something cute and witty, because what else can I tell him that won't put both of us in danger?

My phone lights up with a buzz, and I think how quickly I went from loving when that happens to absolutely dreading it.

How're u feeling bae? It's Mimi.

tired//hungry//great, I text back. The first two items on that list are true, but as to the last one, my plan right now is that maybe I shouldn't tell anyone what I am feeling, because what I am feeling is basically that all my authority figures are liars, and the government wants to kill my sister, and my parents are at least half-fine with that. And maybe if we get Callie where she's going safe and sound, she'll find somewhere she belongs more than with me. Which is great, but also the worst thing ever to have happened. And how do you say that to your best friend, or to the boy with whom you do homework, plus other stuff too? I know that Mimi and Dave only want to help and that they're worried about me. But they can't help, no one can help, because I can't tell them all the things I've just learned.

The one thing I *do* know is that Stan and I have to get Callie and Ted to wherever they're going. I can't think about anything else— especially the part about maybe we'll be killed if Stan and I get Callie and Ted to wherever they're going. And this is what's churning around and around in my head when Stan nearly crashes into the guardrail. We stop abruptly. After I turn to make sure Callie's okay and all buckled in, I whip right around to face Stan.

"What the hell!" I shout.

"Sorry! Sorry! It's this idiot guy! He's been, like, waving at me, at us, viciously. What the hell is he doing?"

I look. A car is parked right behind us, and the driver's side door is open. A guy in his twenties or early thirties gets out, and then I look closer and see a girl sitting inside the car in the passenger seat, staring straight ahead.

The guy approaches and sticks his head in Stan's window.

"Hi!" he says. "I'm Bobby."

"Uh, hey, Bobby," we say, tentative as all heck.

"I see you guys have some Orphans in there," he says, blocking the sun with one hand and putting his forehead against the back window. "Or AROs, as you might call them?"

"Um," we say. Stan looks at me, and all I can do is stare blankly back.

"So let's go somewhere and talk!" says Bobby.

"You want us to *go* somewhere with you?" I say, every protective instinct in me firing up on all cylinders.

"Wait a second, dude. Why would we follow a complete stranger who nearly just ran us off the highway? What do you want?" says Stan.

"Huh! Good point! Fair enough," Bobby says, putting his hands up and smiling. "Let's start over? I'm Bobby, and it's very nice to meet the both of you. I'm a grad student in anthropology. That's Greta," he says, gesturing with a nod toward the girl sitting in his car. We follow his nod and then look back at Bobby. "Greta used to be real close with my younger brother, Alex," he goes on. "But now it's just me and Greta. My stipend covers off-campus housing, so she stays with me. Anyway, the other day, Greta built this amazing *island*." Stan and I look at each other while trying to make it look like we're not looking at each other. "And after that, things got what I'd call vaguely . . . nuts. She dragged me to the car, and here we are, headed north. And your friends in the backseat there have that same look."

"What *look*?" Stan says. I can feel his defensive feathers ruffling.

"Same as Greta there. Sandy blond hair, pale eyes with that look in them that says that language, or what we call language, doesn't mean anything to them. Then of course there's the whole steering the car north thing and all."

"Could you hold on for just a sec?" I say to Bobby, holding up a finger and smiling weirdly, and then I pull Stan out of the car through my door and walk him around to the hood, as far away from Bobby as I can get without losing sight of Callie.

"Who the hell is this guy?" I ask as quietly as possible.

"I don't know," Stan whispers back. "But he's basically narrating our day back to us, minus a bear attack. And"—he doesn't look happy saying this—"his sister sounds like she's probably an Iceling too."

"So what do we do? Just go with him? He could be anyone."

"I mean . . . should we just go get a bite and see what this guy is about?"

"Yeah. Yeah, okay, I guess."

"We'll be somewhere public. With people . . ."

"So if he tries anything . . ."

"Exactly."

Bobby is still whistling inconspicuously. Stan pokes his head out and says, "Okay, dude. Let's go get something to eat. Separate cars."

"Of course!" says Bobby. "This'll be great."

We get back in the car and wait just long enough for Bobby to get his car started, then we pull onto the freeway with this stranger and his sister, his purported *Iceling* sister, in the backseat, and we all head, convoy-style, toward the nearest rest stop.

✳

WE FIND A pavilion that has Burger King and Sbarro and Starbucks. We're all grateful to be stopping to eat and rest, and plus Bobby's buying. It really seems like Bobby wants us to like him. Imagine that.

Bobby tells us he's a linguist. He "got into the field" after something happened to his little brother, Alex, who was incredibly close to Greta, who is currently disassembling her salad on the plate and then reassembling it, piece by piece, on her fork. It's not really clear what happened with his brother, the way he tells it.

And what he keeps repeating, really stressing, is how inseparable Alex and Greta used to be. He tells us a story about how, one day, when Alex and Greta were around eight or nine years old, they wandered off to the greenhouse. After a few hours, their mom asked Bobby to go check on them. And when he did, there was just Greta. But she wasn't at the greenhouse. She was about a mile away, in the woods. Bobby'd seen the start of their tracks and followed them easily enough, but then the wind carried them away. "They found Alex a few hours later," he says, but exactly how they found him, Bobby doesn't seem to want—or be able—to say.

"I'd rather not talk more about that, if that's all right," he says, but then after a few deep breaths during which he stares down at his plate in front of him, he starts talking about it more. "It was winter. I couldn't see their tracks because of the fresh snow, so we had no idea where to start looking for them. All we knew was they got at least twenty feet from the greenhouse. When we got to Greta, she was warm. No frostbite. No hypothermia, no shaking, no loss of color. Nothing. She looked like she always looks. She didn't have a jacket on. It was the strangest thing," he says so quietly, then looks away.

I look over at Callie. "Hey, kid sister," I say. She doesn't turn to look at me; instead she gulps down her Sprite, closes her eyes, then smiles quietly to herself.

Bobby tells us he misses his brother. "Every day, I miss him. And it's weird how you hold on to memories. You know? How you start to wonder if the things that happened happened exactly how you remembered them or if that's just the story you tell yourself to keep going. But I get Greta. And she and Alex were so close, it's almost like there's a piece of him still here as long as she's around. So that's something." He stops, then takes a long gulp of his iced tea, the ice at the bottom of the glass rattling around.

It's hard to tell, only spending the greater part of an hour with her, but Greta seems to be somewhere between Ted and Callie, temperament-wise. If Callie is shy yet sociable, and if Ted is antisocial and rather aggressive when provoked, then Greta'd be categorized as relatively sociable and mildly assertive. She eats more slowly and with more patience than Ted and Callie, who tend to approach their meals in random bursts of hunger. We used to keep track of Callie's eating patterns on these worksheets we got from Jane, which were, apparently, for the freaking government to use to determine whether or not my sister is a monster.

And seeing the three of them together, they look like siblings. Like fraternal triplets. It's weird. Weirder than how it was when I first saw Callie and Ted together. There were so many similarities, but I didn't think of them as brother and sister. But now, the three of them . . . I don't know. I don't know what to make of this.

Bobby finishes his drink and starts telling us how his interest in language and linguistics stemmed from the questions Alex used to ask when he was a kid, about how to better try to talk to Greta. Hearing him talk about it, I realize that Bobby's approach to those questions is something I wish I'd thought of, honestly.

"It just made me think, you know?" says Bobby. "About the roots of language, why we need it, how and why it works. So in the time that I've been the sole brother taking care of Greta, my Iceling—real great neologism, by the way, I'm really cottoning to it—I've tried every sort of base language and permutations I can think of, writing programs to cycle through them endlessly, getting Greta to sit and listen to them with headphones on, electrodes to her temples, her butt in a chair in the living room of the apartment we share, checking to see if anything lights up. She watches a lot of plant docs on YouTube and Netflix and whatever. I started renting some from libraries too, playing them for her one after the other, sometimes keeping the electrodes on and wishing that I had any idea how to quantify, let alone name or navigate or define or even begin to get a glimpse of, the responses behind her eyes."

I've got to say, I admire his dedication to Greta. And the fact that he doesn't seem to blame her for his brother's death, the way you'd think the TV version of a guy like Bobby would. I can tell Stan's listening through his standoffish veneer and that he got especially perked up about the electrodes. I want to know what he's thinking right now. About Bobby and Greta and this whole trip now that we've met Bobby and Greta. And I want to hear what Bobby has to say about as badly as I want us to get back in the car and talk to Stan about what Bobby's saying.

"Like I was saying when I first met you guys, back on the highway, about the island?" Bobby says, and I nod to encourage him to keep going. "Well, just the other day, she started to build this island. Out of dirt and flowers and these sticks she uses to prop up plants. Building, like, *very* insistently. Somehow she built this island so that in the center of it was this kind of . . . *undulating* field. And these blossoms that looked . . . heavy. You know? Like they were about to give birth or something. And after she built it I could just tell that she needed something. She had her suitcase already packed—no idea when she did that, but that was another thing she'd gotten up to lately that was strange: packing and unpacking her suitcase like it was some kind of relay race. Anyway, after the island, with her in the car and looking so worried and scared and excited and I don't even know what, I had this thought: that I might be able to finally help her. The same thought Alex had that night. But he couldn't do it. And maybe I can. So that's why I'm here."

"Well, Bobby," says Stan, "that's exactly why we're here too."

"Yours too?" Bobby says.

"Yup," I say, and then all three of us gaze out at our siblings like proud parents at a dance recital.

Bobby smiles and excuses himself to go to the restroom.

I still don't know exactly what to make of Bobby, but I do know that the scared and suspicious feeling I got when he first flagged us down is pretty much gone now. I watch Stan watching Bobby as he walks, and I can tell that he's still skeptical. A few minutes later, Bobby comes back and then Stan gets up to use the bathroom, which is when my phone buzzes with a text from him that says, Okay, fine. His stories are crazy, but they sound pretty legit. But I can't take someone who dresses like a fancy nerd that seriously. I allow myself a little smile and then take a second look at Bobby's outfit: kinda tight chinos tucked into a pair of duck boots, faded button-down, a lined deck jacket. I don't know many grad students, but Bobby's style doesn't seem so off-base from the language-obsessed intellectual he claims to be. yr just jealous of his sweet all-weather gear, I text back, trying to let Stan know that I'm not worried about Bobby, but that this is first and foremost our journey.

Anyway, if Bobby's attentiveness to his appearance is Stan's only complaint about him, then I know he agrees with me that this guy knows about Icelings. It's clear he's lived most his life alongside one of them, and he knows all about the delicate balancing act you're forced to perform when you're the one pivot point between them and everything else in the whole world.

Stan joins us back at the table, and we share a look and a wink to acknowledge our secret text conversation. Then Bobby leans in, as if to initiate some kind of huddle in which he's about to tell us the game plan.

"I figure," he tells us, "that if *my* Iceling did this, and *your* Icelings did this—building the islands, I mean, and then making us drive north—then probably other Icelings are doing this too. Maybe *all* the Icelings are doing this. Like a mass exodus sort of thing," he says.

Bobby waits a beat, as though he's waiting for us to say something. When we don't, when instead Stan and I both just study him and try to figure out if he's for real, Bobby continues. "If that's true, then that means *something*, something deep in their bones or their hearts or their memories, is calling them home. All of them at once. So we'll probably see more of them, and more of us, out here on the road pretty soon. And what worries me is that someone other than us'll notice too."

"You're right," says Stan, without a hint of mocking or smugness in his voice.

"Yeah," Bobby says, and then we're all quiet as we try to think about what this means.

"Oh my God," I yelp. "Where are they?" Because all of a sudden Callie and Ted and Greta are gone, and I have no idea where they are.

Stan panics. "How the hell did this happen? They were right there! *We* were right there!"

"Guys," says Bobby, "it's fine. They're by the cars. They probably just got impatient. See?"

Bobby points at the window behind Stan and me, and there they are. By the cars. Just like Bobby said. And I don't know how Stan feels about it, but I do know that right now I'm feeling a little bit jealous of Bobby and his skills at being a big sibling.

"Let's get out of here," Stan says, and we bus our tables and head out to where our Icelings wait to get back on the road to the Great Wherever.

Out in the parking lot, Bobby says, "Hey, guys, I got this big old SUV from my parents a while ago. I converted it to biodiesel, so it smells like french fries, but it's got a ton of room."

"Nice sales pitch," says Stan. "You trying to get rid of it?"

"Ha, no, man, you're funny. I just mean that if things are feeling a bit crowded in your car, you guys could always ride with me. Since we're heading in the same direction and all. Plus, I don't know what your situation is, man, and I don't mean to presume, but I do know that I'm not a teenager driving a car in my parents' name, so no one's looking out for me in that kind of way. You know?" I can't tell if what Bobby's saying sounds more ominous or practical—though it's definitely a little pushy, I know that, and I have a feeling Stan does too.

ICELING

"Nah," says Stan. "Even if our parents freaked, and on that possibility we're mostly covered, I think, when it comes down to it, the government's been keeping tabs on the Icelings their whole lives. Once they figure out what's happening, if they haven't figured it out already, they'll be tracking us anyway. So if it's cool with you, let's just do this convoy-style?"

"Hey, fair point," says Bobby, holding his hands up in mock surrender. "I'll see you out there on the road!"

We exchange numbers, get in our cars, and wave to one another as we start our engines and roll out. It's my turn to drive, and I wink at Callie as I turn around to back us out, and then Callie reaches forward and points us north again. It's fifteen minutes before I realize we missed the sunset.

FIFTEEN

BOBBY'S LEADING THE way, mostly because Stan likes the idea of keeping him in front of us rather than behind us. As the traffic builds on this weirdly busy stretch of highway, I start imagining that I'm seeing all these cars pulling into and out of traffic gaps from way up above, their swerves and swoops making up the shapes of their drivers' names. Cars keep passing us, we keep passing cars. Stan nudges me softly and points to a car just ahead of us on the right: a junky Mitsubishi Montero with a Montana license plate that says CORVET. Stan and I started keeping track of particularly strange vanity plates during a particularly boring stretch of New Jersey. So basically when we got to New Jersey. My favorites so far:

- CYCLOPATH
- 9-KIDS (There were only two in the car. What did they do with the other seven?)
- 1WOJMA

ICELING

- TOOTTOOT
- B33PB33P
- F4RTS

I give a small smile to the Mitsubishi CORVET, and Stan adds it to the list in his phone. We picked up some cigarette-lighter-thingy-compatible USB cables for our phones way back when we started this trip, and I'm surprised by how much comfort I get from knowing my phone—and its scary-good GPS capabilities—will never die. I've been wrestling with the idea of shutting off my phone, but I feel weird just cutting my whole world off like that—and I know that Dave and Mimi would completely freak out if I explained to them *why* I thought it best that I shut off my phone. It's been easy to dodge calls from Mom and Dad, and if worse comes to worst, I can always shut it off and chuck it out the window.

Finally, traffic starts to move a little. It's time to pull over to fill up the tank and switch driving shifts. My butt is numb from all the traffic-sitting, and this is the most relieved I've been to trade in the driver's seat for the passenger's. Bobby leans on the side of his car and chats with us as we pump and pay. He doesn't need gas for a few hundred miles; apparently Bobby gets great mileage in his french fry mobile. Good for him. For the past several miles, Ted has had that look in his eyes that Stan has decided means he needs to get out and pace. Maybe he's right, because Ted is currently all over the rest area, pacing up a storm, while Callie finds a patch of grass and plucks out some blades to braid in the car.

Back on the road, we pass another giant diner done up in chrome, and a song I like comes on the radio. I turn it all the way up, lean back against my seat, and let it wash over me. The traffic's building up again, and I can tell we're going to be at a standstill soon. As we slow down, I look over at the diner, which is directly outside my window now. We slow to a stop, and as I'm looking at the diner and the cars parked outside it, a flash of bright color in the diner window catches my eye. It's the sleeve of a high school varsity jacket, worn by a pretty girl about my age who's sitting alone in a booth and putting her hair up in a ponytail. A guy is walking toward her, he's maybe a little older, and my first thought is "Ugh, creep." But then he starts dancing at her. And he's *really good*. And he's totally in sync with the song playing in our car, and I think to myself that this is the most magical thing I've ever seen while sitting in traffic. But the pretty girl in the jacket just isn't having any of this. So the guy steps up his game. He pulls some sunglasses from his back pocket and puts them on, and then he drops out of sight beneath the table, like he did a split, and then a moment later he comes back up and leaps into the air, right onto the table, does a crotch grab and bends his body back, then hops down into the booth across from her.

I break out into wild and ecstatic applause, and Stan kind of flinches as if I woke him up from a trance.

"Stan!" I say. "Did you see that?"

"No," he says.

I look back to the diner as we inch forward a bit. The guy is chugging water, his chest heaving from having given it his all. The girl continues to stare at her phone.

Things like this, you can hardly believe them, even when you see them. But there they are, in front of your eyes, proving that anything can happen out here.

The traffic has barely eased up over the past two hours. We're on a particularly pitch-black and lonely stretch of road when my phone lights up with a text from Dave.

Heard a good joke today.

I hardly have the heart to text him back—I've been pretty standoffish with him, with anyone outside this car, and also sometimes inside it, ever since that awful talk with Mom—but of course I do because he's Dave and of course I miss him a lot.

i could use a joke rn, I text.

Why did Ernest Hemingway cross the road? he texts.

Then, like, a minute passes, and the ghost ellipses keep popping up and dying down, and so I text, idk. why?

To die. Alone. In the rain. I read the punch line, and I actually snort.

aw, that was a good one, I text back. snort-laugh-level good.

Good, he texts. I miss you. How's the road?

Well, let's see, Dave. This is what the road is like: A bear tried to kill us, but we lived, but only because Stan's Iceling brother picked it up, smashed its head into a guardrail, and killed it right in front of us. Oh yeah, and we met another guy with an Iceling sister who also built an island, so they are also headed north, and we are all headed north, quite possibly tracked by the government, which may or may not include our parents, who may or may not have been lying to us our entire lives.

the road's exhausting is what I really type. but we're fine.

Ugh. That felt terrible. Not even the lying-by-omission part— that I'm fine with. What feels terrible is feeling so alone with everything that's happening, and not knowing when that kind of loneliness will end. Or, depending on how big a deal this trek up north really is, *if* I'll ever be able to try to turn that loneliness into something else, something no less melancholic but certainly much less maddening.

And then it hits me. Not that I'll never be able to tell anyone about any of this—I don't know yet whether that's true or not—but that my whole life from before we got in the car is over. No matter what happens with Callie—Callie, who's drinking water from a bottle through a straw in the backseat while Ted squeezes a crayon he must have grabbed from the diner before the bear—no matter what happens to or between any of us on this trip, we can never go back. Because if the government thinks they're monsters, and if Mom tells them about the island, then they'll know where we're going. Unlike us, they know exactly where we're going.

But we have to take them. We told them we'd take them, and we have to. That's it. That's it now.

My phone buzzes. Dave again.

> Babe, I'm sorry things're weird and exhausting. But however weird and exhausting things are, you're doing this for Callie, whom you love. So there's that. And that's something. You know?

And it's not that I start crying. But I do, a little, just a few tears.

"Huh," Stan says.

"Hmm?" I say, wiping away all evidence of an emotional moment.

"Huh," Stan says again, then pauses, then says it again. And then: "Shit." He takes out his phone.

"What?" I say. But he's not answering. He glances at his phone and looks over to the left and behind us while trying to keep his eyes on the road.

"Stan, *what is it*?" I say, way more edge in my voice now. I look back to Callie and Ted, and for the first time in a while there is what looks like fire behind their eyes.

"Sorry," Stan says. "Hold on, we need to call Bobby."

"What? Why?"

"Call Bobby," he says into his phone, which he's put on speaker. It only rings half a ring before Bobby picks up.

ICELING

"I was just about to call you," Bobby says.

"So you noticed the thing with the cars too," Stan says.

"*What* thing with the cars?" I ask, now really starting to feel invisible. I look out the windows frantically, but it's all a mess of darkness, trees, and white and red lights. "Bobby!" I shout. "What thing with the cars? Will one of you tell me what the hell is going on?"

"Hold on," Stan says to Bobby, and he's turning to tell me, but by then he doesn't need to. I'm scanning the road and the travelers on it, and I see what they're talking about. Sitting in the back or passenger seat of almost every single car on the road around us right now are kids, all of them around sixteen years old, all of them staring out ahead, occasionally reaching for the wheel and nudging things north. No doubt about it, they are Icelings, with cheekbones like petals, broad and rising, and that dull blond hair like sweet but dead straw. Through some of the windows I can see that many of the kids are holding objects in their laps, and though I can only see the tip-tops of them, I know immediately what they are.

"They've got islands," I say. "They've got island sculptures."

I spot one that's made of grass, like Callie's, and a couple made of papier-mâché, of which one is way prettier than Ted's and one is way uglier. There's one made of drinking straws and one made of toothpicks and one made of recycled plastic shopping bags and one made of old paper plates that were either used to clean up a murder scene or collected at a backyard barbecue. I see one that takes up the entire back row of an SUV. Some of the Icelings are like Ted and Callie and have come on this trip island-less, and I assume that these are the Icelings who also made sculptures that were way too big to fit in the car. When I scan these cars, I see that Stan, Bobby, and I aren't the only ones getting wise to the situation all around us. I get this weird feeling in my stomach that is either terror or excitement at the fact that we are all here together for the same reason.

"This is exactly what Bobby said," says Stan. "A 'mass exodus.' Of Icelings and . . . *uses.*"

My stomach plummets as my mom's words echo in my head. *Don't die for her.* Is that the choice we're making here? Is that what all these other Icelings on the road are telling us?

"Oh my God," says Stan.

"I know," I say. I snatch up Stan's phone. "What do we do? Do we keep going?"

"I don't know," Stan says, looking from the Icelings on the highway to the Icelings in our backseat.

"I say we keep going," says Bobby.

Stan turns to look at me, then puts his phone on mute. "What do you think?" he says. "Should we trust him?"

I look back at Callie, and Stan's voice fades away. She's breathing so steadily, and her skin looks like it's almost glowing, as if illuminated by moonlight that isn't there because the sky is really cloudy.

"Uh, Lorna?" says Stan. "Hello?"

"Do they look happy?"

"Huh?" Stan says.

"The Icelings. Ours. Theirs. Do you think they look happy? Like people on their way to somewhere wonderful?"

Stan takes a long look at our siblings through the rearview. "They look completely content, Lorna," he says. "But you and I both know that that maybe doesn't mean anything."

"It means we're doing the right thing," I say, without much of a pause. "We're helping them."

"How can you be so sure?" says Stan, who has fought his way into the rightmost lane, clearly prepared to make a swift exit.

"I can't," I admit. "But look around us. Look how many of us there are. This can't be a mistake. All around us are people like us, taking care of their brothers and sisters, making this journey all because of love."

"Okay then," Stan says. He takes the phone off mute. "You're right. We'll keep going." He finds his way back into a middle lane.

"I agree with this," says Bobby, and then I reach over and end the call.

The thing is, I don't feel certain—in the way humans usually mean when they say that, at least. I don't feel at peace or completely free of doubt. Because all of this is a bit scary: all these cars full of kids ferrying their Orphans, their Icelings, their *siblings*, up north, wherever it is we're all headed, possibly just to certain doom. But this has nothing to do with me. It has to do with Callie, and all these kids who know what she knows, and about that I feel certain. So we keep going, straight on 'til whatever morning is out there, off in the distance, twinkling knowingly, like a smug jerk.

SIXTEEN

THE MORNING SKY is gray and covered in clouds, and it's my turn at the wheel. All is calm and quiet, this huge fleet of cars moving at a fairly steady pace, when suddenly a sea of red brake lights starts to blink on all around us. Stan leans out the window to get a better look. The whole highway has come to a stop, so I put the car in park.

"There's a whole bunch of cop cars up ahead," Stan says, pulling his head back into the car.

"Why?" I say "Is there an accident?"

"Not that I could see."

Bobby's one or two cars ahead of us, so we call him up and ask him if he can tell what's happening.

"All I can tell," says Bobby, "is that traffic's stopped. Shit. Hold on."

We exchange a worried glance, then look back to Ted and Callie. I'm expecting to see a pair of anxious frowns, but instead all I see is bright, clear-eyed alertness.

"I don't like this," Stan says.

"Okay, it's probably unlikely that this is, like, a stop to find us, right?"

"Probably," says Bobby, on speaker.

"Like, just a routine thing," I say, as if I believe this, as if saying it could make it real or make me even believe it.

"Right. A bunch of cops stopping northbound traffic. Just your everyday event here on this remote rural interstate."

"Okay," says Bobby, "We don't know that that's what's happening. Do you see any police cars or flashing lights? Let's figure this out." His voice sounds weird and doubled, and then I realize he's walking toward us, turning back and clicking the door lock button on his key ring.

"Hey, guys," says Bobby, leaning into the driver's side window, his phone still on and in his hand.

"Hi?" I say. I'm about to reach over and end the call, but Bobby stops me.

"Not so fast!" he says. "I think we should all just stay calm. I'll go up there and see what's up. It's not likely there's any sort of trouble about you guys, but seeing as I'm thirty and Greta's legal guardian and thus not her kidnapper and all, I think it's better that I go. I'll keep the call open; that way you guys can hear what's going on, and we'll figure out what's up."

Bobby heads up the line of traffic, and soon we hear him say, "Hey," though we can't see him and don't know whom he's talking to. "You guys have any idea what's going on?" Ted coughs, and I mute the phone.

"No, sorry. All we heard was some guy a few cars up yelling about his rights. And, like, the rules of the road. No idea if he was actually talking to someone or just ranting."

"Sounds like a cool guy," says Bobby.

"Hey, why're you holding your phone like that?" asks whomever Bobby's talking to.

"Oh," says Bobby. "No reason. So you said the guy was a few cars up, shouting about rules and rights?"

"Can't miss it," they say.

"Thanks!" Bobby says. Then, more quietly and right into the phone, he says to us, "So, first and foremost, I learned that I need to be less sketchy with my phone. Putting it in my pocket going forward. Second, thought you should know that guy had an Iceling in his car."

Good job, Bobby.

It doesn't take him long to find the car his informant told him about, which we can tell because all of a sudden we can hear the hollering.

"Hey!" we hear Bobby say. "Any idea what all the trouble is?"

A loud, static rustling fills the phone speakers in our car, and the best I can guess is that Bobby's jogging and the phone is rattling around in his pocket.

But then the next thing we hear is this: "What the hell is this? This goddamn phone in your pocket—it's on! Are you goddamn *spying* on us? Who the hell are you?"

"What? No!" Bobby says, sounding farther away than before. "I'm just trying to figure out why there are, like, a hundred cars, totally stopped, with absolutely no indication of when we're going to get moving again."

A new voice—a woman's—says something unintelligible, and then the angry and suspicious guy pipes up again with "Yeah, right, explain that!"

"Come on, sir, have a little faith. These are just my friends on the line—they're in the jam too—and I put them on hold, uh, in my pocket while I came to talk to you. Sir, I swear—"

And then we don't hear anything after that.

ICELING

※

UNTIL TEN MINUTES later, when Bobby calls us back.

"Jesus, Bobby," says Stan when he picks up. "We thought that guy might've murdered and ate you or something. You okay?"

"Man. That guy had a whole lot of what you'd call opinions regarding the rules of the road and his rights as a citizen of the United States in possession of an automobile that he drives on roads his taxes pay for. Good lord. Sorry about that—it was him who hung up on you, not me, by the way."

"But did he have any information?" I ask. "Anything useful and not insane or irrational?"

"No."

"So those ten minutes after that guy hung up on us . . ." says Stan.

"Lucky me, I got to spend those ten minutes listening to a series of lectures about the aforementioned subjects, given while his five-year-old daughter was knocking her head against the backseat window. I wish I knew Morse code, it could have been an SOS."

"Damn," says Stan. "Stay strong, little trouper."

"Anyway, there was one helpful person. I think she just wanted us to shut the hell up and give her some peace, but she was helpful nonetheless. She said that the AM traffic band had been offline for nearly an hour. Apparently it started fritzing out when this big standstill started. Which doesn't seem ominous at all, right?"

"Nope," says Stan.

"Totally not at all ominous in any way," I say.

"Great," says Bobby. "Real glad we're all in agreement here. Anyway, she also said she heard that the AM band would be back up anytime now, so we can stay tuned for that."

"Can't wait," says Stan.

"I'm gonna get back to Greta," says Bobby. "Keep in touch?"

"Roger that," I say, and Bobby heads back to the french fry mobile.

SO WE SIT there for exactly thirty-six minutes. Maybe thirty-six minutes doesn't sound like a crazy amount of time to be stuck in traffic in the grand context of terrible traffic jams all over the world, but when you're stuck in traffic because just ahead of you is most likely a veritable sea of cops in their cop cars, and you're in the car with your siblings with whom you've run away from home, and the government possibly suspects those siblings are weapons who mean to harm our lives, liberty, and pursuit of happiness, then trust me: thirty-six minutes is a *very long time.*

We've been tuned to the AM band with the traffic broadcast, which spits to life after thirty-six minutes. *"The northbound lane is closed,"* a canned voice keeps saying, over and over again. *"Unforeseen maintenance,"* says the radio.

"Unforeseen my ass," says Stan.

I follow his eyes to the off-ramp off the shoulder. I can tell what he's thinking: He could make it. We could all make it, pretty quickly. We could weave through two lanes of traffic and make it to the off-ramp, keep going, to wherever. This is assuming that the cops don't see us fleeing and shoot us on sight. This is also assuming that there aren't helicopters hovering above, filled with a different sort of cop who will see us and shoot at or follow us. That there aren't any passes to head us off at. That this doesn't end like Thelma and Louise did, with some happy, smiling montage of us flashing before our eyes, and whatever images Callie and Ted remember the most flashing before theirs.

Then, suddenly, something starts to move all around me, tearing apart my dark daydream.

It's the traffic. The traffic has chosen this moment, when Stan and I are gazing at the shoulder like it's an oasis and we're dying of thirst, to start to move. Honestly, it's more of a lurching, a crawl. But still. Progress! Stan rolls down the window and leans his head out to try to see better.

"Wait, Lorna," Stan says. "Hold on."

"Look," he says.

"What the hell?" I say, because I look and can't believe this.

The cops are guiding traffic through to the northbound lane, which I guess isn't closed after all. They're smiling and waving and moving cars along.

"So . . . there wasn't any problem after all? They're just letting us through?" I say.

Stan shrugs. "Maybe there was an accident and they cleared everything away?"

But then we get a bit farther along, and it turns out the cops aren't letting *all* the cars through after all. An elderly couple in a Buick is directed toward the off-ramp. A middle-aged lady traveling solo in a small SUV follows after. But then a crappy sedan with two teenagers in the front seat are given the wave-through to keep going north.

They're *only* letting Iceling cars through. Stan realizes what's going on the same time I do, and then . . . this one car.

This one car—one that a cop had just signaled off the road—pulls into the Iceling lane. The cop reacts, and I crack the window a bit so I can hear. The cop tells the driver, a dad-to-grandpa-aged man, to please move his vehicle out of the northbound lane and to direct himself toward the off-ramp. His voice is loud and stern, but he's not yelling. Not quite angry.

"I have a right to be here!" says the driver.

"Sir, please move your vehicle," says the cop, stone-faced.

"Will you please just tell me *why*? This traffic is ridiculous! I pay the taxes for these roads! I have a right to be here!"

"Sir, I am going to ask you to not ask questions and to move the vehicle into the off-bound lane."

"Why can they pass and I can't?" the driver says, gesturing at the hatchbacks and ancient Volvos puttering through. His wife in the passenger seat goes from looking embarrassed, hiding her face, to looking alarmed. She sits upright and puts her hand on her husband's shoulder.

"Would you mind stepping out of the car, sir?" says the cop.

"Excuse me? I don't think that's necessary! I just want to know why *they* can go through and I can't. My mother is sick," he says, gesturing north, where I'm assuming there's a hospital or nursing home, "and I just want to take the kids"—he gestures to the backseat—"to see her one last time. We don't know how long she has, and just . . . Please, officer. This is America! Harry Truman did not intend for the highways to function in this way!"

"Sir," the cop says, unmoved by this poor guy's pleas, "I'm going to have to ask you again to please step out of the vehicle."

"I know my rights!"

"Daddy?" I hear a voice say, very faintly. It's coming from this guy's car two ahead, just in front of Bobby, who we're now directly behind, and one lane over. "Daddy?"

The man turns around to look at his kids in the backseat.

"Sir? Please," the cop says, and the man gives him his attention again. "I'd prefer real strongly not to have to ask you again."

The man looks at his wife, and I can see her nod a bit. Slowly, with not an ounce of resistance left, the guy gets out of the car. The cop steps next to him and begins speaking quietly into his ear. The man's face goes slack. Something in him breaks. A few more cops come around.

"Get back in the car, sir," they tell him.

The little girl who asked for her daddy is sobbing audibly.

"Sir, if you could quiet your child," says a cop, and it's not a question.

The guy asks his daughter to please be quiet through the part of his mouth that's not trembling.

"We're here to serve and protect, sir," I can hear the cops saying, all five of them at once. The guy's just staring ahead. His daughter's kind of weeping still, but she's trailing off a bit. They tell the guy's wife to get behind the wheel and take the car into the westbound lane and to drive along. They help the guy into the backseat next to his daughter and an even younger child sitting in a car seat. They keep their hands on him at all times. He sort of slumps a bit.

"Have a pleasant day, ma'am," they say to his wife, who is looking back at her husband and trying to get the car going, and looking back at her husband and pulling onto the off-ramp that all non-Iceling traffic is being funneled onto, while the cops stand outside and nudge their hats up with their guns.

Now Bobby's up. And we know he's probably going to make it, because the only cars they're letting through are carrying at least one teenager with straw-colored hair and those strange petal-like cheekbones—something I didn't start noticing before this Iceling traffic jam but now can't stop noticing. We are almost 100 percent certain that Bobby's going to make it through, but still, I can hear my heart thumping again anyway, and so I grab Stan's hand.

"He'll make it," says Stan, as the cops signal Bobby forward.

"I know," I say, as the signaling cop holds up his hand for Bobby to stop.

"It'll be fine, and then we'll make it too," says Stan, through what I would guess are gritted teeth, but I can't say for certain, because I'm unable to look at anything but what's unfolding in front of me.

Two police officers are leaning into Bobby's car, at both the driver and passenger windows. My eyes flick up quick to the rearview: There are thumping sounds all around me now, and one of them may or may not be my heart, but one of them is *definitely* Ted's fist, which is pounding against the door. I try to get Callie to find my eyes in the reflection, but she doesn't. Something else I cannot sense holds a claim over her stare. Something else has made it so her eyes are as wide as two bright full moons.

Still gripping Stan's hand, I turn around to face her. I reach out to Callie, needing her without being able to articulate why, my free hand groping for hers, to hold her, to tell her we'll be fine, we'll be there soon, she'll be home soon. This is what I need her to need me to tell her right now, and my heart is crumbling with the weight of knowing she might not need me at all.

"Callie," I say. "Kid sister," I say, softer. I take my hand off her hand to wipe at my eye, and as soon as I do, her eyes snap over to me. She reaches out her hand, close enough to make me believe she's reaching for *my* hand, and my face breaks into an ugly-cry smile. "Hey, kid sister," I say. "Everything's going to be fine."

Then Stan squeezes my hand hard and sudden. I snap my neck around. Two smiling cops are waving Bobby through.

It's fine.

"It'll be fine," I say to both Stan and the Icelings but mostly to myself, because we just need to keep on saying it until it is.

One of Bobby's cops turns back to the main flow of traffic, points his finger right at us, and gives us the "c'mere" sign with his whole hand. Now it's our turn.

"It'll be fine," Stan repeats, and he lets go of my hand and takes the wheel.

We're going to be fine. But this is weird and terrifying. Not the-bear-thing terrifying. But terrifying like menacing and ominous and maybe hinting at things to come that we don't really want to think about.

We pull up next to the officer who waved us over. He's standing on Stan's side, and then his partner comes around to stand on mine. Stan's cop opens his mouth and starts saying something we can't hear, then motions for us to roll down our windows. As Stan rolls down the windows, the cop's voice kicks in: "—oll down your windows. Thanks."

"No problem," says Stan.

"So," says the cop. "You kids going north?"

"Yes, sir, officer. North," says Stan.

"Just the four of you?" asks my cop, peeking in and looking toward the backseat.

"In the car?" I ask.

"In the car, yes," says my cop.

"Yes, sir. Just the four of us," says Stan.

Everything feels like when things won't load on streaming platforms. I have a lag time. I can't really process it all.

"Uh, officer?" I start. "Can you tell us . . . well, what was that all about, earlier? With the man?"

"The man?" asks my cop.

"Which man?" asks Stan's cop.

"Uh, well, the one you removed from his vehicle. Earlier. Just a little while ago."

"Oh, that," says my cop. "Well."

"That's nothing to worry about," says Stan's cop. "Don't let it trouble you, miss. Feel free to move along. North, you said you were going?" says Stan's cop. Their sunglasses are on. What the hell is happening here?

"That's right, officers. North," says Stan.

"Mighty fine direction, north," says Stan's cop.

"Mighty fine indeed," says mine.

"Feel free to move along now, though," says Stan's cop.

Stan takes the hint, and we move along.

WE'RE STILL ALIVE. We plan on staying that way. But we'll still spend the rest of this drive making guesses about what that cop must have whispered in that guy's ear and about what exactly is going on here and why, and I guarantee that no matter how sure we are of any of our explanations, we'll still be 100 percent certain that we have no idea.

SEVENTEEN

WE'RE PAST THE checkpoint, headed north again.

Stan's moving his lips like he's muttering, but he isn't making a sound. A glance in the rearview shows Callie and Ted staring straight ahead. In the other cars, the other Icelings are too. The Icelings in the other cars are all white, and relatively pale, with varying degrees of dirty blond hair, just like Callie and Ted and Greta.

As we drive amid this flock of Icelings, I start to notice that these kids don't just have similar coloring and features. Some of these Icelings really, *really* look alike, like siblings. Could it be that some of them are brothers and sisters by blood rather than circumstance? What if Callie has a sister? A sister in a way I never was, or maybe never could be?

An image flashes in my mind of Callie lounging around with a girl who is pretty in that same chilly way that Callie's so pretty. They're communicating in that easy but complicated way that best friends do, where real language is secondary to a certain comfortable code that years and years of closeness has established and from which outsiders are totally excluded. And Callie's telling her in this way about how sad she was to be stuck with me instead of her real sister, how sad she was that I prevented them from being together. And then I wonder, could that sister be in one of these cars surrounding us, hurtling us toward wherever?

Maybe it was always going to be like this: Callie would leave us for something greater someday. At least I got to have Callie, even if it was only for a little while, in the grand scheme of things. Or maybe this line of thinking is just me spinning my wheels, a kind of selfish distraction from the weird hellscape this highway is starting to feel like. Or maybe I'm just piling on another thing to worry about, to make the whole world feel even more impossible. I want to talk to Stan about this, but it seems like he's in an even deeper existential crisis than I am. He's still muttering silently, worrying away at the handle on the inside of his door, when suddenly he says something that I can't quite make out.

"What?" I say. "Did you just say something about the meek being stuck in . . . squalor?"

"Like sheep to the slaughter," he says clearly.

"Stan," I say.

He shrugs. He says, "It is what it is, Lorna."

And I don't have anything to say to that, because take one look around us. Look at Callie and Ted in the backseat, asleep. Look at the Icelings in the cars moving alongside us, some of them reaching out from their backseat perches, hands pawing at their windows toward the windows of other cars that probably contain their brothers and sisters, whom they haven't seen since my father found them and ripped them apart in the name of rescuing them. I turn and look back to the cop cars behind us, to where we saw the family way back when, a couple of centuries ago, it seems, but it's really only been, like, thirty minutes. The way time passes out here, the way time seems to keep expanding and contracting in alternating fits of bad dreams and sparks of hope . . .

Just take one look around us. He's right.

MY SHIFT IS up, so we pull over at a gas station because finally Bobby needs fuel. We pull up at opposite pumps, and the three of us—Stan, Bobby, and I—get out of the cars while our Icelings stay inside, looking longingly at the road leading back up to the on-ramp.

"Can I tell him what you said?" I ask Stan, and Bobby shoots us a questioning look.

"I don't see why not," Stan says.

"After we passed the checkpoint," I start, "Stan said that we were like . . . sheep. You know. Sheep heading to the slaughter." The gas pump makes a struggling sound and then clicks off, so I remove the nozzle and secure the gas cap. When I turn back to Bobby, he's looking at me like I just slaughtered his favorite sheep right in front of him. "What?" I say. "He has a point. That was way too easy."

"I mean," Bobby starts, then stops. "Listen," he starts again. "They know what we're up to. Stan's right, we'd be stupid to think they don't know what we're up to with all these Icelings. They know more than we do, I'm sure. They know that we're taking them somewhere, and they also know exactly where *they're* taking *us*. They—the government—they're letting this happen. They're letting us do this."

"So . . . how is that not something to completely lose our minds over?" Stan says.

"I don't know," Bobby says. "But we're still standing here, right? We're still okay. They had a wide-open shot at us—a shot to wipe *all* of them out—and they didn't take it. But you—*we*—need to be cautious.

Those cops were *going out of their way* not to do anything to us. You saw that guy who collapsed when they went up to him after he hesitated at the off-ramp? I kept expecting them to just start pulling people out of cars and stomp their faces in. That would have made sense to me. But what they were doing while we drove by, pulling grown men and women from their cars and intimidating them into slumped nothings in front of their children? I mean, in a way that's almost scarier than pistol-whipping them or beating them with their flashlights, you know? That one guy ... he looked *scared*. But when you and I went through? They just stood there. Smiling hard. And moving us all along."

"Man, Bobby," says Stan. "Somehow you've managed to make everything sound even more terrifying."

"God, I'm sorry," he says. "I didn't mean to. But regardless of how terrifying this all is, the most important thing is that they know, the government, about what's happening here. They know where we're headed, *precisely where we're headed*, even if we don't. That's a fact. And it doesn't seem like they want to harm us ... at least not yet."

I widen my eyes as menacingly as I can at Bobby's last statement. "Not *yet*? When, pray tell, are they planning to strike, Bob?"

"I'm not trying to play mind games here, Lorna. And I don't have, like, a cheat code for the future, or copies of any battle plans. I'm just trying to think about this as clearly as possible, from every angle I can. Even *if* they mean to harm us or our siblings at some point down the road, that doesn't change anything. We have to go there anyway. Wherever we're going, that's where our siblings want to be, where they *need* to be. And now we know we won't be alone in this—there are at least a hundred other people taking the exact same chance we are! So we know we need to be cautious and wary. But we also know we have strength in numbers and a prize to keep our eyes on. Okay? We're here, and we're not alone. None of us. Not now."

A tiny noise draws my attention back to the car. Callie has bumped the window, accidentally or on purpose I don't know, because I stop caring which as soon as I see that she's holding up a perfect grass crown, which is what she's been weaving for the past couple of hours. I think it's the most beautiful thing I've ever seen, and then I start to cry a little.

"I'm sorry," Bobby says. "I didn't mean to upset you. Don't think about it like that, like this is some big, serious, apocalyptic, suicidal mission. Look, cops know how scary they are. If they didn't want us to feel freaked out, the government wouldn't have sent cops. They would have done something super shady that we wouldn't have even *seen*."

I consider this and am shocked at how much Bobby's version of logic has cleared things away for me. "That's true," I say. "Only a moron wouldn't be fazed by that checkpoint."

"See? If anything, they're being transparent, which is more than I can say for their methods over the last sixteen years." Bobby takes a deep breath as he secures the gas nozzle to its home on the island and screws on his car's fancy gas cap. "So. Can we agree to keep going, proceeding with level heads and lots of caution?"

"Yeah," Stan says. "I think so."

I turn to look at Callie, who's placed the crown atop Ted's head, adding some cheer to his stoic appearance. I smile and say, "Yes."

"Okay then. Let's hit the road. Greta, you ready, girl?" Bobby opens the driver's side and hops in, then turns to us before closing the door. "See you at the next rest stop?"

We nod and wave and take our assigned seats in the car. Stan starts the engine, and we're off again.

I want to say that everything's different now, that our mission is at once more dangerous and foolhardy yet astonishingly more profound, but I don't know that it is. Or that I feel any different. Maybe it's always been this way, but we just never had the words to say so or the proof to see it. Which makes me think that what's maybe even scarier than the world changing is realizing that the world has always been this way, you just managed to not see it. It's that not-seeing that bugs me. Because what else am I missing? What else are we missing?

I turn to Stan and tell him this. About the not-seeing and how scary it is.

"Man," he says. "I was *just* trying to not think about exactly that."

"Oh. Sorry," I say.

"No, no, don't be. It's actually a nicer thing to think about than the *other* thing on my mind."

"Oh?" I say.

"Yeah. My dad hasn't checked in with me," he says. "Like, not once since I went over to your house. God, when was that? This morning? Yesterday morning? Whatever. Anyway, I guess not hearing from him isn't that strange, but it also is. At least a little. What I mean is that if this were any other day I wouldn't think about this at all. Dad not calling me wouldn't register a tick on my scale, good or bad. But because today is *today*, it's at least a little weird. Right? I guess this could mean all kinds of things, though none of them are very good, I don't think. And the most obvious thing is that it's proof that he really does work for or with whoever it is that's after our Icelings. That or his phone died and he forgot how to charge it, and he forgot my number. Or he got hit on the head and it completely slipped his mind that he has two sons, one of whom is an Orphan who cannot speak. *Or* he met a real nice lady—or a real nice guy, who knows!—and learned how to be happy. *Or* he learned how to be happy just by himself, living all alone, and wants me and Ted to do the same thing."

"Any of those things are possible," I say.

"Yeah, and really unlikely. Anyway, like I said, I don't want to think too much about that," Stan says. "And I think you're right. About the world and how nothing's changed. Or that's not true—something has changed, but it's not the world. It's us. Right? I've spent a good chunk of my life resenting Ted and my dad and just . . . *all* of this, because I blamed them for me not feeling like I have a life or a purpose. And I've always thought that in order to have those things—a life and a purpose—I had to be alone. But I don't think I feel that way anymore. I don't think that's it. I mean, think about what we did back in Pennsylvania. We made this crazy decision, on our own, and now we're on this crazy trip while everyone else we know is just back home watching movies edited for TV and eating bad pizza. And instead of me resenting Ted and thinking he's the problem and I'm just his lame victim, I'm making the choice to help him in a way no one else can. And you're doing the same for Callie, and it feels good and right. I'm not being stupid, I'm not talking about some big idea of *Good* and *Right*, like lit-up words hovering over us, but you know . . ."

"You feel like something in you is sliding into place," I say.

"Yeah."

"Like you found a way of being in the world that makes it a little easier to be in the world."

"Yeah."

"Yeah."

"So we're really going to do this, huh?" he says, his eyes on the road and lit up by the highway lights and the cars around us. "We're going to help them. We're going to give them a shot at feeling this same way too. Is that a selfish way to look at this? I mean, we don't know what they're feeling. No matter how differently we feel about ourselves and them right now, we still have no idea what they think or feel. Or what they want to think and feel."

"Yeah. We don't know," I say. I spy Callie in the rearview mirror, dozing but not quite sleeping with her head against the cold backseat window, a faint reflection of her face glowing out into the night. "But, cheesy as it sounds . . . we can look in their eyes."

"Yeah. We can look in their eyes and know we're the ones best equipped to see the difference between when they feel trapped and when they feel—when they *look* like they feel—rooted. In themselves and in the world." Stan's voice goes dreamy as he says, "I wonder what it's like for everyone else."

I roll down the window.

"Uh," Stan says. "Everything okay?"

I ignore Stan and shout, "Hey!" out the window to no one in particular.

"What the hell are you doing, Lorna?"

I turn back to him. "Finding out what it's like for everyone else. Duh." I turn back to the refreshing chill outside my window. "Hey! Someone roll down their window!"

The kid driving the next car over, Indiana plates, rolls down his window. He has a sister in the backseat, her flower-petal cheeks shining with that glow from the absent moon.

"You okay?" shouts the kid back at me.

"We are, yeah!" I say. "Are you? Anything . . . seem weird to you about any of . . . this?" I sweep my arms out wide to gesture to the entire highway.

"Well," he shouts, "a couple of cops just pulled me over with my sister in the car and didn't ask me what's wrong with her that she can't speak, and *that's* never happened before. So there's that. And, oh yeah, there was that whole thing about my sister building a professional-looking scale model of an island and telepathically demanding I take her on an elaborate road trip to a mystery location. So, yeah. It's been weird."

"For us too!" I shout. "Back in New England, my friend's brother fought a bear."

"Jesus," says Stan.

"A bear?" says the guy.

"Yup, a bear," I say.

"No way," the other driver says.

I unbuckle myself and lean out the window.

"Careful!" both Stan and our new friend shout at the same time, and Stan swerves the car a little. "Jesus, Lorna!" he says.

"I'm fine!" I say. "You just focus on driving." I point to the claw marks on the hood of the car.

"Holy shit," the guy says. "What one guy can do another can do, huh?"

I laugh, loud. I have got to tell you, it feels pretty amazing to laugh right now. Stan isn't laughing. I guess he never watched *The Edge* on cable with his dad.

"I'm Lorna," I say, settling back in my seat.

"I'm Jayson," he says. "That's Chantal in the back."

"That's Callie, and that's Ted, and Stan's driving."

"Hey," says Stan, waving, not taking his eyes off the road despite the fact that we haven't broken thirty-five miles per hour in what feels like days. Traffic's not at a standstill, but it isn't exactly racing.

"That's Charlie in the Nissan just ahead," says Jayson.

"Oh yeah? Did he yell at you from the road too?"

"Yup. Long time ago," he says. "Look around. Do you think you're the only ones who want to know if what's happening is real?"

"I guess it would be pretty crazy if we were," I say.

"Bingo," says Jayson.

Our lane starts to free up, and Stan looks to Jayson apologetically as he gestures to the open space ahead of us.

"Go on!" says Jayson. "Looks like we're all headed toward the same place anyway."

We wave to each other as Stan pulls ahead, and soon Jayson's out of sight. A drawn-out silence fills the space between me and Stan.

"I'm terrified, Stan," I blurt, and then instantly feel so much relief at giving voice to that feeling that I add, "but I'm also kind of excited too." Because it's true.

"Yeah," Stan says. "Me too. All of it. At once. The fear and the exhilaration. I've been feeling that this entire time."

"Phew. I'm glad it's not just me. But we're going to have to try really hard to remember that. I mean, you take everything that's gone down over the last few days—the bear, my mom, the cops being creepy with families at the checkpoint, these cars traveling this road with us carrying the same kind of trouble we are."

"What, those two?" he says, looking at them in the rearview and smiling.

Callie is smiling too, but in her sleep and not at us, and Ted makes a little nose twitch like he's having a dream that he's a rabbit, and Stan and I start to laugh as quietly as possible so that we don't wake them. Then Ted's nose stops twitching and he settles in a bit more, finally finding a comfortable position with his head on Callie's shoulder, and his mouth relaxes into a gentle grin.

Our Icelings, our brother and sister, are sitting right behind us, smiling. Even *Ted* is smiling. And I have to say, it looks weird, Ted smiling, like nobody ever taught him how. Like his whole face is learning it for the first time, seizing this moment when he's asleep to work this problem out.

It's totally possible this will work out *terribly*. But we're here, and they're happy, and something about this feels right. Like we're on the right course. Bobby's right in front of us, and I can see both him and Greta, sitting in the passenger seat, through their rearview mirror. And I can see that Greta's smiling. And I'm thinking we're where we're supposed to be. And whatever this is, we're going to meet it head-on. Grass crowns and all.

Stan points to a sign on the highway.

ISLAND FERRY, 100 MILES

EIGHTEEN

IT'S AMAZING WHAT a police escort can do in terms of getting you up into Canada.

We've been driving for, roughly, forever. At some point we all sort of decided to carpool, or at least the people who weren't already carpooling, like Stan and me, so that we can all sleep in shifts. After our car-to-car chat with Jayson, which happened around midnight, more and more people started rolling down their windows to introduce themselves, sort of like a game of telephone but with really scary life stakes on the line. Anyway, the two things all of us on the road have in common is that A of all, we all have Iceling siblings, and B of all, we are all exhausted.

So for the past long stretch we've been sleeping and driving in shifts all through the night. I imagine this is the kind of thing that, under normal circumstances, would look very suspicious—a bunch of teenagers taking over an entire highway, all of us driving together on the same route with identical siblings in our backseats, not even stopping to sleep in proper beds—but our circumstances are nothing like normal, and it's actually kind of liberating not to have to worry about being stopped and punished just for being under eighteen. I don't know about the other cars, but I know that both Stan and I could really use a shower. Or a rainstorm to stand in for one. Applying drugstore pore cleanser in a truck stop bathroom will only get you so far.

All of a sudden, we glide into a stop. Once again, we've become just one in an expanse of red taillights. All around us, Icelings are opening car doors or else being stymied by child locks, and it's so foggy and packed with cars that I can't see a thing except taillights and Icelings everywhere. So I open the passenger door and step out to get a better look, and then I climb up on the front tire to get an even better one. I shiver and brace myself against the wind, feeling absurdly grateful for the extra parkas and winter gear Bobby had stored in his car—my "warmest parka" feels more like a base layer up here, and in the rush of leaving I forgot about a whole category of clothing called "accessories." I don't care that Bobby's gear is old and smells like mothballs. I tug my new, borrowed fur hat tighter against my ears and squint, then widen, my eyes. We're stopped at the edge of the sea.

This is it.

Not *it* it. But this is where we've been driving to. This is where the road led. To a parking lot in a place (horrifyingly) called Meat Cove. I see a pier, some docks, and a lineup of several industrial-looking and paint-chipped boats and ships and freighters, and everything looks very, very old. Standing on the dock is a grumpy old sailor wearing a peacoat, a watch cap, and, I kid you not, from what I can see from my vantage point, he has an eye patch and a cane.

Callie's going home, I think to myself, and I gasp. I cover my mouth, and I cry.

I turn and duck back into the car to see her, to hold her hand. She's sitting there patiently, looking out to the dock, to whatever lies beyond it. Ted's clamoring at the child lock. Stan lets him out. I go to open the door for Callie, and, as soon as I do, she's off and running, along with Ted, toward the other Icelings who've already bolted and are now down by the pier.

We others, we siblings, bleary- and blank-eyed, as if in a fever, shepherd the Icelings forward, while our adopted brothers and sisters zoom to and fro, from clique to clique, moving against or herding, reminding me of what a high school reunion might be like if you actually liked high school and missed your classmates.

"Huh," says Stan. "They all have the same kind of hair."

"What?"

"That weird dirty blond. Like faded dirt."

"Yeah. I mean, they've got similar cheekbones, they're all the same size." Three run by, all of them about five foot eight, which is to say all of them roughly Callie's height. "They're related. All of them. They have to be, right? They're all the same age and the same size with the same hair, and they all *look* related."

We, on the other hand, unlike the happily reunited, seem to be engaging in a contest to find out who's the most awkward and stand-offish. All around us, kids are comparing notes on what they know, what they don't know, what they think is going on, what they hope is going on, what they hope *isn't* going on. At least three people are walking around replaying voice messages from their parents screaming about the things the government will do to them if they find they've taken the Orphans "back there." It soon becomes clear that some of them have had conversations with their parents similar to the one I had with my mom, but that most of them haven't. You can tell the ones who have from the ones who haven't by how they respond to the rumor that the government is out to get our siblings. Those who've had the conversation react somberly but calmly, and those who haven't have this horrifying look of surprise on their faces. Like the whole world just took off its mask and the real face underneath belongs to a monster.

"Um, guys," says Bobby, sidling over to us as fast as he can through this disoriented mob, "you might want to look at that."

Bobby points, and we follow his finger with our eyes until what we're looking at is so many Icelings.

What I mean is, while we've all been standing around, numb from driving and perplexed by our destination, the Icelings have been gathering. Earlier, they were running around, but swiftly and silently, they slipped away from us completely and segregated themselves on the other side of the marina.

Callie's gone.

How could I lose track of her? Here, of all places, now? I turn around in circles unproductively as heat rises to my forehead, and I get so hot that I almost rip my hat off and expose my skin to this frigid air, but then someone nudges me.

"Hey," says Bobby, and he points.

And there's my Callie.

Over there, with all the other Icelings, who are calmly milling about and among each other, staring up close in each other's eyes. She's moving around like they all are, getting up into each other's faces, looking for what, I can't say. Themselves is my guess. They're looking to see what they can see of themselves in one another's faces. They hold their hands up, as if asking the Iceling across from them to hold *their* hand up too. Sometimes they do, and then both Icelings make this face that says: *Finally*. Some of them don't, and then those Icelings just keep trying.

"They're pairing off," I say. "Right? It's like they're checking to see which person will be their mirror."

"Ho-ly . . ." says Bobby, then trails off as he watches Greta lock hands with an Iceling girl who jumped when she jumped.

"Huh," Stan says. I look, and there's Ted, standing in front of another broody-seeming Iceling. They glare at each other, raise their hands in sync, and then embrace. It's a quick embrace, maybe even warm—in other words, nothing like what I'd expect a hug from Ted to be like. "Well," Stan says. "I guess he's found his other half."

"You hear that, Callie?" I ask, forgetting she isn't there. I look out to where I last saw her in the gathering of Icelings, but she's not there either. I lost her.

But after a minute of frantic searching, there she is. Way down by the landing, standing with a girl who looks uncomfortably just like her. They're smiling, holding their hands up, mirrors for one another. And now their hands are trembling, and they're touching each other's hair (Callie's is long, down past her shoulders, and this other's is lopped off around her chin), feeling it out for all the ways it is and isn't *theirs*.

Someone taps me on the shoulder. I jump and reel around to see a girl around my age, dark hair and curvy, with cool glasses. "Sorry! I didn't mean to scare you," she says with a bit of a Southern accent.

"It's fine, you didn't," I say, not sure whether I mean it or I'm just being polite.

"I'm Emily," she says, holding out her hand. I take it and shake it and tell her my name, and she smiles. "Nice to meet you! Under the weirdest circumstances ever? Anyway, that's my sister over there." She points with her shoulder to where Callie is standing. "Her name's Tara. The girl she's . . . uh . . . talking to. Is that your sister?"

Tara. So that's the name of the girl with whom Callie is, right now, probably forging a bond that's deeper than anything we have ever or could have ever had.

"Yeah," I say. "That's Callie."

"I guess they found their Others," Emily says.

"Their *whats*?"

"Others." She points to the Iceling side of the marina. "That's just what some kids are calling the Orphans their siblings are pairing off with."

"Oh," I say.

"It's like they're . . . sisters," says Emily. "They look so much alike."

"I know," I say, and I can tell she feels maybe as bad as I do about all of this.

"What do you think they're doing? Are they *talking* to each other?"

"I don't know," I say. "But they definitely seem to understand each other." I almost add, "Like I guess in all the ways we never could," but I don't. Something tells me, though, that I maybe could have.

"Yeah," Emily says, then turns from Callie and Tara to fix her gaze on me. "Am I a terrible person for feeling jealous?"

"If that makes you terrible, then I'm the poster child on a series of propaganda ads celebrating war crimes," I say, and she laughs a little.

"Yeah. I mean, my heart's totally broken. But I'm also happy for her," she says.

"Yeah," I say. "I mean, this is all I ever wanted for her—a language she can understand and someone who can understand her. I just wanted it to be me."

"Yeah," Emily says. "Same."

"Hey," I say, "you and me, we could slice our palms open and become blood sisters or something, you know?" She stares at me like I'm some sort of crazed freak.

And then she bursts out laughing, and I do too, and we're so tired from traveling, and sitting for hours and hours and hours, and the ground is so slick that we almost let our legs give way and fall down, but then we hold on to each other and just collapse a bit into the laughter.

"That was funny," she says, her face kind of breaking with this smile, one hand on her stomach and the other still on my shoulder, and if I hadn't just seen her laugh, I don't think I'd believe her. "You don't even *know* how much I needed to laugh like that."

"Not a lot of laughs lately, huh?" I say, my own smile receding back into the furrowed face of concern I've been wearing since we got here.

"Have you heard these voice mails going around? My dad called the other day, right after that completely insane checkpoint. I didn't pick up, obviously. But he left this voice mail that was like, *Emily, return yourself and that Orphan at once. If you cannot or will not return Tara, then at least return yourself. I am warning you. The government is warning you. There will, my child, be consequences.*"

"I had a pretty similar conversation with my mom," I say. "I've never heard her so . . . scared before. It was this terrible combination of serious and scared that I never want to hear again. Except the scariest part isn't that she sounded like that. It's that I haven't heard from her—or my dad—since."

"Oh my God—same. Actually, I'm a little less freaked out now that I know it's the same for you . . ."

"Likewise," I say. I spot two Icelings on the other side of the marina. They start running at each other. Gradually, they slow down, until they come to this eventual, almost eternal halt. They're face-to-face. They look like one guy transformed into two by a mirror, but there's no mirror. One guy moves his arm. The other guy moves the same arm. They do this for maybe a minute, moving different limbs identically, then they stop, and they sort of smile and just stand there.

"They're all so . . . different," I say. "From each other. I mean, that probably sounds really stupid, right? Like, that's like being surprised that a whole bunch of humans who grew up in the same place aren't exactly the same."

"No," Emily says. "I know what you mean. And then our sisters—they're so alike. It's like they're different and alike, but to crazy extremes."

"Exactly," I say, and I feel some kind of strange relief, because it's nice to look around and see a whole bunch of people who know you without you ever having met them.

But it's short-lived. Because, yes, it's nice to look around and see a whole bunch of people who you know without ever having met them. But the reason you feel that way is that you've all spent your whole lives with these siblings who happen to look alike, and move alike, and none of them can communicate with anything approaching the sounds and gestures and inflections we interpret as language, and apparently the government thinks they're maybe some sort of weapon, and you know that the only reason you know that is because your parents told you, because your parents have known it for maybe as long as you've been alive, maybe longer, because your parents are colluding with or in the employ of the government and have been spying on your siblings since forever.

And wherever it is we are out here in the most forbidding swath of Canada, Callie is acting in a way I've never seen. All of our siblings, these Icelings, are acting in a way that *none of us* has ever seen. Maybe this is them coming alive. And maybe it's this weird moonlike place that's allowing them to do it. It's as if something long dormant inside of them is getting up and stretching and taking a look around.

Someone is calling my name. For one completely insane moment, I think, for no reason other than pure and desperate desire, that it's Callie, but then that crazy thought is squashed when I see Stan running up to us, still shouting, "Hey, Lorna!"

"Emily, this is Stan," I say. "We rode up together; his brother is that big guy over there, Ted."

ICELING

"Hey," Stan says, and I can't help but notice a little extra color rise up into his cheeks.

"Emily's sister is Callie's . . . Other," I say, and Emily smiles and nods.

"Ah," Stan says. "I'm still looking for whoever brought Ted's guy up. Anyway, listen. Bobby says someone found a ferry to charter."

"Over there?" I ask, pointing to the fleet of old metal clunkers parked over at the dock. "It's one of those?"

Stan nods his head.

"A ferry?" says Emily. "To where?"

"The island, I guess," Stan says. "Their island."

"Jesus," Emily says. "So this is really happening, huh?"

"Yep," Stan says.

"Are we . . . going over there with them?" Emily asks.

"We better be," I say and exchange a hard look with Stan, who doesn't seem as sure as I do about heading over to the island.

"Come on," he says. "Let's go find Bobby."

We make our way down to the landing, where all those industrial-looking boats and rigs are stationed. Only one looks big enough to carry a hundred Icelings and their hundred adoptive siblings, so I'm assuming that one's ours. Bobby and another guy are standing on the dock in front of this huge barge-looking thing, talking to the grizzled guy I saw when we first pulled up, the one who looks exactly like a cartoon version of a captain, who I'm assuming is the captain. Seeing him up close, I realize he doesn't actually have an eye patch—must have been a shadow—but he does have a cane, which makes me break into a small smile. Stan, Emily, and I push through and join Bobby in the powwow.

"And you're sure you want to go . . . there?" the captain says, pointing to a barely discernible dot on the horizon.

"Yes," Bobby says, and a whole chorus of *yes*es follow, rippling back through the crowd of people.

The captain gives us one more long, skeptical look before he relents. "Well," he says. "So long as you're sure." He lifts up his chin and puffs his chest and puts his hands around his mouth. "All aboard!" he shouts, and maybe it's just the way the cold air is affecting our vocal cords, but I think I hear a little bit of sadness in his tone.

After much corralling and coaxing, we herd our Icelings on board, and now we're traveling again, having traded in our cars for a completely luxury-free boat built to withstand the Arctic. It's really more of a freighter than a ferry. There's a top deck, where the winds are awful. There's below deck, which is still very cold but warmer than up top. It's damp down here, like an old unfinished basement, all wet metal and bad pipes.

The fact that this captain from central casting agreed to take all of us like it was normal . . . I don't know. Either this isn't the first time he's ferried dozens of bizarrely similar-to-identical teenagers and their adoptive siblings across these freezing cold waters or he's the maritime version of the cops who ushered us through that checkpoint. Or he just doesn't care. Any of those answers is unsettling, and I have to actively shove aside the worry that wherever we're going, it's a trap.

Because I don't much see that we've got a choice. This is where they want to go. It's where they have to go. And honestly, I don't see how I could go back at this point. Going forward might kill us. But going back . . . How do you go back to your family after all this? How do you look at your parents like you still trust them? How do you look them in the eye and not spit in that eye?

Stan and Emily go below deck, but I stay up on the top while I can stand it, trying to see as much as I can for as long as I can. Callie's with Tara, and they're holding hands.

hey, I text Dave once I'm alone. Dave's been texting me this whole time, but I haven't had it in me to answer. And since it might be a while until I have another chance to get in touch, I figure that checking in, letting him know I'm safe right now, is the least I can do. sorry i've been gone. we made it up here. we're on a boat now. the reception is weird, i don't even know if you'll get this. but anyway, either way, i wanted to tell you that it might be a while before i text again. i'm in a place right now—mentally, you know—where i kind of need to be present. ok? i'll call when i can. i miss you.

Bobby's up top too, on the upper level, leaning out over the railing several feet away from me. I catch his eye and wave, and he waves back, but then just goes back to staring. I follow his eyes and see that they're on Greta, and there's something wrong with the way he's looking at her. Like he's happy to see her so content and at home with another girl just like her, whom she can communicate with in ways he could maybe only dream about, but there's something else there that makes me think he's worried or scared for her too. Like he knows this joy she's feeling is going to lead to something terrible. And I just watch him for a moment like that, as he leans farther and farther out over the guardrail, staring at the sea and at Greta, his eyes not changing at all.

NINETEEN

I THINK ABOUT going back down with Emily and Stan but decide to go check on Bobby.

"You okay?" I ask Bobby.

"Just fine," he says, dressing his face up like it's full of cheer. Except I can see even more clearly from up here that something's bothering him. He's not looking down at Greta anymore but rather staring out to sea, and his hair's blowing all over his too-stoic face. He looks as though he's ruminating over a mistake he made, one that caused something irreparable. Or maybe I'm just making all of this up because in a way that's really what *I* feel like, but then again I don't know how I feel except still so utterly horrified by the amount of things I'm learning I don't understand in this world.

"Okay," I say. "Do you want any company?"

"Actually, Lorna," he says, turning to face me only after he's said my name, "I'd kind of really like to be alone right now."

"Oh," I say. "Yeah. Of course." And then Bobby doesn't say anything, not even "Thank you."

I head back to the first level, more than a little disconcerted by Bobby. What's going on with him? What was that look in his eyes? Maybe he's just going through what we're all going through and I've been insensitive toward that because he's older and because even he admits that Greta was more Alex's than his. He dedicated his life to trying to find a way to communicate with Greta, and here she is, communicating away with a total stranger in ways he can't fathom or quantify. Maybe that's what's eating at him.

But I don't think it is. Not totally, anyway.

I'm making my way down the stairs when we hit a wave and bounce, and I have to cling to the railing to steady myself, and even then I almost flip over the other side. I finally get my footing back, and the boat's still bobbing with the residual energy of the wave. I take a deep breath and keep going.

Downstairs there are some kids in a corner, crowded around a power strip and punching at their phones furiously with their thumbs. I scan the group quickly for Stan, and when I don't see him I get out my phone and text him.

where, I type.

sitting down, starboard, he texts back.

So Stan and I can text, at least.

I find him sitting alone on a bench with a view of the water out a porthole. "Where's Emily?" I say.

"Trying to find something to eat," Stan says. "She said she was fully prepared to trade half the contents of her backpack for a goddamn Luna Bar."

"Wow. That's a real dedication to Luna Bars," I say. "So . . . I just talked to Bobby."

"Yeah?"

"Yeah. He's acting pretty weird."

"Hasn't he always been weird?"

"I mean weird for Bobby. He says he's fine, and he seems happy for Greta, but . . . I don't know. There's something else going on, I can tell."

"Of course there is. Lorna, what we're doing here . . . everything that's happening right now . . . it's insane!" He gestures to a big group of Icelings gathered near the front of the ship, all of them paired off and engaging in some form of physical contact with another Iceling. They're staring out ahead, to the island we're approaching. He turns back to me. "And maybe really, really dangerous."

"I know," I say. "Of course I know that. And, like, we knew that. Sort of. But I think it's something else."

"Well, he's a linguist, right?" I nod, and Stan goes on. "Well, maybe he had some theory about how the Icelings would be around each other, how they'd communicate, and it turns out he was way off-base."

"It's weird, right?" I say. "How they sort of just . . . ditched us? When we got here? I mean, maybe that's what we should have expected, but still."

"No, I know what you mean. It's almost like—no, it's actually *definitely* like—the Icelings know something we don't."

"Yeah. And now we're the ones who need help navigating this weird place with its weird customs. But they don't seem all that interested in helping us understand." I spot Callie and Tara joining the group of Icelings we've been watching, and I feel my heart fall all over again. Stan follows my gaze over and sighs.

"Don't be sad, Lorna. It's a good thing. It's why we came here."

I nod, pulling my gaze away from my sort-of sister and her new real sister. "What the hell do you think is on that island?"

The island that is now coming into view.

ICELING

We're finally at a close enough distance where we can start to make it out, and it's actually pretty breathtaking.

And now that it's in our line of view, our eyes play tricks on us, making us feel like we're moving more quickly than we were at the beginning of the trip, or like the island is a magnet and we're magnetic and it's pulling us in. The closer we get, the more we can see. There are these mountains that are—wait, no, those are *hills*, snow-capped hills that rise up in a massive line across one whole side of the island. They look like mounds of packed ice and snow and topped with more ice and more snow—layers of ice and snow, like rings of bark on an old tree. The wind is whipping now, and we can see it rolling these big boulders of snow around, and they get bigger and bigger, accumulating with each tumble like snowmen in cartoons. Sprouting up in between and behind those icy ranges are what look like tall, tropical-style trees, almost like *palm* trees, with these low-hanging branches forming canopies covered in more snow and ice. As we cross these final lengths to the shore, our captain steers us around to what looks like some kind of dock or landing, old and odd-looking but maybe recently reconstructed, and then I, along with every other non-Iceling being around me, suck in a terrified gasp.

Because what we see in front of us now is nothing new. We've all seen it before. Our eyes narrow in on the wide-open space beyond the dock: a big, expansive field, trembling. The field from the sculptures they built. And then we get closer and see that the trembling goes even deeper—it's so intense that the hills around it begin to vibrate. Even the air seems to shake. There's this smell of green in the air. Like a greenhouse. Like something living. And something else I can't quite place.

"Holy hell," says Bobby, who is now behind us.

All we can do is stand there, taking it all in. All of the Icelings are crowded along the bow. They look like they'd walk across the water right now. There's an energy building, a hum. Like how the sky gets before it opens up for a summer rain. The sky over the leftmost part of the island starts to get all purple and yellow.

And everything smells like lightning.

That's it. That's that smell from before. The one that wasn't the green one. It's lightning. Just like Dad talked about in the car way back at dinner, forever ago. Everything smells like lightning, and the ground is trembling, and I know this means something, but whatever it is is completely beyond me.

"What the hell is this?" I say.

"Couldn't say," says Bobby, not so much calmly as with an air of inevitability, as if to say that whatever's happening right now is beyond us both in terms of our ability to understand it and our ability to change it. He's staring out to the island like he's looking for something he knows should be there. "Couldn't say," he says again, a little quieter.

The ferry drops anchor right by the rickety yet nearly new dock. So used to rushing to our siblings' side in moments of arriving and departing, we all leap from our places and seek out our Icelings, forgetting that they're the ones who know the secrets of this place, and we're the total foreigners. But then we don't even have a chance to fully make that mistake, because all at once, the Icelings jump. They vault off the boat, none of them wearing jackets, and they hit the water and just light right out for that trembling expanse.

And they're off, they've lit out for a vision they've held maybe since birth, a vision of home, of the kind of home they've never even had a chance to know. And we, their siblings, we stand and we stare.

TWENTY

BOBBY'S GONE, DISAPPEARED in the swarm of shepherds and Icelings, but Stan's still right here, with Emily beside him. The captain, obviously furious and shouting left and right, pulls us in as close as he can and lowers the gangplank, setting it heavily down on the dock, where it scrapes and rattles and bangs because of the trembling.

"EVERYONE OFF!" he shouts, and we file out as quickly as we can, doubling up on parkas and hats and gloves, because this is the coldest any of us has ever been.

The Icelings are long gone, and some of us are rushing after them, while some are lingering, moving real slow, as though they don't want to stray too far from the vessel that might be the *only* thing that can take us back to anything resembling what we used to think of so fondly as "home." Stan and Emily and I shove our way through, leaving the stragglers behind without a second look. Not because we pity or disdain them, but because we're afraid that if we pay them too much attention we might start to understand why they're doing what they're doing and start to do it too. At least that's what I'm worried about, so I keep my head down and push forward.

Cursing myself for all the times I felt scared on this trip, because apparently I had no idea what "scared" meant back then, I look back at the boat so I can memorize exactly where it is, exactly where it'll be waiting for us. I see the captain walking around the second level, scanning the craft for stragglers. He wanders the deck, checking behind benches, and then he ducks down into the stairwell and repeats the process on the first level before heading back toward the gangplank. And then he raises the gangplank and then the anchor. The Icelings are running around and pairing up. They're moving their arms and then standing very still.

"Oh my god, Stan!" I shout, pointing to the ferry, my head swimming with lightning and feeling like I might throw up.

"Hey!" shouts Stan. "What the hell are you doing? You can't leave!"

We're screaming at him, pleading until our throats are raw, but the captain only works to abandon us faster. Some Icelings run through and around us, and we jump back and stumble, startled. The anchor is up, and the captain begins to pull away as the Icelings assemble up ahead, and they stand still, and they sway. People are calling out to their siblings, and some are trying to grab hold of them, but nobody can keep any hands on them; they're in the wind. They're up ahead.

And I'm just staring at the ferry, only registering this in the back of my mind, because what used to be in the back of my mind has now crawled its way to the front. It's the only thought I can hold right now. In that it's gripped me, completely.

"Stan," I say. "They probably knew about the boat. Or even arranged it."

"Who knew about it?" Emily says. "Who arranged it?"

"The government," Stan says, his voice flat and dead.

"What? What are you talking about? What do you mean? What the hell do you mean?" Emily's eyes go wild.

"What I mean is that if we made it this far, it's probably because the government—whoever in the government believes our brothers and sisters are monsters—*wants* us to have made it this far. If we weren't supposed to be on that boat, we wouldn't have been on it. If that guy hadn't been instructed otherwise, he'd be waiting right there for us, to take us safely back to shore, just like we paid him to. And if for some reason we had decided *not* to get on that boat, I'm pretty sure something really terrible, maybe involving bullets, would have happened to us."

Meanwhile, everyone else has just noticed that the ferry's gone.

"Hey!" they shout.

"Hey, come back!" they shout.

"Are you SERIOUS, man? You can't do that! COME BACK!" they shout, they plead.

"We'll die here! You can't leave us here! It's freezing!" they scream.

"Oh God oh God oh God oh God oh God, we're gonna die," they cry. They fall down around each other. Four people have fallen into the sea and are trying to get out. I can't imagine they won't freeze. Did they think they could swim to the freighter that ferried us over as it sails itself away?

"Jesus, people," says a voice of reason. "Get it together. What'd you think would happen? We came out here for them. We came to help them."

"What about *us*?" comes another voice, and I know I need to calm and quiet that voice right away or else everything will fall apart in a way that's worse than I've yet to imagine.

"Hey!" I shout. "HEY. Look at them. They've spent their whole lives quiet, locked up inside themselves, away from home! We get to *live* in the world. We *know* our parents are our parents and our friends are our friends."

Emily, standing next to me, takes a step forward. "We get to make out and drive cars, and when people say things to us, we know what they're talking about!" she shouts. "The least we can do is finish what we started."

We're answered with nothing but grumblings and panicked whines.

"THE WAY I see it," shouts Bobby to anyone who's calm enough to listen, "all we need to do is get enough people to start moving after the Icelings, and everyone else will follow. The longer we stand around, the more time people will have to freak out and worry and come up with reasons to just stand around here and freeze to death."

He's right, I think. I make to turn to the Icelings, to spot them so we can follow them, but they're all gone. While we were all yelling, they lit out for parts unknown that were calling to them like home.

"Damn it," says Stan, seeing what I'm seeing, which is everything but our siblings. "Let's do it. Now. They can follow us, or they can stay here and freeze, but we need to go now."

WE TURN AROUND and follow the path that's been cleared and trampled down by the Icelings, which thankfully leads us right to them—or the smallish speck of them, at least, because they're so far ahead of us. From what we can see, they're running up to this stacked-high pile of what looks like driftwood. But then the closer we get, the more shape and structure the wood pile takes on, and now I see that it's probably not a pile at all but more like a shed. Except the shed looks like it's . . . growing up and out of the ground. There's no snow on it. The snow won't even touch it. The wood looks old, but not at all rotted from the snow and wind like you'd expect. There are no windows. Just two broad gray boards for a roof and four gray walls made of smaller boards and then a small and asymmetrical opening that looks like it could pass for a doorway.

To say this structure gives me the creeps is a real and serious understatement. It's straight out of a horror movie. All it lacks is a creaking door and a pile of fresh bones out back, and I actually can't rule out that second detail just yet. I'm shivering, and it's not from the cold.

I'm expecting this to be the Icelings' first stop, but they breeze right past it—and I am in no way sad about this. I am in no way excited about coming back this way and seeing this place again either. Some of us linger here and check out the shed, but me, I'm going to keep going.

"What the hell was that?" says Stan, who's a couple of footsteps behind me now, the shed having tripped him up a bit.

"Creepy as heck," says Emily, and I just nod, because for some reason even I don't know, I need to get that thing out of my mind. Pretend it doesn't exist, not give language to it at all.

Finally, we're past it; it's nothing but a sinister dot behind my shoulder. We're in the trees now, those tall, tropical-looking trees with the low-hanging branches forming canopies weighed down with ice and snow. Up close, they're not exactly like palm trees, but I've also never seen real palm trees in person before, so the truth is I don't know. They've got these long, broad, flat leaves, and they bend so low with the weight of the snow. I'm looking up at those leaves and the patterns they make in the sky, and my steps slow down, and all of a sudden I'm no longer moving. I can't stop staring at the leaves, because whereas at first glance it seemed that the snow was weighing them down, I see that it's not that at all. They're sloping and drooping at this *willful* kind of angle, like if you brushed the snow off, they wouldn't spring up. In other words, it looks like these trees are bending their branches and leaves low on purpose, for the purpose of holding the snow. It looks like they're built for this strange job, all the way out here. Stan turns around for me and follows my gaze upward. I know he sees what I see, but he doesn't say a word, just nudges my shoulder and guides me back on the path.

We keep walking under this weird canopy for at least half an hour, just following the trampled-down snow to see where our Icelings are going.

"Look!" someone shouts, the need to believe choking his voice. "A squirrel!"

We look, see nothing.

"Oh," says the same voice, this time tinged with sadness. "It was just a gust of wind."

My heart sinks, and I realize how desperate I am—how desperate we all are—to see something familiar. Because not only are there no squirrels around here, there isn't *anything*. No birds, no animals, no lizards, no frigid-water fish. We can hear the water and the wind and the trees as they sigh and bend low under the weight of the snow, but no living things with eyes or minds or hearts. No life, aside from ours, have we yet seen here.

We follow the trampled path until we're finally out from under the trees, and it turns out we were just tracing the coastline, but vaguely inland, and we're approaching another dock. Two docks, actually, both of them newer-looking than the one we used to get on the island—either that or nobody bothered to make them look as weathered as the first one.

STRUCTURES THAT LOOK like storage sheds sit on top of each of these twin docks, and there are these tires that hang off their sides like bumpers. Affixed to one of the docks is an old-fashioned gas pump, painted a bright cherry red, with like what look like functional gauges.

"Huh," says Stan. "This one looks like it might be a refueling dock. And look at all these slips on the other one. For smaller boats to, uh, park."

"How do you know all that?" I ask.

"According to my dad, fishing and camping trips are great ways to bond with your sons," he says, and in what is no longer anywhere close to the darkest part of my mind, I feel relieved at least one of us might know some survival skills. "And these," he says, gesturing at the docks, "are way better maintained than the one we anchored by."

"So the only things missing from this equation are the people maintaining them," says Emily, and we look at her but don't respond, because we don't want to think about what that means.

The docks are in this little rocky cove, hidden and jutting inward in such a way that it was impossible for us to have seen them when we were first circling the island to pull up to the other dock. Hiding them even more is another dense copse of those heavy, weird trees, their stubbornly drooping leaves making a canopy over part of them. The wind blows the snow around, like a smoke screen protecting a fort.

Stan taps me on the shoulder and points to a spot in the distance.

"See that spot of color?" he says. Emily and I shake our heads no, so we get out our phones and try the zoom function, but all I can see is a blur.

"You mean that red thing?" Emily says.

"No," Stan says. "It's yellow. Are you sure you don't see it?"

"All I see are blurs. What do you think it is?" I say.

"I thought it might be a boat," Stan says. "Forget it, though. It's probably nothing. We need to keep going, or we'll lose our way."

"If it's a boat, we need to find it! Otherwise . . ." And I just let the thought drift, because it's terrifying.

"If it's a boat, we *will* find it," Stan says. "Right now we need to keep going. They're somewhere up ahead, and we need to find them."

I take some pictures and a few videos before we go, hoping that I captured enough of the peculiarities of this place so we can find our way back here later. "Hey, Bobby?" I call, wanting to ask him if I've captured enough angles for us to be able to use my footage as a map, but he doesn't answer, and when I look for him, he's not around.

"Hey, Stan," I say. "Have you seen Bobby?"

"Nope," says Stan. "Probably he's up ahead? If anyone knows where they're going, it's Bobby."

Someone calls out, "Yo! Is anyone maybe Hansel-and-Gretel-ing this place?"

Stan gives the guy a thumbs-up, and I hold out my phone and shout, "I've got your bread crumbs right here, champ."

We keep walking the path until it opens up and the trees disappear, and all around us are these low hills. The tracks start to peter out here, though there's still something of a path headed onward. An argument breaks out—some of the kids have had enough and don't want to continue.

Some guy sits down and says, so loud and pouty it makes my frozen skin crawl, "It's goddamn *cold*! I don't even *like* my sister! I wanna go home." A few other guys and girls who share this sentiment join the chorus and plant their asses down on the hostile ground, the definitive sign that this is indeed a collective temper tantrum.

But if it were that easy to just dismiss these kids as selfish whiners, then this would be a different story. People are tired. They're cold. They're hungry. Someone here has driven from Los Angeles, which seems insane to me. To imagine what I went through—what we went through—*in a single day* and just a bit of change, and stretch that out over days or maybe even a week or however long it takes to drive from L.A. . . . I don't know.

"What if they *are* weapons?" someone—whether in the sitting group or the standing group, I don't know—asks.

"They just *ran*. They *left us. Alone*. I never left Jennie alone. Not once in her *life*," someone else sobs.

"So what?" asks someone, and when I see that it's Jayson, a little happy chime rings in my head. Jayson's here! "What, are you gonna swim home? Do you even know which way's land? We're *stuck* here," he says.

"Just because those . . . *things* got me stuck here against my will," says the boy who started all this, "doesn't mean I have to participate in whatever's going to happen. Because *something's* going to happen, and you're an idiot if you don't know that too. It's not like nobody knows we're coming. It's not like *they* would understand the idea of someone setting a trap for them to run into. It's not like they're gonna realize it and then stop themselves from doing whatever it is that's so important they do. It's not like they'd even understand what a trap is if we explained it."

"We have to keep going," says Stan. "We have to leave them and keep going." He's looking out at the Iceling tracks.

"What?" says Emily.

"He's right," I say. "We don't know what's out there or what's waiting for them. And maybe we can't do anything about it, but . . ."

"Yeah," she says. "Right. Okay." It's not the resounding yes I was hoping for, but I know she understands that this is the only option. She puts one foot in front of the other, same as me, and I guide her onward as Stan turns to the seated shepherds.

"We're going," he says. "We've got to. I get why you maybe think you can't, but you can. We can all do this. You're welcome to come with us. Just follow our tracks and you'll find us."

He turns and catches up with us. We trudge on after the speck in the distance we know, in our hearts, to be our siblings. We trudge on and on and on.

SASHA STEPHENSON

※

I KNOW THAT I shouldn't be running like this, toward whatever's to come, happy or horrible. But I can't help it. And it looks like neither can anyone else. At least, anyone else who's with us. Stan, Emily, Jayson, me, and about thirty others are running along this path up one of the low-slung hills, and when we get to the top, we stop and stare.

Because below us is the trembling field of ice. A field about the size of a middle school auditorium, sheeted completely in ice, and it's *trembling*. There's snow all around the ridge of hills bordering the whole island, not so much piled up as somehow shaken off. The ice is starting to look weird. The snow is scattered and heaped in such a way that it's as if the ground is shaking itself loose of things before something shakes itself loose from the ground. I mean that it looks like something's under the surface, and it wants to come out. After several seconds of silent staring, we trudge on again, and as we get down to the bottom of the hill, we see them.

Our Icelings.

And I see her.

Callie.

Callie and Tara and Ted and Greta and all the rest, holding hands. They stand in a circle along the perimeter of the trembling field of ice, and all I can say about it is that they look like they belong there. I zero in on Callie. She knows exactly where she is, exactly whom she's with, exactly what she's supposed to be doing. In other words, she looks a way I've never seen her look before. Like she belongs. Like what I feel like when I walk through Mom and Dad's front door and think—not actively, not even with my brain, because when you belong, you don't really need to think—*This is home. And I feel safe.* They all look like that, like they just got back from a long, long trip, which was exhilarating and rewarding but ultimately really difficult, but they're home now, and they remembered to clean up before they left so that their homecoming could be that much warmer.

Their eyes are closed, and they're holding hands, and they're smiling.

And we stand above them, shivering and numb with awe and terror, and we look at them like we have no idea who they are, and we realize we are strangers here. To each other, to our brothers, to our sisters, to this frigid mystery of a place.

TWENTY-ONE

SAVE FOR THE trembling, all is still. Until it isn't.

Suddenly, the whole island bellows with a chorus of terrible, unfamiliar sounds. We cover our ears and cower, but they just grow louder and closer and louder and closer until they're right on top of us. And it's not the sound of thunder, and it's not the sound of the lightning that we smelled earlier.

Stan grabs my wrist, then Emily's.

"Holy shit," he says, and points skyward. Three winged, needle-nosed aircrafts soaring over the island. On each of the wings is a missile. Which means, I think, that these are drones.

And then we hear what sounds like a fleet of jeeps churning slowly toward us. And then after we hear them we see them, pulling up over the ridge, and from these jeeps pour soldiers, and the soldiers have guns. "Hut," they say. "Hut." They de-jeep, rifles slung low with their elbows straight out, wrists limp, like at any minute they could flick their wrists and spit a hundred bullets at your skull and heart. If they weren't on the other side of the ridge, I might honestly just hand myself over.

But they are. They're over there, and we're over here, and the Icelings are between us. It's a pretty clear *Us vs. Them* situation here. People gasp. Someone faints. A girl next to me pees herself, and for a second I envy the fleeting moment of warmth she must be getting from it, and then I remember where I am.

I feel like I've floated up and out of my own body, and I'm watching myself from up above, and I watch myself look down to the trembling field below. And then I see something that makes me forget all about the drones and weapons and army that has descended upon us.

Because below this ridge of snowy hills, the trembling field is shivering and shaking. The ice is cracking apart. At first it's just the very outer surface, but then dozens of little holes start to crack open, like they're being punctured from below, and then the cracks grow longer and deeper, and it's all happening so fast, like when a nature doc shows the process of a plant blooming from a seed in superfast motion.

The drones move. I can hear this roaring of engines and see snow moving around in their wake. I can hear the soldiers' rifles, and they sound like they're aching.

I feel a little tug and look down to see I'm squeezing Stan's hand way too hard. Just as I'm letting go, I feel and then see a flash of color and movement on the field below. We all look down. Remember how I said it looked like the ground was shaking itself loose of things before something shakes itself loose from the ground? This, I guess, is what was trying to shake itself loose. The ground shudders and shakes like someone's just grabbed it, and there's this sound I can't place as this . . . *hole* opens up. And there's something like smoke, but I know it's not smoke, it's more like a mist, like what might happen when warm air meets Arctic air. And then what shakes itself loose from the ground is this . . . body.

I don't know what else to call it. There are two arms, and they're shivering, and they're attached to a torso that just shoots up, as if the shaking gives it energy. As it keeps rising up it keeps looking like a human figure, and it looks like a him, and then he looks like an Iceling. He's got that flaxy dirty blond hair, and when he walks, he walks like a part of him always needs to feel the ground. I think he's headed toward this big mound of snow. He doesn't once look at the soldiers. None of the Icelings do. But you can tell that they all see them. It's in their bodies. It's the first time Callie's looked like she perfectly understands the world around her.

"Who the hell is that?" asks Stan, but I don't answer him. I don't want to move a muscle, that's how scared I am to lose sight of what's unfolding below.

The Iceling person reaches the mound and steps on top of it. He turns around and stretches out his arms, and all of our brothers' and sisters' body language changes, like they're all deferring to him.

Their eyes snap over and their arms fall to their sides, like an army at attention. The new Iceling drops his arms, fingers tight and hands curved like scoops, palms up. Everyone grabs hands, and the effect is somewhere between the beauty of a choreographed dance and the weird terror of a cult ritual. I don't know how to feel. Mostly what I feel is awe, and terror, and fear for Callie—and for me. So I just keep feeling that.

"Lorna, what the hell is going on?" Stan asks, but again I don't answer him, and I'm not going to, because my legs are moving and I'm heading down the hill.

It's a short descent, maybe twenty feet, to Callie, whose back is to me. I can hear Stan coming down after me, and I can see the soldiers. They started to move down, maybe in response to me, but then someone yells—maybe not a soldier but a commander of some kind—and I hear them stop all at once. "Hut!" they say again.

ICELING

I reach the edge of the field, where I get the strong sense that I'm to go no further. That I don't belong here, and that that's okay. That what's happening here has nothing to do with me and that to cross this boundary made of Icelings would be a trespass of the most awful kind. I move around so I can see Callie. Her eyes are closed, and then they open, her stare fixed on this new guy, who is, I guess, their leader. She looks like she belongs here. She looks like she's noticing and accounting for everything around her in a way that I've never seen her do before.

And it hits me that maybe every time I was tired, or kind of mean to her, and despite that she would just smile at me, like *It's okay, Lorna, I love you anyway,* that maybe that . . . that maybe that smile. Maybe that smile was just something her face did. That nothing I ever did, good or bad or mean or kind, made any sense to her at all. And even if any of it—any of the hours I spent sitting up with her or any of the times I stayed at home instead of going out with my friends because I thought she seemed sad and needed comfort and companionship— did get through to her in some small, simplistic way, it would be nothing like the way this moment right here is affecting her. Is making the purest sense possible to her. And that kind of wrecks me a little.

And as it wrecks me, the soldiers adjust their grips on their rifles, and everyone takes one step forward.

I'm panicking, but I know that if I move I'll only make things worse, so I watch from the outside, keeping an eye on Callie the whole time, making sure I can see her, grab her and run away with her if anything goes wrong. Soon a light—dim yet brilliant, if you can imagine such a thing—starts pulsing beneath the ice. The trembling expanse of ice, around which our Icelings huddle and within which this new Iceling stands, continues to crack open, over and over and over and over, until the field looks like the shell of an egg that's been rolled and smashed but not quite split. The Icelings' faces come alive with what

I read as a sort of nervous excitement. Some of them break rank and look around at each other. They grin, like *Can you believe it?* But it could be something else entirely, something as un-intuitive to me as singing karaoke is to Callie.

And then—*oh my God*—these little . . . *things*, all of them lichen green, start shooting up from the ice. One by one, row after row of them sprouting up with an energy I've never seen in nature before. They've fully breached the surface of the ice, and now they're growing up like stalks, like hundreds of large flowers poking out, and they shiver and shake their way up there, up here, to the surface. Only the more they grow, the more I see that they're not flowers. Not flowers but . . . pods. Jesus. Pods. And the Icelings all look on with awe, their eyes wide, their jaws slack, straining against each other to run out to the pods. I look at Callie, and then at the pods, and at Callie, and at the pods, and I smell the air. I can't explain what the smell is other than to say that it's different from the green one and that I've never smelled it before. It's sort of burnt, and like rain, and electric. There's something else in there that I'm not quite getting, but I'm almost getting it, and before I can wonder about it, I see Callie's face, and it's falling. It's like her heart is breaking behind her face, and I look around, and so is Tara's and Greta's and everyone else's. I look from them to the pods, and that's all it takes to see why.

The pods are all withered and dead-looking, like crushed empty cans, like broken boxes, like corpses. I'm not the botanist in the family, and I don't know how this alien crop is supposed to look, but right now all I can think of is that time Dad bought me a cactus to take care of as a way to help me and Callie bond, and how I was so scared of killing that cactus so I made sure to water it all the time, but then the cactus died anyway because I didn't know that feeding a plant too often could drown and kill the roots. One of the pods starts to open. I think, *Maybe this'll be fine, maybe it'll be all right.* But it's not. The pods are shaped like footballs. They each have four seams, and they're sort of opening from the middle point out, and you can see how they probably should open, how the pod should peel back in quarters, rising toward the sun that's emerging, shining down right on this trembling expanse, the clouds actually moving aside right now as if to make that happen, the sky all around them gone purple, the clouds this steely gray, and you can see in your mind's eye how this *should* play out.

But it doesn't. The plant shudders, like it's coughing, and only one quarter of the football seam peels back, and it's more that it dries up than opens. The whole pod droops, and when it touches the ground, it just turns to dust.

"Lorna," someone whispers, and the sound of my name spoken by another human being feels so foreign right now that for a second I wonder if I'm dead and this is the place my body has chosen to go.

But then I feel a hand on my shoulder, and I turn to see Emily standing beside me, and all around us is everyone else. The rest of us, of the siblings, have come down from up above while I was too engrossed to notice.

Somebody asks what's happening in a desperate voice, and someone else asks it again, even more desperately, and I'm screaming it over and over again in my head, but no one can say anything. All we can do is watch.

The soldiers too. All they do is watch. The drones are moving overhead, and down below more soldiers are setting something up in what looks like a van. Someone's in there, and people are going in and out, like it's a command post or something.

And then suddenly the air is full with that smell, the one other than the green one. The smell of lightning. *So this is what lightning smells like.* It had been lingering this whole time, but I'd gotten used to it. But now it's stronger, and everywhere, the air is choked with it. I remember Dad, after dinner, saying, *"That day . . . that day, it . . .*

just. It just wasn't what we were expecting to find out there. But mostly what I remember was the sky. My God. It was purple and yellow, and it smelled like lightning, but I couldn't see any. Do you know what lightning smells like? Don't. Don't know that. And the clouds were so low and heavy and with a mind of their own, opening a hole in the sky to let the light in."

The smell is more than I can bear, I think, and I wonder if human lungs were built to breathe this stuff in, and then a sudden snap of motion ripples all across the field, and I look. The pods—not dead—start to open.

Oh God.

And then I gasp and choke back tears, because I can't believe how stupid I am not to have seen this all along. Because this is where he found them. This is where they came from. Not some war-torn nation in Eastern Europe or the Balkans, shoved in a boat and swaddled in desperate blankets and left to drift to safety. But here, on a field of trembling ice, in a pod that pushed its way up through the ground. *This* is where they were born. *This* is where the sky turned purple and this lightning smell scarred my father and stayed with him forever. Here. Right here. *Of course* this is where Dad found them. The sky is just like he said, and this smell in the air, like it's electrified, like it's charged with something so *of* the earth that it's alien, and if this quaking, trembling ground isn't basically the *definition* of strange seismic and meteorological activity, then I don't know what is.

This is where they came from. *This* is where and how they were born. And then I almost have to laugh because *my sister is a plant person.*

And then I don't laugh, of course, not at all, because if she's a plant person and this, right in front of me, is how she was born, then what's happening here is that she and her Iceling siblings, they're here to welcome the next generation.

ICELING

The pods are opening more and more, and I try to speak, to tell Stan that *this is it. This is what happened to them, this is where they were found. It wasn't a boat,* but the most I can get out is a whisper that I'm not sure he even hears, because like everyone else he's just standing there, staring.

And then I hear him whisper, "This is where they came from," and I know that he knows and everyone around us knows, even though none of us understand any of it.

We just keep staring at the field, at the pod plants rising up all shriveled and choked. I notice a few kids have their eyes trained on the sky, and then I notice one guy a few people back who's just shaking and peeing himself. Some people are fainting, either again or for the first time. Five people turned and ran but couldn't make it back up the hill the way they came and just sort of slid back down and slumped themselves in balls on the ground. But I'm done with that now, I think. The worst thing that can happen here is Callie dies and so do I. And at least we'll be together.

The pods are almost all the way open now, and as they gape into a field of horrible yawns, a new ripple of fear passes through our group, and the ground, and then the ice, is finally still. They're fully open now, and the Icelings are all closing their eyes, turning their heads away. I try to get closer to see what's happening. I brace myself for the image I've been dreading ever since these pods started opening: a field of perfect, sleeping infants cradled in the maws of these weird blossoms, a flashback to what my sister must have looked like when she was born. But that's not what I see. Not at all.

At first, I don't see anything inside those pods. But then I squint and look closer, and what I see is dust and some gray and clingy substance that looks like mold, and then my view of them is all swallowed up by the icy air whipped up by helicopters and drones. And the Icelings . . . the Icelings are . . .

Some of them, including Callie, fall down to their knees, their mouths open in soundless howls, weeping and weeping and weeping and weeping, their tears hitting the ice and just turning to more ice. The others who aren't wailing like this look just wrathful as hell, their faces and bodies snapping toward the ridge, where the soldiers are, like they'd like to uproot their lives. This was supposed to be the birth of a new generation, I think. They were coming here to welcome the next generation of Icelings into this world, and instead they found a hostile army and a field of dead babies. The leader closes his eyes. His whole body goes limp. Then his head snaps up, and his eyes look for someone on the ridge I can't see. I'm holding on to Stan's hand again, and I squeeze it, and he squeezes harder, and that's when I see Ted.

Ted has broken the circle. He's lumbering forward and straight into the middle of the once-trembling, now-still ice field of shriveled pods, which are so much more than shriveled pods, of course, but what they really are is just . . . unspeakable. Ted lunges violently and picks up a pod, and he hurls it up at the drones, which are hovering low now, flitting in and around as if following him. He makes contact, and one of the drones veers into the rocky hillside it was hugging, and then down and down it tumbles.

But the truly scary thing, the thing that's more shocking and upsetting and so far beyond the word "surprise" that it's actually almost funny, the thing that makes Ted hurling a pod and hitting this drone with such force that it crashes into a small mountain seem like just nothing at all, is that Ted is *screaming*, has been screaming this whole time. The sound is unlike anything I've ever heard, like death whistling through the leaves of a tree, but magnified a thousand times. Blood is falling from his mouth in awful streams.

One of the remaining drones rears up, but instead of aiming for Ted, it's heading right to the Iceling leader. It hovers for a bit, but then we see its gears moving, and it releases a small rocket, which comes soaring out, its aim terrifyingly true. And this is it, I think. This is as far as we go. My name is Lorna Van Allister. I'm seventeen years old. I was born and raised in Abington, Pennsylvania. My sister's name is Callie. I have a boy I won't call my boyfriend named Dave, a mom named Judy, and a dad named Tom, and they probably work for the government, and this is where I'm going to die.

"LOOK OUT!" so many of us shout as we either scatter or lunge toward the Iceling ring to try to drag our siblings to safety, knowing they won't understand but needing to scream all the same. But somebody does understand. The Iceling leader seems to hear us, which I only say because he looks at us, then at the missile hurtling toward him. It's him they were aiming for, we can see the path of the missile clear enough as it's hurtling death through space, and then the missile hits. It smacks his foot against the ice until it breaks, sending violent shards of broken ice and the last remaining shreds of the withered-up pods flying. The Iceling leader—definitely injured but probably not dead—dives down and disappears under the surface of the field.

Callie's down there. My Callie. Where that missile hit. I start to run to her, but I fall back and down, and everything hurts.

TWENTY-TWO

AND THEN EVERYTHING starts to come apart.

When the missile hit, we flinched and took cover, only peeking out from the shields we created with our arms or by curling completely into ourselves when the world-shattering noise from the first missile started to quiet down. It's good the Icelings were in a kind of horseshoe around their leader, because it's only the specific place where he was standing that's completely gone now. In its stead is a smoking craterlike hole. The ice is holding, but who knows for how long.

For a moment, I let myself pretend I live in a world where I get to interpret the lack of an immediate follow-up missile as a sign that the soldiers have decided to lay down their arms and acknowledge the limits of violence to solve anything. But then one of the soldiers shatters that illusion by hollering something I can't make out from here, but by its tone and cadence I can tell it's an order, and my stomach goes sour and drops. I can't make out what the commanding officer said, but immediately after it's said, the troops scatter and fall back into a new line. It's increasingly obvious that everything they're doing is going according to a plan we'll never be a part of, and they file back into the jeeps and start the engines.

The jeeps full of soldiers turn their noses straight for the field, for us and our brothers and sisters, and they drive as a fleet down the hill. Callie, Greta, Tara, and a whole bunch of other Icelings are running to the pods to try to shield them. I want to shout out that they're dead, that there's nothing they can do, but of course I can't, for too many reasons than there's time to explain. Besides, this isn't my world anymore. It's Callie's.

The jeeps go slowly down the hill. All the Icelings who aren't guarding pods are standing defiantly in front of the ones who are.

The jeeps brake and park in much the same formation they had at the top of the hill, and the soldiers, rifles ready, file out of them in less time than it takes to draw breath. They're standing in small groups, their guns trained on whatever they can see. They're moving out, I guess to maximize the area they're covering, to maximize the number of things they can kill.

We have no idea what's coming, but we can guess. I flash back to all the conversations Mimi and I have had while marathoning movies about the end of the world, the conversations about how stupid it is that, when people think about the end of the world, they imagine themselves in the shoes of these characters who are surviving despite all the plagues and zombies trying to wipe them off the face of the earth. When in reality, it's *so* unlikely that the people who are sitting around in the suburbs watching end-of-the-world explosion-death dramas are the same ones who would have what it takes to fight through an actual disaster. So Mimi and I made a pact that in the event of a zombie apocalypse, we'd just do each other in, because there's no way in hell we'd make it past the first wave. But now that I'm here, staring at what looks very much like the opening of the gateway to hell, there's no part of me that thinks anything other than surviving—for my sister, for myself—is an option. And I know that if I give in to the terror being forced upon us, if I end up like that guy wetting himself and going into shock, then I'm done. Callie's done. It's over. So I push all that fear to the deepest part of my soul, and I clear my head and let go of Stan's hand, because it's time to think our way out of this. I know that I might die. That this sad little act of bravery might be my last sad little act ever. I'm not okay with that, not at all, but at least I know I've tried hard to be a good sister to Callie, to this plant person whom I love more than I really know how to say.

But none of this—not my love for Callie, who might not love me back, nor my proving that love by driving all the way up here to face this awful massacre—matters to anyone but me, because to the rest of the world, Callie isn't a person. Any love anyone has for her or anyone like her is rendered invisible, misplaced, insane. And that thought has never been clearer than now, as this wing of the U.S. military calmly walks past us with their assault rifles raised. They make their way through us, shoving us aside and ignoring our cries of surrender. They are, essentially, ignoring us.

"Stay back," one of them says, shoving at us. Nobody does anything about it. You want to think you'd fight back, but they've got assault rifles and U.S. flags on their arms, with the letters *E.T.R.* stitched underneath. They march onto the ice field and start firing, small mechanical bursts aimed toward the ground, at what remains of the pods.

The drones are backing off, maybe because the soldiers are down here. And it actually seems like maybe someone made a mistake, which is the only reason the soldiers are down here now. But maybe that's just wishful thinking. The soldiers are unloading what I recognize as flamethrowers. They're tossing them on like they're backpacks or some kind of trendy vest. Through the smoke and the chaos I can see some of the Icelings wringing their hands as they watch, tears streaming down their faces and turning to ice before hitting their mouths. Stan taps my shoulder and points. I follow his hand, and my eyes find Ted again. He's still fighting back, and now he's got a gang of likeminded Icelings with him, all lined up with their fists clenched, running at those troops like they're about to tear their heads off.

Because I guess what happened here is that the Icelings were coming home to greet the new generation. To welcome them into this world like no one else was able to welcome them. And they got here, and they were ready. They knew, their bodies knew, what they needed to do. And they got here, and all the babies were dead dust.

And now there are soldiers marching among the corpses of the next generation and shooting them and burning them. Ted and his gang are hitting these soldiers in the faces. I don't know whether the soldiers were prepared for what happened here today or for the strength of these Icelings who are pissed about what didn't happen here today. The first wave catches the troops by surprise, but then, once the surprise is over, they start firing. Ted's gang starts picking up the fallen bodies, soldier and Iceling both, and hurling them at the troops, trying to knock them down.

Stan can't tear his eyes away, but I feel like I have to, I have to see what else is going on, so I look to the sky—the drone that fired the missile is long gone, and so are its companions. Hovering in their places are several more drones, smaller than the first ones, that look like roving eyeballs with helicopter blades.

Think, Lorna! Okay. Okay. Okay, okay, okay. There has to be some sort of Wi-Fi or cell network or something going on here that the army is using. How else could these drones work, transmit images? I pull out my phone, and, lo and behold, there is a signal. I open up Twitter and hit record, and all I can do is hope this signal holds long enough for me to broadcast this. Unless this is some secret territory under some secret governance, we're in Canada. And the soldiers have U.S. flags on their shoulders, they're obviously American, and so are we. Someone's watching with those drones. There's no way off this island, or if there is, they're there waiting for us, and we can't hide, because they'll find us. It's not that big of an island. And the Iceling leader came from below the surface, but there's no way we'll figure out how to go down there like he did before they capture or shoot us.

So we need to run right up to the soldiers. We need to tell them we're Americans—not for them, not because they don't know it. But for our phones and whoever might end up seeing this.

I grab Stan and Emily and Jayson and everyone else around and tell them what to do.

"What?" someone says. "Are you *kidding*? That's the *plan*?"

Stan stares down the girl who said it, and then another girl opens up Snapchat, and a guy opens up Periscope, and down the line they go, with Facebook and Instagram and Twitter.

And right when we rush out, phones in front of our faces to try to save our siblings' lives like we're all in some ridiculous ad about how my generation is selfish and ruining everything, someone nearby calls out.

"Stop firing!" He's talking to the soldiers, not us, but we all stop anyway. "That is a fucking order!"

Something about that voice makes me stop and put my ear to the air, and I know Stan hears it too, because he's also frozen in place and searching my face for an answer. I turn around, and then I see him.

Bobby. Bobby from the road trip, Bobby with an Iceling sister. Only he's swapped out his fashionable clothes for a uniform and a baseball cap with *E.T.R.* on it, the same three initials on the helmets and under the flags of the people who are attacking us. He's running into the middle of all this, elbowing soldiers out of the way, and

Icelings too. He's barking cease and desist orders through a bullhorn, and he's just about the only thing we can hear over the bullets, and the drones, and the jeeps, and the flamethrowers.

"What. The. Hell," says Stan. "So Bobby's . . ."

"He's with them," I say.

The guy who bought us dinner yesterday, who kept everyone calm, who kept *me* calm, who claimed to have devoted his life to studying the roots of language so he could find a way to say something to his sister, who lost his brother, this guy, Bobby, if that's even his goddamn name, is one of them. He was with us, getting us here.

"He was the shepherd," says Stan.

"And this was the slaughter," I say.

Bobby's still screaming, "CEASE FIRE!" at the top of his lungs, but the soldiers don't listen. They just keep firing on the already dead pods until they're more bullets than bulbs and ashes, the desiccated bits just floating off into nothing.

We stop in our tracks when the guns keep firing. At no point did I think they'd just fire at or around us when we started running. We're just kids. We're American kids!

"What the hell were they shooting for?" says Emily, quietly, to no one. "Whatever's in there was already dead."

Bobby's ditched the bullhorn and is knocking the muzzles of rifles to the ground around him and screaming, "CEASE YOUR GOD-DAMN FIRING!" over and over until his voice starts to give, only just barely. The guy can shout, I'll give him that.

And that's all I'll give him.

The shots keep ringing out, and I can't look away, because I need to keep my eyes on Callie, I need to make sure they're still only shooting at the ground and not at people. I hear a scream so loud I feel it might shatter the freezing cold air before making its way to my eardrums, and then I realize the scream is coming from me, because in the middle of the field, about a dozen Icelings throw themselves down on top of the remains of the pods, where the soldiers are still shooting. And the soldiers keep shooting, and now instead of just ripping apart the pods, they're ripping apart our brothers and sisters, and I myself feel ripped apart as I watch them get hit by bullet after bullet after bullet. I don't see Callie, and I run out toward Bobby, and I'll kill him if she's dead. I swear to God, I'll kill him. Iceling and soldier blood stains the snow and ice and all that I can see, and then a soldier hurls something at the Icelings, and then they're gone, replaced by a burst of fire.

Bobby tackles the soldier who threw the flamethrower. He punches him in the mouth, repeatedly telling him to "Stand down!"

Some of the soldiers stop now that Bobby has shown he's serious and now that the soldier beneath him has stopped struggling back. The ones who are paying attention reach into their uniforms and put something into their ears.

"Is that why they weren't listening?" Stan says. "They had their earpieces out?" And then I swear I hear a familiar voice coming through the earpieces of the dead soldiers I'm digging through to get to Callie, blood all over my hands and arms, screaming, *"Stop that!"*

And then Stan grabs me. He points. Ted's stopped fighting. He's got Callie behind him. And she's got Greta and Tara. My sister is alive, and I take the biggest breath I've ever taken, and I let it out real slow.

The air smells like burning leaves so much it's choking out the lightning smell. I look around and see Icelings burning, the pods burning, the things that should have been babies in them burning.

"There's someone up there," Emily says, pointing to the top of the hill, where that van from earlier is now parked. I look up. My whole body goes fiery hot and then freezing again, because up on that hill, standing under a military tent, wearing a fur-hooded parka and ski goggles that do nothing to hide the look in her eyes, is Jane.

She's screaming into a walkie-talkie that she holds in one hand, and she clutches a laptop or tablet underneath her other arm. She's stomping around and waving wildly. We're near a valley we hadn't noticed before, lined with trees, leading out somewhere. The hill's maybe as high as a row house, and roughly a half block to our left. Jane's body language tells us she is furious.

"I once had this horrible gymnastics coach," says Emily, and I look at her like she's just had a stroke, "who, whenever we'd go off-routine, would just pace and scream and pace and *fume*."

"Uh, cool, Emily, what the hell does that have to do with us dying out here?" Stan says, the meanest I've ever heard him sound.

"That lady up there looks *exactly* like that gymnastics coach. Like everyone down there did the wrong thing, at the wrong time, in lockstep."

"She's right, Stan," I say.

"Fine," Stan says after a sulky pause. "But what the hell do we do with that? And who the *hell* is Jane really?" says Stan.

I'm shaking. Of course it was Jane. Of course she's been orchestrating all of this, a puppeteer from above. Whether or not she's trying, like Bobby, to put a Band-Aid over this atrocity, I know she doesn't care about what happened, because at the end of the day she came here to kill all of us. She's the villain, she's been the monster all along. Oh my God, do I hate her right now. It's burning white-hot in me. She's studied Callie her whole life just to figure out the best ways to murder her. The government paid her well to do this, and it's obvious to anyone she loves her job, which is to be a complete and utter monster. That's Jane. Heels clicking down a hallway toward a door marked: THE BRUTAL AND INEVITABLE DEATH OF YOUR BELOVED SISTER. Her coat is zipped up over her mouth, but as I look up at her, I swear I see her eyes lock with mine, and though I know it's not true—I know she's up there trying to do what Bobby is doing, only from on high and with a walkie-talkie instead of her fists—it makes me feel better, more fueled with rage, to picture her smiling.

But of course she's not. That's just the easiest thing to think, and it's all wasted because it doesn't even make me feel better.

Most of the troops have stopped firing and are slowly backing away. Bobby's fighting anyone who gets near him. Ted's whole gang is dead except for the ones who, like Ted, ran to stand in front of other Icelings. Icelings are throwing themselves on the burning pods, as if they can put out the fires or save what was inside. Or as if they've given up. But as I've spent my life constantly re-realizing, constantly catching and correcting myself about: I have absolutely no idea what they're feeling. Their actions, their facial expressions, the depths of their gazes—they don't mean for them what they mean for me. Hell, that rule is true even when you speak the same language as the person you're attempting to judge, let alone for an Iceling from an entirely different world. All I can do is guess. All I can do is ascribe the intentions and emotions within my limits of experience to their actions, which, if you think about it long and hard enough, is meaningless. It's an exercise. And it doesn't make anyone feel better—or feel anything—except for me.

My eyes drift to the one lone soldier left who is still shooting at Icelings. His eyes are glazed over, his jaw is slack.

Bobby walks up to him and says, "I SAID, STAND DOWN, SOLDIER."

The soldier doesn't stand down. Bobby shoots him in the head. He falls.

There's no more gunfire now.

In the absence of gunshots, all around us kids are running to their dead brothers and sisters, maybe even feeling betrayed by or scared of their siblings now that they know what they really are, which is something decidedly *Other*, something maybe not even human, but it doesn't matter, because they still care, and they care that they're dead. This is the central truth of their lives right now. That girl's brother is dead. That boy's sister is dead. One of them got shot in the head by a soldier and then set on fire. Another threw her body on a burning pod to try to save it, and then she died because she tried to save a life that wasn't going to make it anyhow.

I see a giant bug hovering and buzzing in the peripheral of my vision, and I swat at it. I miss and swat again, this time making contact, only what I hit isn't a bug at all. It's heavy and manmade, and I go at it again with both hands, and when I smack it down to the ground, I see that it's a drone. I take a step back and start to run, but then the drone rises up again, this time very wobbly, one of its rotors coughing and spitting, and because it doesn't look equipped with weapons or like it was sent to hurt me, I decide to stop and wait it out. It floats itself up to eye level and then a little bit above, and that's when I see it. A smartphone, adhered to the undercarriage of the drone. And staring at me, from the screen of the smartphone, is Jane.

I try to take the phone off the drone, but at the slightest tug, the drone flinches and pulls back, does a little topsy-turvy circle in the air like a bothered wasp, then hovers again with the phone at my eye level, this time just a little bit out of my reach. I look at the live feed of her image on the phone, but either the sound is broken or I can't hear anything in the midst of this military chaos, and all I can see is Jane mouthing something that I can't make out. She goes on like this for a while, and I just shake my head and grit my teeth and keep turning to look for Callie, and I want to just grab the drone and throw it into the middle of the fray so at least some part of Jane can get blown up by her own firepower, but then I see something new flash on the screen. Behind Jane, a young officer holds up a sign that says: I'M SORRY.

"You're *SORRY*?" I scream into the phone, which Jane must take to mean that her message was received, because then she gestures to another officer who then ducks down behind some little device, and then all of a sudden a stream of text pops up on the screen beneath Jane's face.

LORNA. THIS WAS A MISTAKE. THIS WASNT SUPPOSED TO HAPPN. WE WERE JUST HERE 2 CONTAIN + MONITOR. I AM SO SORRY BUT

The words are going blurry from the tears in my eyes. My stupid mind goes numb, and against my will, I start to remember this one time at the hospital. I was waiting for Callie in the front when I heard this noise, like a little crash or an office object being slammed against a desk. And then there was a voice, one I didn't recognize at the time but which I now know belonged to Jane—the real Jane, the monster Jane up on the hill. In the scariest whisper I've ever heard, Jane said, *"I swear to God, if you don't fix this, I'll wear your useless balls as earrings, and your brother will fail out of college, and your wife will leave you, and your student loans will never get paid, and your whole life will be repossessed by the U.S. government, which owns you, you sloppy, useless, inefficient peon in a clip-on necktie."* Part of me, I admit, wanted to find the owner of the voice and shake her hand for being a good role model for girls who need to see examples of women taking charge in the workplace. But that part of me was quickly and easily trampled by a more immediate, cell-level part of me that was completely chilled and terrified. I had no idea what she was talking about or whom she was talking to or what the consequences were, but it didn't matter. I was overcome with a need to see my sister and get her home, and I pleaded with the front-desk lady for forty-five minutes until finally they relented and released my sister early and with a rescheduled appointment.

This is who has been in charge of Callie's whole life. And right now, in the middle of hell swallowing us up—a hell that *she* ordered—she's trying to apologize.

I shake the tears out of my eyes, and the words on the screen blink back into view. THE ICELINGS R A DANGER. LORNA. PLZ LEAVE. PLZ GET 2 SAFETY, IT IS SO V IMPOR—

But I don't want to read the rest. I spit at the phone, and the drone pulls back a bit, flutters around in the air again, then steadies itself and hovers once again so I can see the phone. The camera refocuses on me, and I give it the finger.

Jane gives me a look like she's sighing, but then her face jumps with fear and her eyes go cold, and just as that's happening I feel Stan start beside me.

"Shit," he says. I turn from burning Iceling corpses, whose bodies smell more like burning leaves than meat, and I see the soldiers clearing a path, saying, "Come with us, we'll get you home."

Home? To our parents who lied to us? Who let this kind of slaughter happen? Home with the people who just killed—or tried to kill—the kids we spent our whole lives as brothers and sisters to?

"We're not going, Stan," I say.

"Not even a little bit," says Emily.

And then my body jerks, wrestling between the idea of running and falling to my knees, because before me I see Callie, the one thing that could ever make me think I had any business being a survivor at the end of the world, felled and fallen on the ground. Oh God, please let her be breathing, oh God oh God oh God, and then Ted leaps over and crouches down in front of her. And then I wind up and start to run right over to her, but Stan holds me back and then Emily helps him, and I'm caught in a net of their arms as I watch Ted stand up and break into a full run at a soldier with his weapon ready. Bobby's yelling at the solider, telling him not to shoot, and now Stan's no longer holding me back, because Stan is the one who is running. I'm about to bolt from Emily's grasp when a round goes off, and my heart flutters everywhere, and I cower and crouch down with Emily. I look up and see Stan and Ted, both of them on the ground. Stan is holding his head, covering it with his arms. Bobby's yelling.

"WHAT THE HELL IS WRONG WITH YOU?" he shouts again and again while standing over a soldier he has just thrown to the ground. "DO I NEED TO SHOOT YOU TOO? YOU HAD ORDERS! You had *orders*. Observe and contain. *Contain* doesn't mean *shoot*, it doesn't mean *burn*, it doesn't mean *kill*. It means *restrain*. You opened fire on American citizens, buddy." He kicks him. "Do you understand how much shit you're in? Surrender your weapon and get back to the jeep. *Now*, soldier."

And he does.

And I'm walking toward Bobby with what feels like death in my eyes.

TWENTY-THREE

"THIS IS NOT how this was supposed to go down," says Bobby.

We look out at the decimated field. Callie's safe. The soldiers are backing away, escorting whoever's willing to go back to the jeeps, all of them with that look on their faces like they know they're about to be punished. It's so obvious that they weren't ready for this, for whatever they saw here, just like us. But not Bobby. Not Jane. They were ready.

I look up at the sky, and it's gone. The hole where the sun was—closed up and gone.

The clouds are darker now. They're shifting shape and moving around the sky quickly. They seem to move like the island moves, like when there's trouble below there's trouble above too.

Bobby's trying to move us and our Icelings over to that shaded wooded valley where we were when we first saw Jane. Callie is still on the ground, but she is breathing, and I'm with her now, with her head in my lap and my hand stroking her hair. She was trying to save the pods, and seeing them all dead and burnt up like that just about killed her, I think. I'm staring daggers at Bobby. Tara won't leave Callie's side either, so Emily sits next to her right across from us. Stan and Ted are back on their feet, though Stan has to hold Ted back from jumping on Bobby and removing his head from his body. Greta's here and holding her Other's hand. The hand that is all that's left of her Other.

"Nobody was supposed to get hurt," Bobby says. "Nobody was supposed to blow anything up."

"No? Were they also not supposed to shoot at our brothers and sisters?" spits out Stan. "At any living thing that might have been about to come out of those pods?"

"Look, you can give me shit," Bobby says, his sternness from the battlefield coming back into his voice, "or you can listen while I try to help save you. Take your pick."

"I think you're a little late for that, buddy," says Stan. "Coulda used your help a long time ago, like when we were still on our way up here? Coulda given us a heads-up."

"I know you're pissed. There's nothing I can do or say that will make you feel better, so just trust me that had I come clean with you back on the road? Things would have turned out a lot worse. What happened here? This is the second-worst-case-possible scenario. Believe it or not, things could be worse. And it still could get worse, so you need to leave." And he's right. He's a monster and an asshole and a liar, but he's right. He gives us a beat to figure this out, then he tells us, "You need to take Greta with you and leave the island."

"And why the hell should we trust you?" says Stan, and Bobby immediately jumps to respond, but Stan won't let him. "No, I get it. We all saw you with your megaphone, trying to wave off those soldiers." Bobby looks at Stan in confusion, as if to acknowledge that yes, he was trying to call them off, and yes, he did do all of those things, so can Stan just try to give him the benefit of the doubt? "But who gives a shit? What does any of that prove? That it bothers you that your men, the people you've been planning this *whole thing* with, tried to slaughter our brothers and sisters? That's great, it's great that you give a shit about them slaughtering Icelings after it happens. But what about your role in everything that just happened should make us feel safe right now? That you were a spy this whole time? That you were prepared to take an order and then kill Greta and Ted and Callie and Tara and whomever else at a moment's notice? That you never really told us what really happened to your brother, Alex, who was the one who was actually close to Greta, the one who was *actually* her brother, and that it's awful convenient that she's stuck with you now that he's out of the picture? That it's one thing for you to come up here and get involved with a group trying to exterminate all these kids, but to use your *sister*, who is one of these kids you people think are monsters, as a way of studying and getting closer to that group, so that you'll be able to carry out your orders to kill them that much more easily? It's great. It's really super compassionate of you. No, I can tell. I can tell how, like, the death of your brother really made you and Greta super close, really made you want to bond with her and look out for her like the sister your brother always saw her as. No, dude. You're super compassionate. I get it." And I place my hand on Stan's arm, because I can see that this is going to get us somewhere, though I don't think it's anywhere we really want to go.

"Don't talk about Greta, Stan. Or Alex. You wouldn't dare talk about either of them or make presumptions about my love for my family if you'd seen her that day, lying next to his body, his nose and fingers and toes black, his skin way too pale, and Greta staring at him, and Alex staring at nothing at all because he was dead. She didn't kill him. She had nothing to do with him dying. It was a stupid accident— he was walking to a friend's house in the middle of a snowstorm, and he got lost. He didn't tell my parents he was going. But Greta found him. She found him and tried to save him. She gave him all her warm clothes, her coat. But he was already gone. He was eleven."

The way he says all of this, it makes me think he means it. But even if he doesn't, even if this is a lie like everything else anyone claiming any authority has ever told us, I can't help but think about being eight and wanting to Rollerblade like my babysitter, and going to the garage and illegally strapping on my dad's pair, which were way too big, and falling as soon as I hit the driveway, skinning my knee, and Callie running up to me and holding me and trying to grab the hose, and me getting it together enough to stop crying, to wash it with the hose. I think about Callie tugging me out of the bathroom when I slipped in the tub, about Callie holding me at night when we were four and five and eight and ten. And I think about losing her, or her losing me, what that would be like for either of us. And I look over at Bobby, and a part of my heart just breaks.

"So don't talk to me about Alex, Stan," says Bobby. "You wanna hit me? Fine. But remember that one of us knows where and how to hit a bone so that it breaks in an instant, and the other one is just seventeen and righteously pissed off."

I can tell Stan was moved by Bobby's story, which is why I feel so ashamed of him and his stubbornness when he actually responds.

"Back at that rest stop," he says, arching his shoulders up like he's trying to shrug off Bobby's story and everything he felt about it, "you were trying to take Callie and Ted. Weren't you? When you kept talking about how your shitty car had so much room? You were hoping we'd be stupid, that we'd either leave you alone with them or fall for your nice-guy act and let them ride with you."

The look in Bobby's eyes says *yes*, and now Stan's the one who looks like he has the right to feel right about everything.

"What?" Emily says, standing up and inserting herself into the argument. "What the hell? Is that true?"

Bobby sighs. "I thought maybe I could do something so that you guys wouldn't have to see this. I thought maybe I could help. I'd been sharing the road with you guys since you left Pennsylvania; you were the first ones I saw. I thought . . . I just wanted to help. I thought I could help, honestly. But that doesn't matter now. And just . . . this is currently the second-worst-case-possible scenario, and you need to leave. Now. You need to take Greta and leave the island. Listen. There's a boat docked out there. It's got sails and a motor and gas. I left it there during recon. As far as I know, nobody's thought twice about it."

"Why?" I say. "Why do we need to go right now? What will happen if we don't? You said it might get worse. What's the worst-case scenario?"

But he just says it again. "You need to leave the island. Please. I need you to trust me. Please, take Greta and leave the island." And how he says it, the pleading in his eyes, how he's trying so hard *not* to answer me . . . I get a shudder all over.

"Bobby," I say. "You need to tell us. If you really want us to leave, we need to understand why it's so important."

"Bobby, what is the worst-case scenario?" Stan asks.

"The worst-case scenario is a full-measure attack to ensure that no AROs ever leave this island."

"What are you saying?" Stan asks. "They're going to pick them off one-by-one? Isn't that what they were doing just before you and Jane called them off?"

"It'll be worse than that," Bobby says, looking down at his boots now.

"Worse?" I say. "Worse *how*?"

"If Jane gives the okay, if she thinks it's necessary . . ." he starts, then lets out a heavy sigh before bracing himself to go on. "If she thinks it's necessary, she'll press a button that will blow up the entire island. I don't mean an explosion like the one you saw during the drone attack. That was nothing. I mean a catastrophic measure that would neutralize all biological entities on and beneath the surface."

Emily's face goes slack. Stan just stares out at the ice field, at the rows of destroyed stalks and their ashes.

"But why would Jane need to do that?" I ask. "All those pods came up dead and empty, and even if they hadn't, they're blown to bits now. Why would she risk all the bad press, all the questions back home, just to kill our Icelings, who have been living with us pretty peacefully for the last sixteen years? Why would she risk all of that to kill *us*?"

"It's not the pods, or your Icelings, or you they're worried about."

"Then what?" I shout at him, clutching Callie's hand tight.

"You saw him," Bobby says quietly. "The one that was here already, the one they came to meet." The Iceling leader. The one the drone was aiming at. But the drone missed, because . . . "He went back. Under the ice. He's down there, and he's still alive. And he's—they think he's the one who makes it happen. The pods. He's the original Iceling."

"Oh my God," I say, and then a starker realization hits me. "And we . . . we saw it all." Bobby nods. "The Icelings can't say anything about it, but we're witnesses."

"Yeah," says Bobby. "So do you get it now? Do you see why you need to go?"

"Where in the hell are we supposed to go from here?"

"You know where to go, Lorna."

What the hell? Why do *I* know where to go? Why does he keep looking at me like I know what's going on?

"You've got no reason to trust me, I know," he says, speaking now to my expression of incredulity and confusion. "But I just told you that the goal is to kill you and everyone else on this island. I'm the one person here who has not shot at you, or at anyone other than soldiers who risked and took lives because they were too stupid and too scared to follow orders. I'm trying to save your lives. I'm trying to save my sister's life. And if you have trouble believing that, then just think about what you would do to save Callie, and then put yourself in my shoes." He looks up, and we follow his gaze, and we see drones circling overhead. "You need to go now, and I need to get back to Jane. Stan, I need you to do me a favor before you go."

"Are you serious right now?" Stan says, looking from Bobby to the drones to Ted to all of us and then back to Bobby.

"I think you'll be okay helping me out with this one," Bobby says, then asks Stan to punch him as hard as he can, to make him look injured so he has an explanation for where he's been and why he's late, and I can tell Stan is happier than he should be to help him out with this one.

Stan rears up in front of Bobby and swings at him, landing right in the eye with a punch that draws blood. "Thanks," Bobby says, clutching his face. "Now get out of here." Bobby turns to Greta. He doesn't have time to hug her, but you can see in his eyes he wants to. He holds up his hand and brings it down. Greta does the same.

She stands there like that, staring at Bobby as we try to drag her away, and she's smiling and then frowning furiously, like she's trying to get her face into a shape that means what she wants it to. It's Callie and Tara who get her to move, finally, once Bobby is out of sight.

And then we run, as fast as we can, through the trees and up a path to the top of the hill. Maybe ten or fifteen people went with the soldiers. There are maybe five kids shot dead and fifteen or twenty collapsed over their dead Iceling brothers and sisters. The rest are holding on to their Icelings, and their Icelings are holding on to them. The drones have pulled way back, and the jeeps are making their way back up the opposite hill.

We look around in every direction, no one sure of which way to go. I take off my gloves and reach for my phone, braving the frigid air as I flip backward through my photos. I find the one I was looking for and call out "Left!" and we head left. "Past the low trees!" All is still around us, same lack of animal life we found on the way over to the ice field, which strikes me as odd, since I would have thought the guns and explosions would have set off some kind of shakedown in the trees and shrubs and rocks, would have sent some animals running. But there's nothing.

Nothing except us, and now we're running back through those trees. The giant leaves are still holding the snow just so, and it's barely moved at all in spite of the missiles and the bullets and the ground shaking and then going still. The wind is whipping all around us, we can feel it on our skin, but it's completely silent. Completely terrifying. And though we know it's there because of the way it chills our bones, there's no other evidence of it. No rustling of branches or leaves, no whistling. No howling, no roaring, no nothing. All we can hear are bullets and fire. We can hear screams, but they don't sound human. All I can think is that it's the Icelings, mourning. It feels strange and cruel not to stop and turn around, to find the sources of the screaming and see how we can help, but we all heard what Bobby said, and we know we can't.

Finally, we're out of the trees and into the clearing.

"There are the docks!" shouts Stan, and here we are, at that newish-looking set of docks with the fuel pump.

And there aren't any boats.

TWENTY-FOUR

THE DRONES LOOM overhead, heavy with missiles, and probably with cameras too. Callie's slowly coming back into herself after everything that just happened, but *slowly* is the primary way to characterize this evolution. She and Tara lean on each other, physically support one another, and in that way they're able to keep moving. And they seem to know how important it is to keep moving. Ted and Greta are with Stan, and Emily and I are up in front, trying hard not to look at our respective sisters becoming more like sisters for each other than we could probably ever be for them. But now I know that whenever this is over—in whatever form being over takes—I'll have done right by her. I brought her home. I found her sister. She can be understood and maybe at peace. Even if it's not with me.

I look up to the sky, and darkness creeps in from all around, and it feels like all I can see now are bombs and missiles growing larger and larger as they circle us like birds of prey.

"No boat," says Emily, and I shake my head and come back down to earth.

Nobody says anything, because what is there to say? There is no boat here, no way to get off the island like Bobby said we need to do, no way to get to the place Bobby said I would know about but don't, and in a few minutes this island is going to get blown to hell.

"Shit" is all Stan says. He looks around, his face contorting in angles that tell me he's trying to hatch a plan and having a panic attack all at once. "Ted," he says after many moments of this. Emily and I just stare at him until he repeats, "TED!" again and then grabs his brother.

"Wait," Emily says.

"What?" I say.

But Stan doesn't answer. Instead, he looks to Ted and starts tearing up the docks. He starts at the furthest edge and works his way back in, getting a handhold and levering each board up with his whole body, kicking whatever he has to whenever he has to. After several minutes of Stan going at this alone, Ted joins in, making better and faster work of it than Stan, kicking at the planks and supports.

Callie and Tara stop and look at Ted, but they don't do much else. Greta gets up, maybe to help, but whatever she does doesn't help much. But still, she got up.

"Over there," Stan says, grunting and pointing to a distant spot in the water, "I saw a boat. Lorna, do you remember that weird shed we saw on the way out?"

"Yes," I say, shuddering to remember it.

"Good. See if there are any fuel containers inside it."

"What?"

"Look," he says, kicking the demolished dock, grabbing a plank with his hand and trying to tear it up. "This wood isn't rotten, not quite yet, so it'll float a bit. Long enough. And if that *is* a boat over there, we'll need fuel." And all I can do is stand there, staring at him, staring at Callie, who looks so empty and in that way so heartbroken.

"Are you saying," Emily says, "that we're going to use that old wood as a *raft*? To take us over there, where there may or may not be a boat?"

"It's either that," Stan says, "or we just stay here and admit we're going to die. And I, for one, am not really good with that option."

✳

SO EMILY AND I go to the shed.

On the way there I look up to the sky. The clouds are swirling again.

But in the eye of it all there isn't sunlight. There are drones. The ones with the missiles. They're rising up and spreading out, and I can see how they'll bank around and settle in. There's just two of them. The smaller one that fired the first shot—I can't see it anywhere. But it was pulled back as soon as the missile was fired. And as much as I hate it, this means we need to hurry.

I nudge Emily and point to the drones. "We need to—"

And Emily says, "Hurry, yeah, I see. Jesus."

So we run to the terrifying shed.

There it is, right where I hoped we'd left it, as in *behind us*, as in *for good*. There's that roof, still completely bare, as though even the snow won't touch it. I don't want to go in, but I have to.

So I close my eyes, and we duck down and make ourselves as small as possible so we can fit through that makeshift entryway. It doesn't take much maneuvering before we're inside, and I'm some-how further unsettled by how surprisingly easy it was to get in. I open my eyes, and Emily reaches out for my hand.

We scan the space frantically, our eyes lingering and then pass-ing over a bunk bed, a desk with three surge protectors and a mini fridge under it. There's an axe and a cabinet mounted on the wall. How so much stuff fits in this space I don't understand, but it's almost like it's just slightly bigger on the inside than out.

"There," Emily says as she ducks down and dives for the corner, where there are a bunch of red plastic jugs with capped yellow spouts—what anyone in any country would recognize as fuel containers.

"Emily, you're a genius," I say, and I duck down to help her.

There are six containers, which is probably as many as we can carry between the two of us. They're empty, so now there *has* to be fuel left in those old gas pumps, or we're screwed. We gather them all up, and then Emily grabs the axe on the wall to take with her. She winks at me as she does, and I do something I never imagined myself doing inside this little shed of horrors: I laugh.

But the joy is short-lived, because as we scan the room one last time to make sure we have everything we need, I notice something weird with the floorboards that the containers had been sitting on.

It's a trapdoor.

I set the containers down and crouch before the door.

"Lorna!" shouts Emily. "What are you doing? We have to *go*. I can hear the drones from in here!"

"Just one second!" I say. "Do you see this? Emily, we have to open it. We can't just leave without seeing what's in—"

A crack, like a gunshot, rings out. I can tell it's not right outside the shed—we're probably not even in target range—but it brings me back to earth all the same. I can hear the drones hovering, and so I stand back up, pick up the containers, and let Emily drag me out of there.

We move fast, Emily just in front of me. The drones are nearly in a firing position right above the shed, but once we've run a bit, we can see that the drones don't seem to be following us. Maybe they're keeping their distance, sure, but maybe they also aren't after us. Maybe they're after the shed and whatever was under that door in the floor.

ICELING

Stan and the Icelings are in sight, so I just dig in and keep going. We're hurtling toward the docks, and when Stan sees us and what we're carrying, he smiles for the first time in a while.

"Hurry!" he shouts, but we're going as fast as we can. As we approach I see that another pair of drones is hovering and shining some kind of spotlight over what was once the trembling field, where everyone else left on the island still is.

"How do we know if there's still gas in that pump?" I ask, forcing the drones out of my head so that I can keep moving forward.

"I already got what we need out of it," Stan says, pointing to four red fuel containers at his feet, identical to the ones we brought from the shed.

"What the hell?" I say. "Why did you make us go over to that creepy shed then?"

"*These* are for fuel," Stan says, pointing at the cans at his feet. Then he looks up at us and nods at the extraneous empties in our arms. "*Those* are for the raft."

"What?" Emily says. "You mean we're not going to use these to carry fuel over to the other boat?"

"No," he says. "We're going to use them to float the raft."

Emily and I look at each other as if in agreement that this is it, this life is over, our death warrant has just been signed by this one massively terrible idea.

"Just trust me," says Stan.

We take the containers and screw the caps on tight, and Stan and I fasten them to the bottom of the raft, while Emily works on calming the Icelings and keeping them together so we can get them on the raft when it's time.

Stan ties off the last knot, and together we glide the structure into the water, tying it to the dock first, to test it. It's all the way in, and I'm holding my breath, and then my heart both soars and sinks to see that it works, it floats. Stan smiles and leaps up onto the shore, where he takes the containers filled with fuel and piles them onto the raft one at a time, securing each of them to the dock wood with the rope that had been used to lash the tires hanging off the docks as bumpers.

We can hear gunfire.

"Ready?" says Stan.

I nod, and he holds the raft steady as Emily and I coax Ted, Callie, Greta, and Tara onto the raft. But Greta won't leave. Callie and Tara take her hands and sort of tug her along. All I can guess is that she doesn't want to leave Bobby. Then there's another round of gunfire, loud and cracking, and Greta jumps, first up, then out onto the raft. When it doesn't shatter and capsize, I give Stan a thumbs-up.

Callie was never super big on baths at home, so I'm a bit surprised she's not kicking up more of a fuss about the raft, which is just planks tied together on top of tires, with the empty fuel jugs acting as buoys. Stan's gripping a makeshift paddle, which is just a jagged plank.

Now, finally, we're all on the raft, every last limb just barely fitting within the perimeter of our close quarters. Stan pushes us off. The water around us is perfectly still, weirdly still, save for the modest wake our craft makes. Callie and Tara lean over the side and touch the water, and I flinch even though I know they can't feel how freezing cold it is, that what is freezing cold to me is something else entirely to them. I can't read their faces. Can't read their bodies. But I try, because I can't not. Here is what they say to me:

Greta hates leaving Bobby. Ted hates leaving the island. Callie and Tara are still, I think, too stunned by all the death to really process this. They finally got home, and then everything around them died. What would that feel like? To have spent your life wanting to go back to the place you were born, and from where you were stolen, and then finally you get there! And you're there for the most wonderful reason: to meet the next generation! And then the big event happens, and they're all stillborn. And then come the people with guns, who don't understand you, and they burn all the babies' bodies, and they shoot your family. And this person pretending to be your sister drags you away from it to save your life, but for what?

Callie, kid sister, I wish I knew. But there's a chance we might still find out.

✳

IF IT WAS freezing before, it's now the kind of cold that there isn't a sufficient word for. Out here on the water, with not a single buffer between the icy air and the frigid water, it's scary-cold, and I think but I don't say it: *We'll freeze to death before we make it.* But Stan knew exactly where he saw that dot of color. And it's right up ahead. We're getting closer now, close enough to see that it's really more shaped like a boat and not a dot, and though the cold is closing in on me and my eyes are getting tired and my head is feeling so light that it's heavy, the closer we get the more sure I am that the dot is indeed turning into something that can only be a boat. Emily says she can see it too, and I force myself to believe her. We have to see it. That has to be what we see. Because if it isn't, then it's just us, on this raft, in this freezing cold water, which is perfectly still.

In the distance, we see the beginning of a sunset. But then, in an instant, that light turns from pale to angry orange, and for a second I wonder if Arctic sunsets are somehow sped up, if the sun works differently way up here on the top of the world. But then I watch the looks on Stan's and Emily's faces as they watch too, and then I look again and realize it isn't the sunset. It's fire. And then there's this hiss in the air and a loud, low, ominous whistle, and then at least a dozen more, and the whole world howls and shakes, and the raft breaks, and we're thrown headlong into the sea.

SASHA STEPHENSON

※

WE COME TO after who knows how much time has passed, and the pain is piercing hot and striking me at every angle. At first I think I must have washed ashore, that my body is frozen stiff and the piercing pain is actually just the process of my body freezing over. But then I force my eyes open, and the first thing I see is water, and then I take a weak look around to see more of the same, and then I realize that this is still happening. It's not over yet. We still have to keep going. Our raft is smashed to pieces, and we're still hanging on to planks, bobbing up and down. At first I think I am alone, but then Emily bobs into view and then Stan. But I still don't see Callie or the other Icelings, and if my heart could beat any faster—assuming it can even keep beating after this beating we're taking—it would be pounding out of my chest.

Just about the only thing I can reason out right now is that this should have killed us. We should be dead. But we're not. Why aren't we dead? And then I see a flutter on the surface of the water, and that flutter turns into Tara, and she's swimming from Emily toward me. And then I see a second flutter, and it's Callie, swimming from Stan to Emily. And then Greta, and Ted, swimming all around from one of us to the other. Tara closes in on me, and I try to move but can't, and then she makes contact, and all at once I'm hit with a very faint sensation of warmth.

The Icelings go on like this, taking turns wrapping themselves around us, kicking and pushing their way toward us and then away and away and away. This makes no sense, I know it makes no sense, but somehow . . . they're keeping us warm. They're keeping us warm, and I can tell by the way they kick and breathe that they're not at all cold. It makes sense how Greta could go out after Alex like that. Could try to keep him warm and save him. It's what they're doing right now.

I'm feeling warmer by the second, slowly regaining my ability to take in the world around me and try to make meaning out of it. The sea is no longer calm. My ears are roaring. I open my mouth and try to say something, a test to see if my ears still work, but then a little wave bobs up and my mouth is full of water, cold and salty and I'm almost choking on it, so I start spitting it out. I have no idea why I had to think about it in order to do it, or why my eyes and brain and muscles couldn't work together to see the wave and react by closing my mouth so my lungs didn't fill with water, and then I try to close my eyes against all these thoughts, because if my brain and body aren't really working right now, then I don't want to waste what energy I have worrying about why and how my brain and body don't work. I'm worried that if I worry anymore, then I'll lose my grip on this plank and plummet to the bottom of the sea, because it's just too overwhelming for my broken brain, the sheer amount of things there are to worry about right now—like drowning, or hypothermia, or death by bullets or fire or U.S. military missiles, which we might have avoided but which might still be seeking us out right now, there's no way to tell because I can't hear anything except my own thoughts, which are screaming, screaming about things like how many people and Icelings Jane's team just murdered, or why we didn't just stay home, why we thought this was even a good idea to begin with. *Why did we think this was a good idea?*

And then there is a splash and another swirl of movement and motion around me, and I can feel more of it this time, because I just keep getting warmer. I look over, and there's Callie, leaving Emily's side and making her way over to me, and then she reaches me, and then she's embracing me, and the warmth increases tenfold. And now I remember: That's why. Callie is why. We did this because of Callie, and Ted, and all the other Icelings, because it was the only thing that could be done. They needed to come here. We didn't know this—any of this—would happen. I try to smile at her, but her face is not at an angle where she can see mine, and anyway I can't hold my face like that for too long, and then a new wave of cold settles in and I start shivering and shaking.

And then the roaring in my ears dies down a little, and I can hear something, a calm sound, soft and low, and I try to stretch my neck up as far as I can to see if I can make it out any better. I follow the faint sound and find Emily again. She's awake, and right next to me, closer than I would have thought, and the sound is coming from her. It's louder now, and I make out that she's urging Stan to kick. I realize I can hardly feel my toes, an improvement from when I first woke up and couldn't feel anything but pain, and I start trying to kick too. Emily sees me and gives me as much of a smile as our bodies will allow right now, and then we kick together, trying to move toward Stan, the Icelings still clinging to us and moving along with us. We close in on Stan and Greta, who is wrapped around him, and we nudge him with our legs as best we can until he starts to kick too.

Our world's on fire, or maybe it's drowning. We're on fire, and we're drowning. And because we don't know which disaster is the right one, we stay like this for a long while, silent and treading water, half-conscious and drifting in and out of it all, blinking back and forth between flashes of the dock wreckage, the island, what we thought of as our lives until now. Our Icelings and Bobby's Iceling continue to take turns keeping us alive until we're warm enough to look around and think about what to do next. My periphery's on fire. Flames lick at the fuel depot by the docks, all lit up and spitting sparks and burning bits of metal and wood and gas all over the sea. My ears are still roaring, though thankfully it's quieted down quite a bit, and now I can hear the splashes our own bodies make in the water.

When my vision starts to come back and I no longer have to blink and squint to tell the difference between Emily and Stan, I begin to take stock of our surroundings. We can see the boat. We know we can make it now. Emily's the only one with a backpack. I'm sure we'll regret it later, but our parkas were weighing us down. Thank God for layers, but still. Floating on a plank that Ted's holding on to are two of the five containers of fuel we brought. I twirl around to see if the others might be near, and I see a flash of red bobbing up and down a little ways off. I try to swim to it but can barely make it a foot under my own strength. Then Ted grabs me, not ungently. I start to point to the big red-and-yellow container, but before I can he's already gone, swimming out to the bobbing beacon, and Callie's got one arm wrapped around me and the other holding on to the plank that's holding the other two tanks. Ted comes back and plops the third container on the plank with the rest of them, and Callie lets go and brings her other arm around me again. I look over to the island. And every inch of it that I can see is on fire.

And I guess that was all too much, because I'm exhausted again. Emily was apparently on the swim team *and* the gymnastics team, because she's looking strong against all the struggling. Stan's beat but mostly breathing, and me, I'm in shock and shocked that I'm still breathing. And so we're quiet again for a while, and we all just let ourselves drift, let ourselves be held by the Icelings and the freezing water, clinging to whatever's left to cling to, while the home our siblings have been dreaming of their whole lives burns to the ground.

When I'm warm enough to cry, I cry. My tears mingle with the water. But I didn't have to tell you that.

TWENTY-FIVE

AFTER AN UNKNOWN stretch of time during which I'm hovering in and out of various states of consciousness and feeling, I come to, sharply and for good, when a drone with spinning helicopter blades crashes into the sea about fifteen feet away from us. Its propellers smack the water first, and the water smacks back, forcing the fighting blades to send a few sad sparks into the air, like a flare gun to its friends, and then slow down to a desperate stop. In movies, things explode on impact. But in the water, nearly drowning things just sort of spark a bit, and then the blades try sadly spinning, but they can't do it right, and it just kind of floats there, partially submerged and whirring until it can't.

We're rocking in the wake of the fallen drone, Stan, Emily, our Icelings, and I, all awake and alert now. Callie's fine. Maybe in shock, but she's physically fine. She's floating and breathing, and I'm just so glad to see her, and my face is so wet I can't tell if I'm crying. The boat—the boat that is definitely a boat—is still ahead of us and close enough that we know we'll make it. I'm about to ask if everyone's okay when a high whistling in the sky, way out toward the island, sends my gaze upward and out, and I see two more drones faltering in the air above, heading right toward each other. They crash, nose to nose, smacking into each other, and then they explode in the air and fall, on fire, down to the sea that stretches between us and the still-burning island, where they fizzle and smoke.

I have no idea how long we've been adrift, but my body is screaming like it's been hours to days.

"We only left about an hour ago," says Stan. He's pointing to his watch, which I noticed as far back as the hospital, noting that it was probably too fancy for a teenager but having no idea that it was a real nautical instrument that could go through all of this and keep on ticking.

"Jesus," says Emily. "It's still burning."

"And there are still little drones in the air—the ones that haven't crashed into each other or the water, at least. And honestly, they're getting a bit too close to us for my comfort," I say.

"You think they're aiming for us?" asks Emily.

"I think right now I'm going to say yes and hope I'm wrong rather than say no and hope I'm right," Stan says. And everyone gets quiet for a minute.

"The boat's maybe fifteen, twenty minutes away, based on how we've been going," Stan says finally. "That's assuming no one drowns and no one gets any sudden bursts of energy."

"Let's go," says Emily.

※

SO WITH OUR Icelings, who just saved our lives and kept us living, still hovering around us like angels or ghosts, we swim. Bits of drones bob and sulk around us as we make our way toward that dot of color, and I'm bracing myself because I keep expecting to see other kinds of debris—nonmechanical debris, *human* debris—in the water, but so far we don't, and I'm quietly, ashamedly grateful for that.

We're silent as we go, and the sea is silent too, the only noise around us the sound of our own breathing. All of a sudden the boat comes bobbing into view in between the waves and dips of our journey, and I feel a surge of energy and start swimming faster. We all swim faster, and we're all trying so hard not to swallow more water than we can choke down and out.

Suddenly, Emily starts to falter, and the plank she was holding on to slips from her grip. Her body slowly plunges down into the water, but Tara's there for her before her lips can even touch the brine.

"You okay?" I shout.

"Yeah, fine," she says. "Just exhausted." She turns to Tara, who's holding her around the waist and propping her up. "Thank you," she says, and Tara does and says nothing.

But then, without warning, Ted takes a sudden dive into the water.

"Ted!" Stan shouts, but Greta keeps a strong grip on him and doesn't let him follow after.

I keep expecting him to resurface any second, but he hasn't; he's still under there. Stan's freaking out, using all the energy he has left to dart around in place as much as Greta's grip will allow, searching the water for his brother. Finally, full minutes later, Ted comes back with a huge plank, the biggest piece of the dock raft, which I'd assumed was long gone. He swims back to our group, holding the plank above water, then sets it down to float.

"Ted, you're amazing!" I say, and Stan just grins like a proud big brother.

Without taking a beat to pat himself on the back, Ted scoops us up, one by one, Stan, Emily, and me, and puts us on the plank. He takes the smaller plank with the fuel containers on it and grips one board in each hand, then the Icelings take turns pushing and guiding us along toward our destination. And as we go, up on the planks now instead of freezing in the water, they keep trying to hold us, or maybe just touch us to see if we're still there, still breathing, or some other thing that I can never know. But whatever they're doing, it's nice. Or I'm choosing to interpret it as nice, or what it makes me feel is nice. Not that any of this is nice—the world is on fire, and hundreds of people might be dead mere feet away from us. But what I mean is that it's nice to feel something other than cold water and cold legs and cold bones wrapped in cold veins.

"Hey," says Emily with some effort. She's beside me on the plank, her body sort of slumped on mine for support. "You okay?"

I look over at Callie. She drifts around until she finds a spot with a good view of the island, and she just treads water there while she watches it burn. She stares at it for a while, then turns back around. I turn away, I can't even look at her right now, because I'm afraid of how much it'll hurt.

"Nope," I say.

"Cool," she says. "Me neither."

I smile. I smile, and then, with some pain in my chest and gut and arms and legs, I laugh. I laugh because clearly my body needs to laugh so badly that it channeled all the energy it has into producing one tiny guffaw, regardless of the pain it sent shivering through my bones. And then Emily laughs too, and our laughter sounds so ragged and sick that I can't help but smile again, and then the whole cycle starts anew. Stan's pushed up next to me on my other side, and when I feel his body start I think he must be laughing too, but when I turn to him I see that's not what he's doing at all.

Stan is sitting, stick straight and rigid, staring straight ahead with his mouth half-open and his eyes peeled in shock.

"Stan?" I say, and he doesn't answer, and then my heart starts to flutter, and then, slowly, I brace myself and turn to face whatever horror he's seeing.

But then my jaw goes slack and my eyes go wide, because the thing that Stan sees is what I'm looking at now too.

A floating dock. And tied up at the side: the boat.

THERE IT IS, a real boat, and it's right in front of us, and it's not made from old planks and empty plastic containers, and it's going to save our lives. And it has a ladder on the side.

And even though it only takes a few more minutes of paddling and Iceling life support to get to it, it takes *forever* to get to it.

But then we do. We're all paddling, stupidly, our hands in the freezing cold water, the Icelings slapping them away even though we keep putting them back in, and now we're here. The dock is square-shaped, and like the boat, it also has a ladder, which we grab on to one after the other. The boat is bigger than an SUV—definitely big enough for all of us—and I guess Stan can predict from the model that it'll have bunks inside. It has a motor and sails, just like Bobby said. And if there's fuel on board, we can get somewhere on that combined with the fuel we brought and the sails.

"So . . . does anyone know how to drive a boat?" asks Emily.

"Stan does," I say.

"Yeah," says Stan. "I can pilot this. I can get us where we need to go. Assuming Lorna knows."

"I'm really sorry, you guys. I could name a place, I could think of somewhere that might make sense. But I have no idea what the hell Bobby was talking about."

"Think, Lorna!" cries Emily. Like that'll help.

"Trust me, I have been. In between worrying whether or not

we'd make it to the boat alive, and about what's going on with Callie, or about how the hell she and the others kept us alive, or anything that's happened since yesterday—which is a hell of a lot—I've been thinking about where we need to go next. I don't know. Maybe once we're on the boat, when I'm freaking out a little bit less, maybe I'll figure it out then. For now, we can go south. Somewhere that's the opposite of here. That's the only thing I know for sure—that I want to get away from here."

"South sounds good," says Stan.

Almost as if he understands us, Ted starts climbing up the ladder on the boat. We follow his lead, and he's helping the rest of us up, which is when I notice that Stan needs the most help. Emily and I trade a look that lets me know she has noticed too.

"He dove for us," whispers Emily to me. "After the first blast."

Oh, God. That's when he must have gotten hurt, saving us all again, and because it's all I can do right now, I just send her a look that I hope says, *We'll keep an eye on him together.*

It's not until we're all in the boat that I realize how freaking weird this is, this boat that fits seven people comfortably, tied to a floating dock in the middle of an Arctic sea, like it's been waiting here for us. Sure, Bobby said he left it here, that he did it on purpose during recon, but for what purpose? And why *didn't* anyone from his team pay it any mind? It seems like a pretty big thing to overlook—especially when it's tied to an area they didn't want anyone coming out of alive. I understand what a terrifying thought this is and acknowledge it completely, but right now my body won't let me be terrified. Maybe I already used up my daily allotment of terror, or maybe my body just knows that right now it needs to be solely focused on staying alive and getting the hell out of here and its survival instincts are completely blocking out all of its fear instincts.

Stan takes the fuel containers and goes to explore the inner workings of the boat so that we can get going right away, while Emily and I explore every other aspect of the craft to determine what kinds of supplies our guardian angels or demons have left for us here. In a trunk down in the lower level we find a whole bunch of towels and blankets and dry clothes—sweatpants and sweaters and fresh woolen socks. In an unlocked metal locker we find a whole bunch of food—ready-made emergency meal type things, packed in tins and foil bags.

"Jackpot," Emily says.

"Stan!" I shout. "You have to come see this!"

Stan limps over, and his eyes go wide and he smiles, and then he practically collapses on the floor beside us. We sit there on the floor of the boat and we eat like we'll never eat again. It tastes *awful*—like budget prepackaged health food meals, but drier and staler than usual. But it's filling, and it's warming me up, and some part of my brain is saying, *Hey, all right, things are gonna be okay*, and I'm actually listening to it.

The Icelings pick apart the rations to try to see what's in them, and they eat things they find. Ted pops a whole fun-size candy bar into his mouth. Wrapper and all. He winces. I noticed he's limping, and his eyes have been wired, but now he looks sleepy and exhausted.

Emily and I pause in the middle of eating to change into the clothes we found, but Stan doesn't pause until he's downed two of those emergency meals. Once we're all changed and shivering a little less, we dare to look inside our pockets and Emily's backpack to survey the damage. Both Emily's and Stan's phones are completely wrecked, but Emily still tosses them in a sack of basmati rice we find in a cardboard box in the back of the locker, "Just in case." She zips open her sodden and soaked backpack, which is completely full of Luna bars. Stan smirks.

Since I'm my father's daughter, I had my phone packed in a

weird plastic case that's supposed to be waterproof. I pull it out and it seems mostly dry, but the battery's dead. I have no idea if my charger still works or if there's anywhere to plug it in.

I'm still hunting around the boat for an electrical outlet when I notice Callie sitting down on the floor of the boat, leaning against the side wall and looking out across the sea. The other Icelings join her, and then I do too. Stan and Emily follow, and we all sit together, and we watch the island burn.

We watch those weird trees burning from the roots up, the ice that cakes their branches turning into steam, which then fizzles out and dies. Those hills, craggy and rigid in places like mountains, are crumbled and all aflame with a fire that probably started with the jet fuel from the crashed drones and was sustained by the final blast that shook everything down at once. The hills are lit up like a sunset, or like hundreds of sunsets. We can't see any people, but I know we're all looking for them. I know we're all hoping we don't see any people, in whatever state anyone over there could possibly be in, but that we're all also hoping that we *do* see some people, because despite all the fire and ash we can see from our little haven in the sea, we still have no idea what actually happened over there.

"Could anyone have survived that?" Emily says.

"No," says Stan without a single pause.

"Jane, Bobby, the army," I say. "The Icelings . . . those *kids* . . . all of them . . ."

"They're dead," Emily whispers.

We stand there, stunned, the fire playing off our eyes like a song. The Icelings are just staring. Then they look away. They can't, or won't, watch this anymore.

Suddenly and without any words of warning, Stan grabs hold of Ted, buries his head in his shoulder.

"I'm so sorry, Ted," he says. "I'm so sorry. You saved my life, Ted.

You saved my life so many times—the bear, the soldier. From drowning and hypothermia. And I've done nothing for you. Nothing that even comes close." I have to stop looking at him now, because it hurts too much to listen, to see Stan start to cry, but it also hurts too much to keep looking at the island, so I just inch myself closer to Callie and stare down at the water below lapping sadly against our boat. "You're my brother," Stan goes on, still talking into Ted's shoulder, his voice muffled. "And I can't do anything except be so completely sorry. I'm sorry for when I hit you because my friends couldn't come play, and I'm sorry about when I told you hated you—I don't, I don't hate you, Ted. And I'm sorry about Mom. I'm sorry she left, and I'm sorry about Dad, about everything about Dad, and I'm sorry about everything. All of it. And it doesn't do anything, it doesn't mean anything, I know that . . ." And then he just slowly goes quiet, his voice giving way to quiet sobs and gasps.

I look up. Stan is still buried in Ted's shoulder, but Ted is still staring at the burning island. He stares at the place he came from, his home, a place he'd seen before, when he opened his eyes for the very first time sixteen years ago, but probably didn't remember, and now he's finally seeing it, for real, and it's on fire. Everything in and on and beneath it, everything that makes it a place, burning. His face is screwed up like he's crying silently, but he's not. He's just watching it. His eyes are wet, perhaps just from the wind, and his jaw is set, and he stands, staring. And when Stan finally lets go and looks up at his brother's face, he still keeps standing, the expression on his face unchanged for what feels like forever.

Then Ted lifts his arm. He lifts his arm, still staring at the island, eyes still wet, the reflection of the flames burning in them. And then he takes his lifted arm and puts it around Stan, and then he holds Stan to him. And they stay like that.

And now Callie is burrowing up to me and holding on to Tara, who is holding on to both Callie and Emily. And Emily is crying, and now I'm crying too.

And Greta is alone. And though I have no way of knowing, when I look in her eyes, I just feel that she's looking for Bobby, waiting for him to come back. And then Tara looks over at Greta, then Callie looks over at Greta, and then they both let go of us. They go over to Greta, and one after the other they touch her on the shoulder, and the expressions on their faces don't change: They set their mouths in lines; they still won't look. But my face changes, and Emily's does too. I see the way I feel reflected in Emily's face: We're alive. We brought our sisters home, and they found new sisters, *real sisters*, and then their home got blown up. And despite that, they saved us. And now we're here. And we all need each other now. Regret, and awe, and fear, and pride, and terror—it's all mixed up there.

And then Ted collapses.

※

FOUR DAYS LATER, and Ted is barely breathing.

Stan, we're not so sure. He's piloting the boat, refuses to teach me or Emily how so that he has an excuse to be stuck there at all times. We're going south. We haven't spoken in two days. Nobody knows what to say, and Stan won't talk. He checks the rigging, he leaves a steady course to check on Ted for a couple of minutes at a time. He checks our course, he checks on Ted. He checks the engine, he checks on Ted. Ted, who carried us all here. Ted, who saved us from a bear.

Ted, who sometimes scared the hell out of me, is dying. No part of me wants to believe this, but what choice do I have? We can't pretend anything anymore. We stopped having that luxury when we saw plants carrying babies bursting out of the ice while our government tried to blow up an island.

I don't know why it's happening, and I really hope I'm wrong. But what I think—what I feel—is that Ted is maybe going to die soon. And I don't know what'll happen to Stan when he does. I don't even want to imagine it. These past couple of nights, Callie has come to sit with me on the deck while I watch the stars dance across the water, somehow without drowning. Emily tries to talk to Stan, and when that doesn't work, she comes and sits here too.

I want to try to tell you what I think about when I sit here and look out.

I want you to imagine that when you were very young, you were taken from your home. Really imagine it. You're barely old enough to be able to recall a home, a family, an unparalleled warmth and deep-down knowledge that you *belong*. You can't remember too many things about your home or the people who were there, but you can remember just enough—just enough of a *feeling* about the place—that you know it is your one and only home, and the place you are now is not your home. And then imagine living your whole life with the soft sadness of being so far away from that home—and the less soft sadness of not being able to tell anyone about how you hurt, because even if you could, they wouldn't understand—but also with the hope and trust that, one day, in some better future, you'll be able to return to that home again. And then when that day finally comes, when you can finally go back to that home that's been the one bright beacon in a life that is otherwise filled with a lot of murky, lonely darkness, you're so happy. And then you get there, and the people you were born with get there too, and you're so happy. But then it's gone. In the worst way possible, it's gone. And now it's worse than before, because that little bit of hope that makes all the pain maybe tolerable has been snuffed out. And you know you'll spend your whole life trying to understand this, to understand yourself, trying to tell anyone at all why it is that you hurt, but you're scared because you've never been able to before, and you're pretty sure you'll never be able to now. Now that your home is gone for good and there is no place in this world that you belong.

Really. Imagine it. You are a person who hurts. Deep down and forever. Because something, when you were very young, was taken from you. And there's nothing you can do about it. And you dream of that home you can just barely recall every single night. You wake up sweating so hard, like your whole body is crying, like every single inch of you is wracked with sobs, and you can barely stand to move, and you lay there like that, not wanting to sleep, because when you sleep all you see is the home you'll never get to see again. But at the same time you're terrified of never seeing it again, and you hate yourself for not wanting to sleep, for not wanting to see it. And then, slowly, after years and years of this, you just sort of stop dreaming about home. You sleep more easily, you wake up every morning and feel emptier than you thought possible, in ways you can't even begin to articulate to yourself, let alone to another person. And you start the whole process over again, of trying to tell people, in the right words, the right tone of voice, the right body language, what it is that hurts you, what it is that pains you, what it is that feels so unrelentingly *absent* from your life, why you don't ever feel like anything resembling *whole*.

But you can't.

You can't ever get the words out. The people in your life, they're there every day, and while you know they care about you because of the looks they give you and the way they keep poking you to get up and join them even when you're so sad you can't even move, they'll never be anything but strangers. You can't ever seem to know them, and they can't ever seem to know you.

It's the same for everyone you meet. Even when you get a glimpse of some kind of connection between you and someone else, you can't figure out what it is, what made the spark, or how to hold on to it. And they can't seem to do this with you either, and you're more or less completely alone.

And then one day you start dreaming of home again.

You don't sweat, you don't cry out, and it doesn't hurt. You're floating over it. It's not the vicious, gut-cutting sensation of being able to see things from your eyes, from your memories. It's like you're above everything, floating there, seeing where you came from, where you belong, and you can feel, somewhere deep down, that your family is there. That people who understand you are there, and they're waiting for you.

And then you wake up.

You wake up, and you can remember the dream of home, but you can't do anything about it. But you still try. Every day you try to find a way to get back there. And every night you dream of it more clearly than before. You dream bigger. You dream like the movies. You zoom in, you zoom out, you focus on specific details so that you capture their essence exactly as it's meant to be captured. You see boats, and trees, and gardens, and mountains, and lions and tigers and bears. And you also see where you live now, where this life you're stuck in has stuck you, and how far away it is from where you need to be. But because you can see all of this, you can see how to finally get *home*.

And then you do! You get home! You get home, and you see your family, and you see the land that made your life possible, and the whole world comes rising up to greet you. And your heart feels full up with everything. I mean *everything*. You can hardly stand how alive you feel right now, how connected to all of this you feel, to life, to the lives of others, to the whole entire world.

I want you to imagine having gone through all of this.

And then I want you to imagine watching it burn to the ground.

Your aching heart, your fallen face looking back at you in the mirror: That's what my sister looks like right now.

TWENTY-SIX

WE'RE FIVE DAYS out. Ted's below deck, and it doesn't look good. His breathing is ragged and shallow—when he's even breathing at all. His skin is paper-white, past pale. Like the life's being drained out of it. His hair's turning yellow and brittle at the edges and crumbling up and away and off. When Stan goes down to see him, everyone else leaves, even the Icelings. Like they know. I try to look at him, but he doesn't want to look at me. Not now, anyway.

Stan is working with an average of maybe four hours of sleep a night. And that's spaced out throughout the night, too, in increments of fifteen to thirty minutes. He doesn't want us to get off-course, and he still won't teach anyone how to do anything without him. But Emily and I just let him. There's nothing else we can do. I think he's putting everything he has into this, into having a skill that might be able to get us somewhere. I think it's all he can think to do, all he *can* do, right now. He needs to be needed. He needs to feel he has a purpose. He needs to keep going.

But at some point he's going to need to stop running. The body gives up. I'm so worried about him. And there's still so much to try to think about, to try to figure out.

Emily and I do what we can to look after Ted, but really it's Callie and Greta and Tara's thing. All we can really do is check on things, just look at our sisters and try to see what's in their eyes.

IT'S EARLY MORNING. The sun's just starting to think about dragging itself out of bed. Callie's up here with me, and I'm trying to figure out where we're supposed to go.

But mostly what I've spent my time figuring out is this: Callie, my sister, is a plant person. I mean that she was brought into this world by a plant that rose up from a trembling field of ice, and she was plucked from the pod of that plant by my father and brought home to me.

Or that's my guess. But everything he said, about the ground shaking, then going still, about the sky smelling like lightning, the clouds low and heavy and with a mind of their own, opening a hole in the sky to let the light in . . .

He didn't know what he was doing, I tell myself. I hope to myself. I hope so hard that he didn't know that he was stealing—*kidnapping*—dozens of infants, robbing them of their home, their families, the lives they were supposed to lead. And maybe he didn't mean to. Maybe he really thought he was saving them. But even if he thought he *was* somehow helping them, saving them, I still have got to wonder: Why would he take them away from their home? Their *habitat*, the place that literally nurtures them. They came *out of the ground*. *In pods.* What would make him think that they'd belong somewhere else? That they'd *survive* somewhere else? Was it because of me? Did he take them because of me? Did he miss me so much that when he saw Callie, a perfect alien baby, his parental instincts just went haywire and took over? Did something go wrong with the pods, and was it his fault, and was he afraid for their safety? Did something go wrong and it *wasn't* his fault? Did he understand at *all* what he'd done? And if he did, and if he took them all away more out of love than anything else, would that even start to make it okay? Or was that his mission all along?

And then I always come back to the fact that if he hadn't done what he did, I wouldn't have Callie. And right now, I don't even know how to ask if that would have been a good thing or a bad thing. For either of us. And I especially don't know how to think about the more likely and infinitely more gut-punching possibility: that Dad never bringing Callie home would have been a bad thing for me but a good thing for Callie. Everything is so wrapped up in itself right now, I don't have a clue *what* to think. I mean that just . . . I mean that if I was going to sit here and wonder what would have happened if none of this had happened, then I wouldn't be of any use to anyone.

And then there is this: *What if Callie's an alien?* And what if she's not the nice kind of alien? Or what if she's not an alien but just a plant-based fluke from the middle of the earth who can withstand extreme climates and who looks like a human but isn't? What if Callie is dangerous? What if Callie doesn't really love me at all? Not because she hates me or wants to harm me, but because she can't? Love me or hate me, she just *can't*?

But you know what? So what? Who cares? What I know for sure is that in this life, Callie is my sister, and I want to help. She's my sister. And I want to help. I *have* to help. Right?

But in the tired, calm quiet that has settled in on this boat, as we sail our way across the sea, the realizations of the day keep flooding in, crashing and re-crashing like a recycled wave. My sister, *my sister*, is a *plant person*. Or, more specifically: My sister is a plant. Who looks like a person. Who came out of a *pod*. That *rose up out of the earth* in a *trembling field of ice*. And then I think about it some more, and then I look at Callie, still the sweet-seeming and sometimes-quiet, sometimes-giddy girl I grew up with, and I try to feel startled and shocked and like the world as I know it has been changed and ruined forever, but then I kind of have to laugh at myself, because of *course* she's a plant person! And I'm the dummy who didn't see it before! She's always had a thing for being close to the ground, has always needed to sleep on the floor, sit on the floor, touch the ground and the soil. And when she walks, it's like she needs to be as near to the ground as possible. She needs to be able to touch it, if she has to. This deliberate, low-armed, shifting gait.

And it's even right there in the official ARO literature! All AROs are *required* to be near to and have access to a garden or greenhouse. Required! And she loves the sun, loves rainstorms and showers and sprinklers and Super Soaker fights, and she hates taking baths, just refuses to do it. And her crazy diet, and her naps by the window, and her sluggishness during spans when the sun hides behind the clouds. And the way she practically glows when she's healthy and happy, but when she's sad or going through a rough time where we're always back and forth between home and the hospital, she looks so miserable, so physically wilted and worn, that I feel like I'd do anything—something dangerous, violent, unthinkable—just to be able to climb inside her mind and ask her what's wrong in a language she understands.

My sister is a plant person. Who was stolen from the only place on earth where she knew how to belong. By my father, a scientist, who—I hope—thought he was doing her a favor by taking her away from the weird, silent winds and the snow-cradling trees and the rocky hills and cliffs and putting her in the suburbs, in a house that was warm and dry and safe, with cable TV and microwave ovens and telephones to connect her to anyone in the world except the only ones she wants.

And then I remember that . . . guy. That Iceling who looked like their leader, who was there to greet our Icelings in the Arctic, who disappeared underground, who might have survived the genocide. Where the hell has he been these past sixteen years? There was no way for me to tell how old he is or what kind of Iceling he is, but whether he's very old and was around when my dad was there or was one of the babies in Callie's . . . crop who somehow managed to hide and cling to the Arctic when the others were taken, why the hell didn't he *do* anything? Because whether he was already there when Callie was born or was born at the same time as Callie, it means the same thing: Someone survived. And if he couldn't find a way to rescue Callie and the others earlier, then why did he let it happen again? Why did he allow them to die? Why wasn't he prepared?

But Callie is the plant person, not me, which has been the problem all along and which is the reason why it's stupid for me to be asking these questions, because there's no way for me to know. Callie might know. There's no telling all the things she knows that I can't know because of my human limitations, because I am limited to merely five out of the probably infinite number of senses there are in this universe.

But there's one thought during this exhausting and trauma-fueled loop I'm on that I keep coming back to, the one that keeps rearing around and triggering me back to the start all over again. And that thought is represented by one stark, horrifying image, the same image I would use in the encyclopedia entry for this completely surreal experience: the pods. The crumbling, shriveled-up pods that were dead before the government could kill them. If that Iceling, the leader, the one who was already there . . . if he survived . . . if he had at least sixteen years to plan for the next trembling field, the next generation of pod people . . . then why would he mess it up so badly? Why wouldn't he do everything to make sure the island—the field, at the very least—was protected? Bulletproof. That the island was uninhabitable by anyone who was not born from a pod?

But more importantly, why were the pods empty? Why were they already dead?

Were they dead on purpose? Was that the whole point? Were they meant to draw the military here, draw its fire? Was the island supposed to burn? And if the answer to any of these questions is yes, then who was in on it? Was Callie? Her brothers and sisters? Or was it just that one Iceling, the one who disappeared into the ground?

Whoever planned it, maybe they knew, or at least thought, that whoever took the babies was one day going to come back? Maybe they figured they'd make sure that what happened there, what happened to Callie and Ted and Greta and Tara, would never happen again? I know this is crazy. I know I'm trying to solve a mystery that may as well have happened on another planet, in another time period, to a bunch of characters in a TV show aired in another dimension, one that was cancelled before fans could get any answers. But I can't help but wonder if maybe an Iceling—or all the Icelings—rigged this whole entire thing to happen exactly as it did, because they felt like it would be better if everyone thought they were dead. Because I have to think that if I were in Callie's shoes, or in the shoes of an Iceling who was left behind, all alone, while his family was stolen from him and taken somewhere hostile . . . I wouldn't trust anyone ever again. I would want to disappear, to make everyone think I was dead and gone so that they could never hurt me or anyone I loved again, because in their eyes there wouldn't be anyone to hurt.

I look over at Callie. I think as hard as I can about everything she's been through. I think about her whole life, as far as I'm equipped to imagine it, and then I kick myself for thinking I could even *begin* to

ICELING

do that. For the sheer vanity, the fucking *arrogance* of thinking that I could *ever* even attempt to speak for a person whom I have never heard speak, and who has never acknowledged in any definitive way the words that I speak. That I could presume to know how she looks at the world and feels about anyone, especially me. And for the first time, I don't feel sad because there's no way to know if she feels anything at all about or for me. Instead, I feel guilty and foolish for never choosing to look at Callie or our relationship in any way besides the one that fits with *my* world, the one that Callie can't be a part of.

I close my eyes. I see Callie smiling at me and shoving a Ritz cracker in her mouth. And I see her braiding flowers into my hair and my hair into a crown before every first day of school until I was twelve, when I picked her hands up and put them down at her sides and just left her there, because the girls at school were brutal, and wearing your hair down was the thing. And I see her weaving crowns of grass the other week, and sitting in my empty car for days on end, waiting for me to take her somewhere I didn't even understand it was possible to go to. And I can see her smiling! And I can remember her being scared about going to school, and I can remember when she didn't go back to school, when Jane determined there were better ways to socialize and educate, and I can remember not knowing how scared I should have been, how I was just hurt everyone thought Callie was so different. And I can see her throwing her whole room into a suitcase, a look of determined panic on her face, and I see her hands building an island, building her home. I see her sitting in my empty car, day after day, waiting for me to take her somewhere I didn't even understand it was possible to go. And then I see her watching that place, her home, burn to the ground. And I remember when we took baths together when we were really little, and Callie was so confused and terrified by the water, and me, at four years old, holding her hand, patting the water, wanting to show her it was okay, that even if some-

231

thing was scary to her it was all still going to be okay, and taking her hand to pat it, and we patted the water, and it was okay, it was, at that moment I felt it was okay, that I had made her feel okay, but it's not until now that I see that okay for me and okay for Callie have never been the same thing.

I can hear Emily waking up. Stan checking the motor. I know that Callie's lying on her back over to my right, in the morning sun. I know the wind's coming from the aft and blowing a bit toward starboard. I know the water's a little choppy, but that's how it gets sometimes.

I close my eyes, and when I open them, what I see is the sea. And a clear sky. And when I turn my head, there's the sun, and I let it warm my whole face. And what I know right now is exactly what I've always known: Callie is my sister, and I love her. But I know something new now too. I know I would die for her. I would. I know that I don't partic- ularly want to die but that I would die for her. And I'm crying. I touch her face, just to touch it, just to . . . I want to tell her that I'm here for her. I want to tell her that I'll always be here for her, and that I love her so much, and I want to tell her that I don't know how to tell her this. So I touch her face, and she lets me, and that's all either of us can say right now. And if I told you it was enough, I'd be a liar.

TWENTY-SEVEN

WE'RE SEVEN DAYS out when Stan finds a note hidden somewhere on the boat. It is typed. It isn't signed. It says, *Good luck.* And it took us a week to find it.

"What the hell?" says Stan, holding it up. It's the first time he's spoken in five days.

"This is so creepy," says Emily. "Do you think . . . did someone know we were coming?"

"Maybe someone knew *someone* was coming," Stan says. "But that doesn't mean that we were the ones they were expecting."

"But they were expecting somebody," I say.

"So can we even trust any of this?" Emily says. "And who is 'they'? And where did you even *find* that thing?"

"Does it matter who they are? And I found it in Ted's blanket. We put him in there first thing, because he looked so awful, and then I didn't see it until today when I was changing his blanket and it fell out."

"Stan," I start, and he shoots me a look, and I change the subject pronto. If this gets him talking, this is what we'll talk about. I turn to speak directly to Emily. "If whoever wrote the note is with the same people who did all of this . . . if it's the government . . . they could track us. They tracked us before. Bobby told me that I already know where we need to go. Which is nonsense, but . . . if Bobby thought that, then maybe they did too. Maybe they already know exactly where we are at all times and can find us no matter where we go. Maybe it doesn't matter."

"What do you mean?" Emily says. "We go through all of this, and then suddenly it doesn't matter?"

"She means that we're just kids," Stan says. "We're not terrorists or revolutionaries. We don't have military training, and we don't know how to outsmart the government. We can try. But if trying slows us down from getting wherever Ted and Tara and Callie and Greta need to go? Then why bother?"

"Yeah," I say. "I mean that maybe we're screwed, but we're alive. Maybe this boat is bugged. Maybe we'll all die. But right now, we're here, and we're not dead. And neither are the Icelings. And it doesn't matter how smart we are or how much we care, because that won't keep a boat running forever. But we can try to take it where we need to go."

"And where's that, Lorna?" Emily says. "Where do we need to go?"

"I don't know," I say, and I can tell Emily's about to jump down my throat, so I do what I can to calm her. "But I'll know soon. I'm working on it. I'm close."

EMILY AND STAN leave me alone to finish my turn on watch duty. I lean against the deck, thinking about everything I don't know, and the world feels like it's slipping out from under me. I told Emily I was on the brink of a breakthrough, but the truth is I'm so far from the brink that I don't even know which direction it's in.

ICELING

I'm so tired, and all I want to do is sleep, and then, all of a sudden, there is Callie. She's standing right next to me, somehow having made it over to me silently, and her hand is on my shoulder. She smiles, and I choose to believe she's smiling at me. She takes my binoculars and leans against the deck next to me, and I lean against her. I lean against her because if I don't I will collapse. I rest the side of my head against the side of hers, and then I squeeze her around the middle, and then I leave her to take over on watch. I go down below deck and get some sleep. It's not any good, the sleep. But I get it anyway.

WHILE I WAS sleeping, Stan sketched out a map of the ship and diagrammed the steering board with instructions. He's opening up a bit again—I hope, at least. He's still not sleeping, but I guess I can live with that if it means he's back to talking. I know his talking again is a gesture he's making for me and Emily, and I'm glad for it.

For a while, I study the diagram, which was beside me in my bunk when I woke up. But after a couple of minutes, I can no longer see or make sense of the images in front of me. All I can see is that bear. How it looked so eager to kill us. And then I see Ted killing it. And I see the soldiers. And their rifles are raised and spitting sparks that are actually bullets at the already-dead pods, just making them more dead than they already were. How did they not know they were already dead? Maybe they didn't even take the time to notice, because they were there to kill them, and then once they were satisfied that they had, they shot them up until they were literally nothing any-more, and then they burnt them up. Then *they* died too. They died when those drones spun around each other, like it was a dance, and then collided, everything exploding and on fire. And then I have a terrible thought, which is that all of that happened because Ted, who was so furious that the pods came up dead, flung all that fury at the drones, those instruments of death hovering above us.

Up on the deck, I hear what I think is Stan teaching Emily how to tie knots. And from Stan's tone and cadence, it sounds like Emily's a quick learner. I start to make my way up to the deck, and as I go I can hear their conversation more clearly. I guess Emily's such a quick learner that she's through talking about knots altogether and is now telling Stan about how she's seen somewhere between fifty and two hundred dolphins in her lifetime.

"I hope we end up somewhere tropical," I hear her say. "I'm ready for a complete change of scenery. Cabana boys and everything."

Right, like a trip like this could ever end with a piña colada and cabana boys.

Oh my God.

Cabana boys.

Oh my *God.*

I know where we're going.

I run up the stairs as fast as I can. Stan and Emily look up at me, like "Hi, Lorna, did you figure it out?" *Guess what, guys, I totally did.*

"We go to the Galápagos."

They're still sitting, but they're staring up at me, as though to ask, "Um, what?" And I'm grinning like a genius who just discovered something I didn't know I knew, which was that I know where we're going. I know where to find more Icelings.

"The Galápagos?" says Stan finally.

"The Galápagos," I say.

Tara and Greta come up from below deck, which I choose to interpret as a heraldic sign of my discovery. I know it isn't, but still.

"Why?" Emily says. "How do you know?"

"Because that's where my parents are."

"Let's try again," Emily says. "*How* do you know?"

"Listen," I say, and then I tell them.

I tell them about how it was my dad's research crew that discovered the Arctic Orphans. I tell the story he tells about the boat and the infants, which they'd all heard before, but maybe not exactly like this. I tell them how, just one night after I saw Stan at the hospital the night Callie had her scariest fit yet, my parents took me to dinner to tell me how proud they were of me for taking such good care of Callie. That they were so proud, in fact, that they'd decided to leave Callie home alone with me while they both went off to the Galápagos to investigate a bizarre meteorological/seismic confluence. I tell them how, after that dinner, my dad got all funny, almost trancelike, and told me a story—a memory—about how when he found Callie and the other Icelings, he saw a trembling field of ice. And that the sky was purple and yellow, and it smelled like lightning, but he couldn't see any. He asked me if I knew what lightning smelled like, and then he told me, "Don't. Don't know that."

"He told me—like he's always told me—that he found them on a boat. But everything he described—"

"It's what we just saw," said Emily. "On that island. That's . . . that's what . . . wow."

Stan's and Emily's eyes are wide. Because now we all know. We know that the weird new details my dad slipped into his old story after the restaurant were what actually happened when they found the baby Icelings, and the boat story was just a cover for that. The trembling field of ice, the sky going purple and yellow while the clouds moved with a mind of their own to shine the sun down on a field of baby Icelings. It's the same thing that happened when *we* found the baby Icelings, only the ones we found never even had a chance.

"So do you believe me now?" I ask. "That if that's where they are, then that's where we should go? Because if the unusual activity that they're there to study is at all similar to what we just saw . . . then that must mean there are more of them there. Right? If that's true, then we have to go. That's where Bobby wants us to go, that's why he said I knew where to go. I don't know what will happen when we get there. It's not like we can save anyone, but . . ."

"No," Stan says, cutting me off.

"What?" I say, terrified and, frankly, totally shocked that he's not even going to consider it. "Are you serious?"

"Oh, wait, no," he says. "No. That's not what I meant—I didn't mean *no*. I meant *no*, we can't *not* go there. But also *no*, we can't think that by going there we're not going to be able to help. Not after seeing what we just saw, going through what we just went through."

"All right then," says Emily, her smile wide. "Let's do it."

Stan starts charting the course. He asks if I know which island, and I remember my phone. I finally got it to charge, and miraculously it still turns on. But I can't call or text anyone or do much of anything else with it either, because the only apps that open are the ones that don't require access to Wi-Fi or a cellular network, neither of which we have out here. But I do have the address of where they're staying and where their office is, written down in my notes app. I bring it up to Stan, and he grins at me, then puts his head back down to complete the course.

"We've got a plan, kid sister!" I shout triumphantly at Callie. I know she doesn't understand what I'm saying, but after I say it, she smiles. And I don't know if it means what I want it to. But right now, I don't care.

And then, down below deck, a phone rings.

TWENTY-EIGHT

"**WHERE THE** *HELL* is this phone?" shouts Stan. He's running down the stairs faster than Emily and I can run down the stairs, which we are also doing.

We're pulling apart the beds, flinging boxes of cereal and tins of rations all over. There's an upended jug of water on the floor, and in the haze of all this frantic looking I indulge in a half-formed thought about how I hope the cap doesn't come unscrewed, sending all that drinkable water all over the carpet.

The phone keeps ringing, each new ring sounding to me like a gun going off, except we can't see the gun or who's shooting it. *RING* and we flinch. It's not on the table. *RING* and we shudder. It's not in the cabinets. *RING RING* and we gasp. It's not on the floor.

It's in Emily's hand.

"I found it!" she shouts.

She hands it to me, a brightly colored satellite phone just like the one my parents have, and I spin around to Stan so that we can all answer it together.

Except Stan's not there when I spin around. He's by Ted's bunk. And the phone is still ringing.

"Hey, Ted. Hey," he says, gently trying to shake loose a look from him. And the phone's still ringing in my hand, and my hand is shaking. "Hey, Ted. Hey," Stan says again, and tears are streaming down his face, and Ted's not doing anything. Callie and Greta and Tara come running down. They stop in front of Ted and stare and reach toward the floor with claw-like hands, and as I watch them I name what it is they're doing: weeping.

The phone's ringing. It's ringing and ringing. Emily takes it from my hand and sets it on the table, and we let it ring for a little while longer until it stops on its own and goes silent.

TED DIED IN his sleep tonight, while all around him we flung open the inside of this boat, looking for a phone that kept ringing. Whoever left us the phone is a mystery, the answer to which is residing on the other end of the call we missed.

Stan's kneeling beside Ted. We put our hands on his shoulders, and he looks up at us in response to our touch, but then turns his face away again. His face is dry now, and his eyes are red. "Ted's dead," he says. His voice sounds like it's coming from somewhere else.

Oh, Stan. We move to sit down by him, but he gets up. "I'm okay," he says.

"Okay, no I'm not," he tells us once he's up. "Wait," he says. "The phone call . . . did you get it?"

"We found the phone," says Emily, flicking her eyes at me, "but not in time. Whoever it was hung up, and it's been silent ever since. It's on the table," she says, pointing. "In case they try back."

"Oh," he says. He kneels down again and puts his hand on Ted's shoulder, then moves his hand to Ted's face. He stares at his brother, his dead brother, for what must feel to him like forever.

Emily and I go above deck. Stan isn't alone. We're still here. But Ted's gone. And whatever Stan needs, we just have to find a way to be there for him.

He lets loose a scream like I've never heard.

FINALLY, AFTER SITTING up with Ted for so long I start to worry he might never leave, Stan sleeps. Emily and I stay on the course he made and taught us how to follow.

He wakes up, at sunset, announcing that he needs to use one of the two lifeboats and some of the gasoline. Emily and I look at each other, both knowing without asking that he's going to use them to give Ted a burial at sea. It seems like something he needs to do himself, but we stand by in case he needs us.

"One thing that always calmed Ted was Vikings," Stan says. "Looking at actors dressed as Vikings on TV. Touching books about Vikings. So I'm giving him a Viking funeral." His hands are shaking as he tries to pour the gasoline on his brother, who is lying really peacefully in the small lifeboat. I dart my hand forward and help him hold the can steady. Emily grabs the rope that lowers the lifeboat. Stan's got some matches. His hands are trembling as he and Emily carefully lower him down. Ted's in the water now, and Stan takes a deep breath.

"Ted," he says, "I wasn't the best brother. And maybe sometimes you weren't either. I was scared of you, and a lot of the time I resented the hell out of you. But I always . . . I always loved you. You're the only brother I ever had. You were a loner, Ted. A rebel. And you saved my life. The only reason any of us are here right now is because you were strong enough, and smart enough, and had a heart big enough to save our lives. And I miss you. I really, really miss you." He clears his throat and wipes his nose on the back of his hand. He lights a match and flicks it below into the lifeboat, the flame carrying what we can remember of Ted's life off into the great beyond.

It catches quick. The flames stretch and grow and dance over the water and our eyes. Greta and Tara are standing by Stan. Callie takes hold of my hand. Emily's crying. I'm crying.

TWENTY-NINE

THE SUNSETS WE can see from this boat are so beautiful you wouldn't believe them. Which is nice, because sunsets—the way they shiver their way down into the edge of the water while all the warmth leaves the world—are pretty much all I'm comfortable talking about right now. Sunsets and sunrises. I can talk to you about sunrises all day, how they come up over the water all pale yellow and dusky blue, like the sea is the lip of a table, or your life. How the water extends and multiplies the just-woke sun's glow. You see things like this and you can understand how people once thought the ocean was the edge of the world. You see how you could entertain the notion that, if you sailed out a little bit farther, everything would just fall off.

After two weeks out here, I'm starting to think those the-world-is-flat fanatics might have been on to something. From where I'm standing, the horizon looks exactly like the edge of a map nobody's figured out how to survey yet. Maybe that's where dragons are. Maybe we'll be swallowed up by something too terrifying to even put into a sentence. Maybe *that's* what dragons are. Maybe we'll learn something new about ourselves, and maybe we'll die. Maybe we'll end up in the Galápagos after all. Maybe turtles will swim up to us—Icelings and all—with tropical drinks and snacks balanced on their shells, and nobody will shoot anybody, ever, forever. Maybe my parents will take our side, and we'll bring down the government together, or at least get them off our backs. But maybe I'm just seventeen years old and terrified. And maybe all of this is a dream with no edges to tell me where it stops and the world begins, like a horizon line hidden by sky and water that are the exact same shade of blue.

Except that I know that it isn't a dream. And I can always make out the horizon, no matter how monochrome everything gets. And every time I open my eyes, we're still on a boat, aiming for the Galápagos, where the government has sent my parents to hunt for another group of Icelings on behalf of the government, which just tried to annihilate us along with an unknown number of others.

We didn't get to that phone in time. Or we did, but then we saw Ted, and Stan mattered more than the phone ever did. We don't know who called. Maybe it'll ring again, and whoever's on the other end will tell us something terrible or wondrous. Or maybe it will never ring again, and we'll just keep going like we were ready to before we even knew anyone had a way to reach us out here.

It's been over two weeks since I told Mimi and Dave that I'd call them as soon as I was safe, and I have to force myself not to think about how worried they must be that they haven't heard from me. I miss Dave. More than I thought I would. And I miss my life. And at this point, I'm pretty much positive that there's no going back. That whatever happens after this, that's the rest of my life now. There's no option that'll take me back home, to the time when Callie was just solidly weird and nothing more, and Jane was just a creepy doctor who lacked social skills, and my parents were just nerdy people who loved me. Because Callie's a plant person. And Jane murders children. And my parents stole Callie from her home, from her family, from her whole entire life. And that's my whole world now, and I'm not even sure I have a place in it.

STAN TELLS US we might have enough fuel to make it, but that it's a good thing that this boat also has sails, just in case. He thinks we're maybe about halfway there. He wants to make sure we keep some reserve gas on the boat no matter what, so when there's a good wind, we ride that, even though we move at roughly a third of the speed that we do under the engine. But Stan would rather get there late than not get there at all.

Stan tells us this in a steady monotone, and Emily and I agree that he must be in some kind of shock. Like a sort of fugue state. Like he needs this project, to make an elaborate plan for our voyage at sea, because now that Ted is gone he needs another reason to keep going. But Emily and I are worried about him. Because I look at him and all I can think about is how grief will change things in you. It'll change how you see things, and how you think you used to see things.

The boat is quiet now with Ted gone, and the solitude between us makes the whole world feel urgent. Like it's a bomb covered in water and land. Like our heartbeats are ticking out the seconds until we meet the next horrible thing that will rise up to bite our heads off. And the longer we're on the boat, the more time we have to start to wonder if maybe we're walking into the same trap all over again.

"Even if we are," says Emily, "at least it'll be warm."

Stan doesn't turn from the wheel, but I can still see his cheek move up in a fraction of a smile, and I feel I could kiss Emily right now for making that little joke.

SASHA STEPHENSON

IT'S NIGHTTIME NOW, and it's clear out, so I set myself up next to Callie, and we lay down under the stars, and I tell us stories about them.

My eyes catch on these two stars, one small and bright, one big but softer and more glowy than the other, side by side in the sky and linked by a delicate chain made of tiny twinkles. Those two stars, I tell myself and Callie too, if some part of her can listen, are two girls who grew up together. Though they've never spoken, they are like sisters, and they love each other very much. They love each other so much that they are bound together—not in their hearts, but literally by a rope tied around their wrists by a stranger. Because they've never spoken, they can never get unbound, so they've just adapted to life like that. But eventually, one of them will die. And the one left behind will carry the other's weight around with her forever.

IT'S NOW BEEN sixteen days since we got on the boat. We cross the days off on the wrong month on a calendar that's three years old. Nineteen days ago was the last time I slept in my own bed, the last time I woke up with anything resembling a sense that the world was something I understood.

In the distance there's a storm. There are these strange clouds way, way off, acting like they have a mind of their own, storming along all heavy and low. I look at them and can't help but think about everything we've seen, everything we know.

Callie knows about the storm too. I'm sure of it. She keeps milling about on the deck with me, sticking her nose up to the sky, like there's something in the air she can smell. Like there's something she can hear, way off in the distance, that she needs to get to.

ICELING

I go below deck. I stand in the doorway and lean, holding the top of the frame with my arms, and I sway a bit. I ask Stan and Emily if they've noticed the clouds too.

"Yes," says Stan immediately.

"Yeah," says Emily at the same time. Then they look at each other. Then they look at me. We don't even need to specify which clouds we're talking about. We know which clouds we're talking about.

Stan gets up, slips past me, and jogs over to adjust the engine.

"He's going to speed up," says Emily. "I don't know if we have the fuel. But he was saying he thinks we're a few days out. Like, maybe no more than three. Maybe less now."

We follow him up to see if we can help, but we don't make it up. Because, below deck, that phone. It starts to ring.

THIRTY

EMILY'S THE FIRST to the phone. She snatches it up immediately and presses the green button, because we're not going to let ourselves miss it a second time. Stan rushes down from above and joins us, and we all stare at Emily as she puts the phone to her ear and says, "Uh, yes? This is the . . . uh, boat speaking. Who's calling?"

My heart starts pounding as I stare at Emily while she listens to whoever's on the other end of the phone, and Stan edges up closer to her as if to try to listen too. Emily's brow furrows up, and then her face lights up in either shock or realization, and I'm doing all I can not to reach out and grab the phone from her, and right when I think I can't hold out any longer, she thrusts the phone out to me.

"I . . . it's for you," she says.

"Hell—" I start to say, but I cut myself off, because I realize that the person on the other end of the line is still talking, and at first I think whoever this is must still think Emily's on the line, but then I stop thinking that entirely when, half a second later, I recognize the voice.

". . . and anyway, sport," says my father. "Like I said, I'm just leaving you this voice mail to check in, ask you to call back, see how things are."

What? Why the hell is my dad calling me on this creepy satellite phone hidden on this boat? Why is he pretending this is a voice mail? "Dad," I say, "what the—"

"And also to tell you," he interrupts, "I heard from Mom that you guys had a party after we left, which I can't say I'm surprised by, and in fact I have to say I'm a little proud." And then I hear a door closing on his end.

"Listen, Lorna," he says in a hushed voice just above a whisper, "very, very carefully. As far as I know, Bobby and I are the only ones who know about this phone. I don't know how much time I have, so just listen. Don't talk."

And, as much as I want to talk, as much as I want to demand answers to questions worth asking, I hear the tone in his voice, and I bite my tongue. I take a deep breath and give the thumbs-up to Emily and Stan, who are watching me with terrified eyes.

"I know you talked to Mom before they started herding everyone north. Reports about what ultimately happened have been scarce, so I'm guessing whatever it was, it wasn't good. The last broadcast we heard said that one of the AROs tossed a pod at a drone, and then some kid soldier fired off a rocket without orders. I swear to God, I thought you were dead. Your mother worries you might be. Me, though, I didn't see the champion of my heart getting blown up in a governmental cluster, no matter what sort of payloads were involved." He pauses now, and I almost venture to say something, but then I miss my chance. "I just want to tell you," he says, "everything. About that day, about Callie. We were up there to check on those anomalies," he says, "which you already knew. And I'm sure you noticed those same anomalies for yourself when you were up there. We were there on a grant, a government grant, which is also probably no big surprise to you now.

"There weren't any docks there back then. We had to beach the boat, and I made two interns stay with it, planting themselves in the frozen sand, clinging to ropes, with nothing but the vague hope of getting course credit tethering them there. We landed where the new docks are now, which is why the new docks are there now. There was this hole in the ground, and we heard some sounds coming up out of it. Did you see the shed? They built a shed over it. Not even I know what the hell they found in there or what they were looking for. But we made our way there, among those goddamn trees, covered in snow and ice. And we stayed for a while, taking photos. We made it past the hills. The hills sing. I don't know if you heard them. They sing. Not like a song. They resonate around the trembling expanse.

"And the ice field is trembling, viciously. I go out, and I test it. Because the readings don't make any sense, and the sky doesn't make any sense. It's purple and yellow, but only over the field. We can see the sky going gray all around this, just normal and flat and endless like the sky gets out there. And the air smells like lightning. Which I told you I hoped you would never get to smell. There's always a change with lightning around. It's this sort of math you can't predict. And it always, always alters something. Irretrievably. And then this guy . . . this guy just pops up out of the ground. He stares at us. All he does is stare. And the ice is breaking apart, and I'm standing on it, because the readings don't make any sense here, because even though it's quaking, it's more than stable enough to stand on.

"The guy stands there and stares on and on, and then the pods come up. All at once, they poke out through the ice. It was like watching one of those time-lapse films of plants pushing their way up out the soil. Except the soil is a field of solid ice staying solid above a core that's just barely not magma. Just barely. They look like flowers. Like flowers wrapping a gift. And then they unwrap. They open. One pod at a time. And the sound of thunder is everywhere. And I see, at my feet, a baby. And my own baby girl, she's back home, safe in southeastern Pennsylvania, on Carpenter Street. I pick up the baby girl in front of me, and I look in her eyes, and I have no idea what I'm seeing, but I can't look away from her. And I can't leave her there. If I am to believe the readings, then I should believe that the island is falling apart, but when I look around and feel myself standing there on that troubled earth, that's not what I believe will happen at all. That guy is still there, staring at us. He looks like he's about thirty years old, give or take a couple of years. And like he doesn't know a thing about babies. And I just go. I run from pod to pod, my students hustling along beside me, helping me grab these babies. Some of them, Lorna . . . Have you ever seen premature babies? How small they are? Some of these kids just . . . they were like dust. Their skin looked like it was built to never see the sun. They were so pale it was like I could see through them, see their little hearts not beat but just give out. Just give out right in front of me, Lorna.

"We kept running, and we grabbed as many as we could, tucked them in our jackets. I had maybe six in there, holding them close, trying so hard not to crush them, to just keep them warm and alive.

"We saved them, we thought. That's what we thought we were doing. And Callie. I couldn't leave her there. I couldn't. Maybe that's selfish as hell. I think it is now.

"Nobody else knows this. My assistants, my students, I don't know what happened to them. I can't. I don't think about it—that's how I live with it. Your mom knows. Now you. Jane doesn't know. The main way I know your mom still loves me is that Jane still doesn't know. She loves me enough not to go to her. Lorna, I love you, and I'm sorry." His voice quivers a bit, and I find I don't even want to say anything to him. I just want to get off the phone.

"After that, Lorna," he goes on. "After the plants came up, those perfect little infants nestled in the mouths of those pods . . . the things we saw were just—"

And the phone call ends.

I don't know how or why it was allowed to last that long.

I know my dad. I know he thought he was being a good person. I know he thought he was doing the right thing. And I don't know what happened after that. I don't know what happened to my dad. I don't know if the dad I know is just his story of who he thought he was going to be before that day.

His voice was so strange on the phone. My mouth is moving and moving, trying to tell Stan and Emily what happened, and I can't make a sound. I can't. I can hardly breathe, and there is this weight, like my heart is a rock that just dropped into my stomach, and I just want to throw it up, to just get it out of me and breathe, and I can't. I can't. I don't know how right now.

I run up above the deck, and I fling the phone into the sea. I want so badly to hear Dad's voice again, to have him tell me that everything is okay. But I don't know who else was listening. As much as Dad may believe that he and Bobby are the only ones who know about the phone, there's no way to prove it. Someone could have been tracking it—and us. I throw my regular phone overboard too, because it might still be pinging out a signal. Then I put my face in my hands. I put my face in my hands, and I stay like that for a while, not wanting to see or hear anything else.

I hear a sound like a whisper, near my ear. Callie's holding me. I know it's Callie because she smells like Callie, because I have smelled Callie every day for almost every day of her life. She peels my hands from my face slowly, like she's unwrapping a present. She wipes my tears away, and I just make new ones. She looks at me. She makes her face look like mine. She sits there with me and makes her face look like mine, and I have my first funny thought in a while, which is: If that's what I look like, I should stop that. So I try to. And she smiles at me.

We sit there like that all night, watching the sea. Dolphins do this thing where they have to breathe, but they also have to sleep, so they sort of float there like logs, turning and breathing and turning and breathing. The water's mostly calm. The wind has been getting warmer over the past several days. The air smells like it always smells: wet, and salty, and like fish living and dying and breeding all around us.

THE SUN'S COMING up. It's dawn, and the sky is anything but clear, and a fog is rising and settling all around us. I'm wracked and ragged from last night, from this whole life, which is, I am now realizing, mine. So here I am. On the deck of this boat, and my sister is here, holding my hand and watching the sea with me. Our feet are dangling over the edge, getting damp in the foggy mist. Callie reaches into her pocket and pulls out two crackers. She puts one in her mouth, and she puts the other in mine.

I don't know what comes next, and I couldn't even begin to imagine it without screwing it up, but whatever it is, it's my sister and me. Here. Now. And with this—with this—I say, *Fine. I can take it. I dare you.*

ACKNOWLEDGMENTS

Thanks to Liz Tingue, without whom this book wouldn't be here, and to Rebecca Novack for the notes and attention. Thanks to Nalini Edwin, Sarah Hallacher, Andrea McGinty, and Lauren Wilkinson for their friendship and eyes along the way. Thanks to Maggie Logan for being the best, and to my parents and brother for their endless love and support.